GU00857829

The Girl of Diamonds and Rust

Book 3
The Half Shell Series

Susan Ward

ISBN: 1511412984
ISBN-13: 978-1511412988

"Maybe this is love. Protecting the part of yourself most important to you and knowing when to let go so that you can keep a small piece of that person alive and real in your heart." ~~Chrissie Parker

PROLOGUE

January 1993

I wake to the sound of glass hitting glass.

I ease away from Alan and gaze up at him. It's barely morning, and he's wide awake, when Alan hardly ever wakes before noon. His posture tells me he's been sitting there quite a while, drinking and watching me.

"You are not returning to Berkeley," he snaps.

All drowsiness leaves my flesh in a nerve-popping jolt. I scoot away from Alan, dragging the sheets to cover me, rapidly searching his face, and then my heart drops to my knees because his eyes are hooded as they burn into me.

He says, "You still talk in your sleep. Do you know that?"

No, no, no! Why did he ask me that?

"I didn't know that," I whisper, sounding surprisingly calm even though every part of me is frantic and afraid.

He takes a long swallow of his drink. "Neil hasn't mentioned it?"

Oh God! "I stopped seeing Neil."

Those black eyes fix on me, unblinking. "When did you end it with him?"

My body chills and then heat rises on my cheeks. I try to stutter out a safe response and somehow manage to say

1

nothing. His eyes lock on me again.

"When did you end it with Neil? Don't lie to me, Chrissie."

I sit up in the bed, struggling to meet his gaze directly, though the way he is staring at me makes it an unbearably painful thing.

"I would never lie to you. I ended it with Neil because I love you."

He sets down his drink, running a hand through his hair. "Goddamn you, I ask you not to do it and you rip out my heart anyway," he says through gritted teeth. "You won't be straight with me even when I ask you to and yet you just answered me, Chrissie."

The phone rings and it makes me jump and kicks up Alan's temper. He reaches out and grabs the receiver.

"What?" he bites off into the phone. "I'm in Malibu. I'm taking a couple days downtime at the beach. No, I'm not discussing that."

My stomach turns. I can hear Nia's voice through the phone. I can't make out the words, but everything inside me grows cold. I don't know which is worse: how Nia sounds talking to Alan or that he let me hear them talk because he is angry with me and wants to get in a blow during our fight without even being focused on me.

"OK," Alan says. "That's fine. Tell them I've agreed to that."

He hangs up the phone and I stare at him, shaking. "You're such an asshole. Why do you have to be so mean when you're angry?"

I scramble from the bed, go for my bag and rapidly

start packing up my things.

"That's it, Chrissie. Run. Give you an excuse to run, not to have to face anything in your life directly, and you take it. That is what you do, isn't it, love?"

"What the hell is that supposed to mean?" I hiss.

Every line in his face tightens in extreme anger. "You ran off in New York, and you fucked up everything for both of us. You fucked up my life, too. You don't have a right to get angry today."

"It didn't sound fucked up to me on the phone."

"I haven't lived with Nia since six months before I came to see you in Berkeley," he says, almost inflectionless. "I have told you that, Chrissie. We've reached a settlement. I gave Nia everything she wanted so I can finally get out. That call was her bleeding me one last time before we sign the papers. When was the last time you fucked Neil?"

He holds me in an unrelenting stare and his gaze is brutally intense, shards of fury and despondency and hurt. It's too much, from everything uncertain and dangling, to possible and disintegrating in a horrible, unimaginable way; slamming together, brutally, all at once.

I continue to pack, my body shaking so fiercely I can barely grab hold of my clothes and shove them in. "I'm not going to answer that. I think it's better I don't. I think I should leave before we both say things we'll regret."

His eyes harden and some still functioning part of my brain warns that I've just fucked up big time, as Alan calmly grabs his pants and pulls them into place.

"That's how you want to deal with this?" He shakes his head, not bothering to even look at me. "You can leave if you want to, but if you do we're over, Chrissie. Or you can come to the patio, and if you are honest with me I will listen and we'll see where we go from there."

With that, Alan walks away. I stare at the door and sink down on the bed. He's angrier than I have ever seen him, so angry he's quiet. I shouldn't even try to talk to him. The way he is now, this could spin out of control in any direction.

Alan wants honesty. My inner voice reminds me of all the reasons why this is so important to Alan, of all the times people he has loved have lied to him, and warns me of how dangerous it will be for us both if I tell him everything about Neil.

The distraught look on his face as he left the bedroom shames me. I was so unkind to him in how I behaved in this...will he forgive me...will the truth be enough? I don't know, and that scares the hell out of me and I am more afraid than I have been at any other moment in my life.

Somehow I manage to go to my duffel, pull out some sweats, and dress. I open the door. The house is quiet when I step into the hall, and it surprises me that it is. I don't know what I expected, but not this heavy, waiting silence.

I go toward the wall of glass and I find Alan on the patio just as he said he would be. Then I slide open the door and step out.

After a minute or two, Alan pushes off the wall and stomps out his cigarette on the concrete. His jaw is clenching. His gaze shifts and his eyes lock on me.

"Even after this I'm not sure I want us over," he says, sounding frustrated with himself, but he is pulsing with anger even more strongly than he was in the bedroom. "You didn't answer me when I asked before. When was the last time you fucked Neil?"

I stare at him, the tightly held arrangement of his long body parts, and with aching despair I know I shouldn't have come out here to try to talk him. We will both end up bloody, hating each other before this is through.

"We should wait to talk until you're calmer."

Alan's eyes flash and widen. "Not today, Chrissie. That is the worst thing you could do for either of us. Walk out that door without answering every single question I have and we are over. That is the only thing I am positive of today."

I stand frozen in place, searching his face. I can't tell for certain if he means it, but I do know if I stay he will rip us to shreds. We don't have a chance if I stay here.

"No, Alan. If we try to talk this out now, that's when we will end up over. You are just too angry to see it."

~~~

By the time I reach Berkeley, I am something beyond numb. I don't even have the sensation of having driven here. The scenery passed in a blur, unreal, as disjointed moments of my life rose in my memory, now connected, unkind and too real.

All through the drive, my senses were only claimed by the flashing images of all the mistakes I've made. The mistakes I've made in how I love Alan. The mistakes I've made with everyone in my life.

I pull into the carport, grab my bag, and somehow manage to get into the elevator. I look at myself in the mirrored squares, and it's a strange thing that I should look normal, exactly as I always do, and yet there is nothing comfortable or familiar left inside me. I hurt the man I love. I hurt my best friend, and yes, Neil is my best friend. I didn't realize it when we broke up, but it is painfully present inside me today.

Inside the condo, I drop my bag, and without turning on the lights I go to my bedroom. I rummage through my drawer for my mobile phone, flip it open, stare and start to shake.

It fully sinks in at this moment. It didn't completely have the feel of realness before now, though it probably should have and I don't know why it didn't.

My legs are no longer able to hold me, and I sink on the bed and stare at the phone. Ten hours and not one message from Alan. Nothing. Not a single call. This time, I should have stayed and fought for him. Even if it bloodied us. Even if it hurt too much. And even if it ended this way.

Chrissie's Journal

There are times I truly hate the phone. There are times I truly hate Alan. And there are times I truly hate myself. I'm sick of staring at the phone. I'm sick of waiting for Alan to call me. And I'm sick of feeling pathetic for repeatedly calling him.

I knew it in January when I walked out on Alan; I'd made a catastrophic mistake, the kind you don't repair with a guy. It shouldn't surprise me that Alan ignores my phone messages. It shouldn't surprise me to see him splattered across the tabloids with a new girl every week. It shouldn't surprise me that he's self-destructing in print and ignoring me.

I've lived this horrible moment before. I seem to live the horrible moments of my life over and over again. It is all exactly like it was after I left Alan in New York in 1989. Only this time, I wish I could undo it, take back my mistakes, because this time I really could use Alan being here with me.

There is nothing about the past three months I don't get...or blame Alan for...or forgive myself for. I am the one who fucked us up big time. I just really wish Alan would call, so I could tell him what's going on with me because I don't know what to do. What I'm supposed to do. What he would want me to do.

Crap, Chrissie, stop lying to your journal. You know exactly what Alan would want you to do. You just want *him* to say it so it won't be something *you* do, something you own totally on your own.

Shit, how can someone's life get so fucked up in three short months? January was awful and it keeps going downhill from there. One minute my life is OK, survivable, and then everything changes too quickly and my life is anything but OK.

Three little words and the world has changed. Time has lost the feel of realness. I have lost the feel of realness. I don't know what to do, and I hate that I'm in this mess alone trying to figure out my life by myself.

Fuck, Alan, just call me. We're over. Message received. You don't need to continue behaving like an asshole so the message is sent to me every day via the tabloids. Your silence says it all. So now, can you please answer a single phone message?

Accept the fact, Chrissie, he's not going to call. I need to stop calling him. Maybe it's time to let go of him the way he has definitely let go of me. Only a stupid girl runs to a guy, who doesn't want her, with her problems. This is my problem and I need to fix it on my own.

Maybe this is what being an adult is. This awful aloneness with life-altering decisions you are too terrified to make.

Still, when I left Malibu I didn't really believe Alan would end us. I thought he'd be pissed off for a few days and then break down and call me. He called and sent me letters for a year after I left him in New York, but after Malibu, nothing. I really didn't expect this.

Maybe there are some hurts love can't fix. Maybe there are some things people are not supposed to be able to forgive. Maybe it is better to walk away from someone rather than to try to mend your heart after having someone rip it out.

That's what Alan said to me. I *ripped out his heart*. Oh God, the memory of the way he looked at me still makes me grow shaky and cold inside. Maybe it's all better this way, with him walling me out in a way that makes it abundantly clear that I fucked up and we are over forever.

Maybe this is love. Protecting the part of yourself most important to you and knowing when to let go so that you can keep a small piece of that person alive and real in your heart. Maybe this is the only way Alan can keep from hating me.

And really, that's not such a bad thing. As awful as *this* is, as much as I need him now, it would be worse knowing that Alan hates me. Maybe the best two people can do when they've loved each other badly, is to walk away before hating each other.

Maybe someday we'll get past this and be friends. That would be nice. But I don't think that's ever going to happen.

It's probably better this way.

CHAPTER ONE

April 1993

I sit at the kitchen table, hunched over the typewriter, staring at a blank page. Damn, I've been at this four hours and I still haven't written a single word. There is something so intimidating about a blank page. Some people think only black represents nothingness, but white does as well. The absence of everything, just in a gentler, less-frightening-looking way.

I feel my eyes mist up and I focus on staring at my fingers ready on the typewriter keys. *The absence of everything.* That's how my life has felt since I walked out on Alan. I don't even know how I've made it through the last three months of school. I feel blank inside like this stark, white typing paper, and numb, as if the world in all its bright spring color in Berkeley exists in total absence of everything.

But it doesn't. Life, and the world, is marching into the future around me, same as always. Time goes on whether my heart is broken or not, or I'm panicking inside because I've got decisions I have to make being forced upon me whether I want to make them or not.

I push away my thoughts and type my name in the upper right hand corner of the blank page. There. That's

"Visit home for a few weeks, see the family, and then back to Seattle."

"Things going good for you?"

"Really good," Neil says, and he sounds upbeat and very happy. For some reason that makes my emotional distress more jumbled. "We'll catch up when I come to Berkeley to grab my stuff."

"I'm looking forward to it."

"I miss you, Chrissie."

His voice is so soft I almost didn't hear him and I debate with myself whether to pretend that I didn't.

I let out a steadying breath. "I miss you, too."

It's the truth. Why does it hurt for me to admit it? Neil is always so calming to be with. My still-water pond. It would be nice to have him here for a while, especially now that every part of my life is a disaster.

"Maybe we can go out, Chrissie. Kick around. If you're not too busy with your finals."

Emotion makes it impossible for me to answer him.

"Just as friends. OK?" Neil continues. "I'm not going to push you for anything more."

With the tips of my fingers I press hard on the end of my nose to keep the tears back. "OK. I'd like that, Neil."

"However, if you want to push me for something more, I want you to know, that would be OK with me."

The way Neil says that makes me laugh even though I don't feel like laughing.

"Sorry. Bad joke, Chrissie. But I really do miss you."

For some reason, I feel a little better. My laughter intensifies, leaving my body in a more comfortable flow.

"It's OK. I like it when you're a conceited jerk, Neil."

I can hear what almost sounds like a sigh through the receiver.

"Good night, Chrissie. See ya in a week or so."

"See ya, Neil."

Click. I stare at the phone, and fight to rein in my scattered emotions. Blending with the chaos that's been consuming me for weeks is now a strangely good kind of feeling, an *I've talked to Neil* kind of thing.

I push the hair from my face, rise to my feet, and set the cordless back on the receiver. After I drop onto my chair at the table, without hesitation, I start to type again. I can finish this paper. I can make it through my last days at Berkeley. I've come this far, and I'm going to finish. I may have fucked up big time, I may be knee deep in mess, but I am not letting my mistakes take one more thing from me that I don't want to give.

I can make it through all the things I have to so I can put the last three months of my life behind me forever. I continue to strike the keys, only this time my fingers are pounding against them with the force of my determination. Two hours later I am done with my paper. I staple together the sheets, shove them into my folder and scoop up my stuff from the kitchen table.

I wander down the hallway to Rene's room and knock. "You can use the typewriter now," I say through the wood door.

I don't wait for Rene to answer. I go quickly to my room and close the door behind me. I sink down on the ground beside my carry tote and shove my folders into it.

I know he's still in love with me. He hasn't said it, but I know it. I can tell by how he speaks to me. I wonder what it will be like to see him again. We haven't been together for four months. I wonder if it will feel good to be with Neil or just grossly uncomfortable for us both in that *we used to be together but now we're not* kind of way. Neither of us knowing how to act around each other, or what to say or do. God, that would be awful. I hope it's not like that.

Maybe I should have stayed with Neil, even though we were only close, almost perfect, but not enough. It would have been better than where I am today; alone, frightened, and brokenhearted.

I set Neil's picture back on the nightstand and switch off the light. I curl into a tight ball, hugging his pillow. I loved Neil less than I love Alan and tonight I wish to God I had loved Neil more. Loving Neil less is what's gotten me into this, my latest nightmare. If I had loved Neil more than Alan, I would still be with him, and be the *Chrissie* I am when I'm with Neil.

A better girl than I am today. A girl I sort of started to like. Not the girl lying here alone and afraid, or the girl I will be tomorrow. The girl I always seem to become with Alan. My worst *me*.

CHAPTER TWO

A soft rap on the front door brings me awake and I open my eyes. I slowly sit up on the couch, pausing a moment to take a deep breath, and then rise to my feet praying that the change of position doesn't make me start throwing up again.

Damn, why does every little movement of my body make me vomit today?

Feeling that nagging warning in my stomach, I swallow hard and fumble to unlatch the door. I open it and somehow manage a smile. "Hey Mr. Next-Big-Thing, welcome back to Berkeley."

Neil's warm green eyes claim me like a gentle hold and he laughs, shaking his head at me. "Next big thing, huh?"

I stare up at him, wondering if he'll kiss me, and I can feel that my eyes are sparkly in that way they get when I'm really happy. Neil gazes down at me, neither of us move, and belatedly I note that it was my turn to talk and I didn't.

I flush and say quickly, "Yep, you are Mr. Next-Big-Thing. I saw you on TV a few days ago, and that's what the interviewer said before they cut away, that the buzz is you're definitely going to be the next big thing."

Neil gives me a pained, sweetly exasperated look. "That's Ernie Levine's publicity machine. You know how managers are. It's just bullshit, Chrissie. I'm more like *Mr.*

broke, tired, glad to be off the road, and really glad to see you kind of a thing."

I laugh. "I'm glad to see you, too."

Neil relaxes casually against the doorframe, his green eyes twinkling in an *oh-so-Neil* impish way. He touches my cheek and says, "That's probably because Rene is giving you shit about when my stuff will be out of here."

"She is not. She's going to be thrilled when she gets back from class and finds you here." I tilt my head toward the living room. "Come on in."

Neil ambles into the living room as I close the door and re-attach the chain. He stares at the disorderly room, and his laughter comes loudly this time as his chestnut waves dance on his shoulders when he shakes his head.

He turns to smile at me. "Rene is going to be thrilled? Is that why there are boxes stacked floor to ceiling against the wall?"

I scrunch up my nose, making a face at him. "Those aren't for *you*. We move out next month. You know Rene and her lists and her hyper-organized tendencies. She made us start packing a week ago."

"Yep, that definitely sounds like Rene."

Neil sinks down on the couch and I settle close beside him, legs bent beneath me, my bottom resting on my heels.

"So how long are you staying in Berkeley?" I ask.

"Don't worry. I'm leaving in the morning," Neil teases.

He says that in the familiar tone we banter with, but for some reason it makes cold needlelike pricks run the surface of my flesh. "You can stay as long as you want."

Neil's expression changes and the smile leaves his face. He gives me a sharp once-over and frowns. "Are you OK, Chrissie?"

I nod. "I'm great."

"Well, you don't sound great." His frown lowers and it looks like he's seeing me more thoroughly and not liking what he sees. Inwardly, I cringe, and then he says, "And you don't exactly look great either. In fact, you look really not good, Chrissie."

I flush and give him a pointed stare as I anxiously straighten my frumpy, oversized Cal sweats. "Thanks a lot. I've been throwing up all day. I think I ate something bad last night."

He crinkles his nose. "Sorry. I probably shouldn't have said that, right? Not one of my swifter comments."

"Definitely, not one of your swifter comments. I didn't feel like getting dressed today, but it's nothing. Food poisoning."

He grimaces and then asks, "Do you need me to get you anything? Do you want me to make you some tea? That might be good in your stomach if you have a touch of food poisoning."

I shake my head, though Neil's wanting to try to help me is unexpected and overwhelming. Even after everything that's happened between us, he is still kind and caring Neil. How stupid I was to worry even for a minute that he would make this terrible for me.

"I'm OK, Neil. You don't need to make me tea. It's not that bad right now. I'll be better by morning."

He looks relieved and smiles. "Do you want me to

come back tomorrow to get my junk? You look like you're feeling pretty lousy. If you need to rest, I'll get out of your way."

He doesn't wait for an answer and starts to rise from the couch. I grab his arm. "No. Don't leave. I'm fine. It's not that bad. I thought you were going to stay here tonight, hang out so we could catch up."

His eyes widen and he looks surprised.

"Really? I thought you wouldn't want me here so I planned on grabbing a couch at a friend's in the city."

For some reason I'm unexpectedly hurt by that. We parted in a good place. Still friends. Didn't we?

"Well, I thought you were going to grab my couch," I counter quietly. Something in how he looks at me makes me anxious and sad. I add, "I really want you to stay here, Neil."

I can feel him watching me in that way he has when he's trying to make sense of me. A few seconds pass. He sinks back down on the couch.

"Thanks, Chrissie. If you are sure you feel up to it and you're cool with it, I would really like to stay here tonight."

"Good."

Neil sighs, closes his eyes and lays his head back against the couch. "Fuck, it feels good to be here. It's quiet here. I can breathe. I'll probably be terrible company tonight. I feel like I could sleep for a week."

My anxiety fades and I take in more detail of him. He definitely looks exhausted. Neil is such a gorgeous guy— tanned skin; tall, long, lean-muscled body; messy sun-streaked shoulder-length chestnut waves framing a strongly featured face with brilliant green eyes—I often miss details, like the fatigue lines beneath his eyes and around his lips.

"You look really tired, Neil. Was it awful out on the road this time? You didn't make it sound awful whenever we talked on the phone. You always sounded really good. Happy. "

Neil chuckles in a tired, loose way. "Worst four months of my life, ever. Trust me, Chrissie, it was miserable every day. The larger the venues, the more shit. Everything went wrong that could go wrong from the first day out of Seattle. And the fucking band fought almost the entire time. The minute things start to go good everyone goes crazy."

His eyes open and I make a pout of sympathy.

He reaches out to lightly touch my cheek. "It feels good to be here with you. I missed you so much, Chrissie. I kept thinking about you. What I did wrong. I know I fucked up. Why you dumped me. I get it."

"You didn't fuck up," I say contritely, guilt flooding my digestive track. "And I didn't dump you. We are just going in different directions and it didn't seem fair to you or to me for us to try to stay together. It was the right thing for us both, Neil."

His eyes burn into me, and the heat increases across my cheeks.

"No, Chrissie. It wasn't the right thing for me. Not by a long shot. You always thought I was joking when I asked, but I really did think we'd end up married someday."

"I thought you weren't going to do this, Neil."

He runs a hand through his hair in an aggravated way. He looks impatient and annoyed with himself. "You're right. Sorry. I won't do it again."

I stare down at my fingers, digging into my knees. "I'm not someplace where I can even think about us. I just want to hang out. Keep everything light. I could really use that, Neil. OK?"

"I said I won't do it again," Neil counters, and I can't tell if he's irritated with me or himself.

This moment just got extremely awkward, to the point of feeling almost smothering, and I'm starting to feel really badly when the front door opens with enough force to hit the wall with a boom. We both turn to look as Rene pauses in the doorway, hands on hips encased in too-short Cal shorts, her pretty face awash with pretend irritation.

"When the hell did you get back?"

Neil laughs, pulling his body away from me to settle with more space between us on the couch.

"About twenty minutes ago. How ya doing, Rene?" he says, amused.

Rene closes the door and crosses the room in a flurry, dropping down on the couch on the vacant spot beside Neil. I watch her lean in to give him a sloppy kiss on the cheek, and their easy closeness gives me a sharp stab in my stomach. They hated each other when Neil first moved into the condo, and now they are more comfortable as friends than I am with Neil.

Rene's pretty face fills with a dazzling smile. "Really. How long are you staying?"

"A day. Maybe two…" He makes a face in my

direction. "…or I might just stay until Chrissie kicks me out."

They laugh, and I fight not to let show how much that jab hurt me. Neil was only teasing, messing with me like he likes to do, but I still feel badly about how I treated Neil. I miss him more than I ever thought I would, and every lighthearted taunt seems to hold an edge and bite today.

Rene taps Neil on the chest with an index finger. "I've got plans tonight, but your ass is mine in the morning. I don't have class until noon. Why don't we go out, grab some breakfast, kick around Berkeley for a while?"

"Deal," Neil says as Rene springs up from the couch. He follows her with his eyes until she disappears into her bedroom and then turns to give me a heavily exasperated look. "I will never get used to it when Rene is being nice."

"I told you she would be glad you're here."

His expression changes and something about his eyes makes me tense. "Are you glad I'm here or is this hard for you? I can't quite figure out what I'm feeling from you."

Crap. I take in a deep breath to steady myself. "I'm just going through some stuff, Neil. It's no big deal. It doesn't have anything to do with you. I'm really happy you're here. It's just me. OK?"

Neil leans into me, his eyes filled with concern. "Anything serious?"

I struggle to hold back my words. For some reason, the second Neil walked through my door the urge to blurt out my problems to him has been almost overpowering.

I shift my gaze away from his. "Nothing serious. I don't want to talk about it. I don't want ruin you being here with my lame drama."

He lifts my chin so I have no choice but to meet his eyes. "Lame drama, huh? Nope, not buying it, Chrissie. Tell me what's wrong. I can tell when something is pretty fucked in your world. I'll help however I can."

When I don't answer him, Neil shakes his head, exasperated, and pulls me against him.

"God, you're really frustrating at times. Most girls can't wait to tell you their shit, and it's like pulling teeth to get you to say anything about anything even when I ask you to."

I roll my eyes, and try to manage a *don't make a big deal of this* kind of face. "I'm just fucked up that way."

"You're not fucked up in any way." He lets out a long, sort of angry exhale of breath. "I hate that you say that about yourself. I'd like to kick the shit out of whoever said that to you and made you believe it."

I can feel my eyes start to burn with tears and I don't want them to. I don't know how he can think I'm not a fucked-up girl after how I treated him, but then Neil has never known me the way Alan does. It was Alan who said that to me—*you're a pretty fucked-up girl*—but he said it for a good reason, to try to help me, back when he used to care about me.

I bury my face against Neil's chest. Into his shirt, I whisper, "I've fucked up big this time. If I told you everything, you would hate me. And I don't want you to hate me. Not ever."

Neil's arms tighten around me. "Nothing would ever make me hate you, Chrissie. Whatever is going on it's going to be OK. Talk to me. I want to help. We'll figure out together how to fix whatever has got you so worried and afraid."

Worried and afraid? How can he see that? That's how I feel today. I just didn't know it showed.

I turn in his arms to put space between us. His eyes are lush green and unguarded, and something in his gaze nearly makes the words spill from me.

"I'm sorry I'm such a pain," I whisper.

"You're not a pain. We're friends. Friends help each other during the shitty times. I'm glad I'm here at a time when you need me. It's one of the things I did wrong. One of the things I regret. Not being here for you as much as you were always here for me. Tell me what's going on, Chrissie. There is no point pretending things are OK. Not with me, and I want to help. I owe you a lot."

Neil means that, but somehow it makes being with him so much harder.

"You owe me nothing, Neil."

His eyes burn into me. "Then let me be here for you because I love you."

"Neil, please..."

"I won't pretend I don't love you when I do."

He reaches up and wipes away a tear from my cheek with his finger, those callused fingers that touch with their own sweet type of velvet care.

"I love you and I'm going to keep loving you even if it's just only as your friend," Neil whispers.

The tears come harder; I can't stop them. The sensation of Neil's rough fingertips brushing my flesh floods my heart with the memory of Alan. When Neil touches me this way, it is Alan I think of and feel, and I don't want to.

Why can't life be as kind as Neil is? Why can't I love Neil the way I love Alan?

I don't pull back when Neil takes my body against him and wraps his arms around me. I know this is wrong, dishonest and unkind, but it feels so good to be held. Really, really good to let Neil hold me.

~~~

I wake in the wrap of Neil's limbs. My bedroom is filled with faint light, and it feels like early morning. I don't know if I should stir and let Neil see that I'm awake. His breath teasing my ear has the shallowness of sleep, but I'm not sure if he *is* asleep. I can't tell by the way his arms are holding me, and I can't see his face.

Somehow last night, we ended up in my bed together. I'm not exactly sure how it happened. It just happened.

I shift my head and my hair falls across my face. Unfocused moments slip by. I know why it happened; last night Neil was exactly what I need from a guy right now. For hours he just sat with me on the couch, holding me, caressing me, saying nothing, not probing into my fucked-up life with a whole bunch of questions, and by the time we went to bed everything about my predicament felt a little less scary.

It's no big deal. It was a fuck. Nothing more. No harm, no foul to either of us.

More snippets of the night come to me. The way Neil looked at me. The words he spoke. The expression in his

29

eyes as he made love to me.

Oh God, why did I let it happen? I try to console myself with the thought that it was just one of those things girls do when they are overwhelmed by their worries, when the guy they love will not love them, and there is a different guy, giving and wonderful, ready to be what you need him to be.

I cringe. That's a pitiful rationalization. Well, there's no point in panicking over this now, it's done, and I really don't need another thing to feel badly about.

I look down at Neil's arms and try to figure out a way to slip out of bed without waking him. I need some alone time to get my emotions back in check. I've got to get the right amount of distance between us again.

Jeez, I don't even know if that's possible after last night. The temptation to tell him everything was painfully strong, even before we went to bed together. But I can't do it. I can't dump my shit on him. It wouldn't be right, not on any level.

Having sex with Neil and waking with his flesh all around me reminds me that, as good as we are together, he is only *almost everything* I want and I won't ever be in that place emotionally with Neil where he is *everything* that I want. Neil deserves that from a girl—for him to be *everything* that she wants—because he's an amazing guy. I can't give him that, and it would be wrong not to make that clear to him today.

Why did I take him to bed and fuck him?

I feel Neil move behind me, and then he starts kissing against the back of my neck and I tense. I can tell by how he is kissing me, touching me, that he is definitely in the mood for a repeat of last night.

I untangle myself from his arms and turn onto my other side, facing him.

Neil's sleepy eyes hold me like an embrace as he reaches out to lightly touch my cheek. "Hi."

My heart leaps against my chest since he says a single word—*hi*—in a way that tells me this wasn't just a fuck for him.

"Hi," I reply, tense and awkward.

His darkly tanned, nicely muscled arm lifts and he pushes the hair from his face. "I don't think I have enough strength to get out of bed today. I think I'll just lie here while you're at class, thinking of you."

"I don't have class until four."

"Everything is going my way today." He smiles and starts to lightly brush his fingers along my arm. "Fuck, I've missed being with you, Chrissie. I wasn't sure until I saw you lying beside me that I didn't dream last night and that I wasn't really on the couch."

He leans in to kiss me and my entire body stiffens before I pull back. He eases up on an elbow, gaze rapidly sharpening, and I wonder what has slipped into my expression.

The languidness leaves him in a jolt I can feel. "What's wrong?"

"Nothing." I scooch away from him to recline against the headboard. "Look, Neil..."

His eyes start to flash, trapping my words inside me. "What do you mean *look, Neil*. Look, Neil, what?"

Oh crap. I try desperately not to look flustered. "Last night was good. Really good, but…" I halt for a minute, searching for the right words since it's not easy to tell a guy you've just gone to bed with that having sex with him doesn't mean you want him back. "…but I don't think we should change anything about us."

He pulls away and sits on the edge of the bed. "Not change anything, huh? Excuse me, but fucking you last night kind of seemed like we were changing things about us."

My face burns, and I lower my gaze. "I don't want us to get back together."

In a moment he is rising from the bed, jerking on his pants.

"Where are you going? What are you doing?"

"I'm just putting on my pants," Neil growls through gritted teeth, and I can feel he's pulsing with anger and other things. He turns to face me. "What was last night? Did you just want to get laid or was that some kind of pity fuck for the guy you dumped?"

I cringe. "Jeez, Neil, pity fuck? Really?"

The way he stares at me makes me regret those words. OK, they were lame, but I never think fast on my feet.

I stare up at him, wide-eyed and pleading. "I care about you. You care about me. It just happened. That was what last night was. Can't we just leave it at that?"

His jaw clenches and unclenches, and his expression changes several times. His gaze locks back on me, furious. "Are you seeing someone else? Involved with someone?"

Betraying color floods my cheeks and he lets out a

ragged sigh as he rakes a hand through his hair.

"Fuck, I know I didn't ask you that, but why didn't you tell me?"

"Because I'm not involved with anyone. I'm not even dating."

He searches my face. "Are you telling me the truth?"

I nod and he looks relieved. I can tell that a part of the relief is that he's wondered if I broke up with him for someone else.

He sinks down beside me on the bed.

"So do you want to start by telling me what's going on or maybe just explain why you fucked me if you're not interested in getting back together?"

I shake my head. "I don't want to do either."

Neil makes a small laugh. "That wasn't an option. I'm only letting you choose where we start."

I take a moment to try to organize my thoughts into a disclosure that won't amplify Neil's uncharacteristic, volatile state.

"I was involved with someone else for a while, but it's over."

That seems to calm Neil a little and he nods.

"Are you in love with him?" he asks, his voice rough.

I shrug. "We're over. It doesn't matter. I don't want to talk about that."

"How long were you together?"

Fuck, why that question? There is no way to answer it without telling Neil things I don't want to tell him. After several minutes carefully crafting the best way to answer, I'm trying to sputter out my response when all words take flight and I am knocked off my feet by what I am feeling.

I scramble from my bed and run into the bathroom to the toilet as the bile pushes upward from my stomach to mouth. I almost don't make it and I barely manage to lift the lid and lower to my knees before the violent spasms start.

Oh fuck, oh fuck. Oh fuck. Not again. It's getting more intense each day, as intense as it was yesterday. Over and over again I throw up, until I am sure there is nothing left in my stomach.

Struggling against my body, I pull myself up in front of the sink and splash water on my face. I breathe in and then out, hoping it's passed, but I can feel my stomach take over again and I slouch over counter.

I can't stop the spasms. There is too much rushing through me all at once.

I start to pant and splash more water on my face. Please, I don't want to be sick all day today. Not now. Crap, how is it possible for there to be so much acid-tasting yellow bile?

Just the smell of it makes the sickness intensify and I vomit again. Panting heavily, I reach out, grab a hand towel, turn on the water, and once it's soaked I hold it against my face.

I sit on the floor beside the toilet. Oh please, let that be the last. Breathe in. Breathe out. It goes away faster when I stop fighting it.

"When were you going to tell me that you're pregnant?"

Oh no!

I look over my shoulder to find Neil watching from the open doorway. He waits until my labored breathing subsides.

"When were you going to tell me?" he repeats, more harshly this time.

The anxious and alarmed arrangement of his features warns me that he thinks he's responsible for this. I say, "I hadn't planned on telling you."

Something changes in his eyes. It is something I've not seen before. The lines of his face harden in front of me inch by inch.

"Are you saying you weren't going to tell me because you wanted to take care of it privately or because it isn't mine?" he asks, his voice faint and emotion-roughened.

Crap, I didn't want to tell Neil this, not like this, not this way, not ever. The answer will hurt us both too much if I allow it voice in the room. The truth will also make abundantly clear the parts of *our* history Neil doesn't know and I'm suddenly desperate for him never to know that I was with Alan while we were together. Even though Neil and I understood we had an open arrangement, I don't want him to know this.

My silence intensifies his anger.

"Fuck, Chrissie, don't you think I deserve an answer to that?"

The knot in my throat is painful. "Yes, you deserve an answer. It's not yours, Neil, and yes, I planned to take care of it privately, and yes, I didn't want to ever tell you or anyone."

His lower teeth cut into his upper lip, and it looks like

he's struggling with something only loosely internally contained.

Finally, he sinks down on the floor beside me, close but not touching. Minutes pass in heavy silence and it feels like neither of us knows what to say to each other.

Neil looks at me. "Does the guy know?"

I shake my head and his eyes flash at me.

"Don't you think he deserves to know, Chrissie?"

"He doesn't care and he doesn't want to know. He ended it with me. We're over. He doesn't care about me. OK?"

My lips tighten as I struggle not to let surface how those words hurt me, but the words rip at my heart since they force me to remember that Alan doesn't love me anymore. I set my washcloth down on the tile and lean back against the tub.

"How pregnant are you?" he asks.

I shrug. "Three months, I think."

Neil looks alarmed again. "Think? Haven't you been to see a doctor? If you don't know how pregnant you are how do you know it's not mine?"

I give him a hard stare since I'm not explaining that one to him. "I just know, Neil. It's not yours."

He shakes his head again. "You need to see a doctor."

"I'm going to the clinic tomorrow. I'm doing it all in one appointment. Go to the clinic, get a pregnancy test, exam and termination all in the same day. According to Rene it's no big deal. She's had two abortions."

"Fuck. I could have gone my entire life without knowing that about Rene. Is that why she's so happy I'm here? She thinks I knocked you up? Is that why she wants to have breakfast with me this morning?"

I grimace at him saying *knocked-up* and murmur, "No, she doesn't know and I'd really appreciate it if you didn't tell her. You're the only person I've told. Jack doesn't even know."

His eyes fix on my face. "Are you going to tell me who you've been seeing?"

For a moment I debate whether I should and then I wonder why I am being stupid about this. Neil knows practically everything. Why not just be honest? Why not tell him everything? I already feel better, more calm inside, after the little I've already shared with Neil. Maybe if I tell him everything I'll stop feeling awful and alone and afraid.

"I've been seeing Alan Manzone for almost three years. The baby is his."

My voice is so quiet I can barely hear myself, but I know Neil heard me because his entire body tenses.

"Three years? You've been fucking Alan Manzone for three years?"

The way he repeats that makes me flinch.

"Is that why you broke up with me?" he asks.

His eyes burn into me and reluctantly I admit, "Yes."

"Fuck, Chrissie."

His legs come up in front of him, knees bent, and he plants his elbows on them, his face resting in his hands, his fingers tightly clenched in his hair.

"What else don't I know? You might as well tell me everything, Chrissie."

I'm so ashamed.

"You know everything, Neil. I've told you everything."

He takes a slow, deep inhale of breath and then looks up. "Do you want me to stay longer? Go with you? Be with you during the appointment?"

I can't believe Neil just offered to do that for me. "I was just going to go alone."

"No, Chrissie. And I won't let you. Fuck, I'm staying in Berkeley as long as you need me. I'll go with you."

"I can't let you do that."

"You don't have a choice. I'm staying. I'm doing it. You're not going alone," he announces stubbornly.

I drop my gaze to my clasped fingers resting in my lap. "Thanks." I'm barely able to choke out that word before I turn into him and start to cry. "I'm sorry. I'm sorry about everything. I don't know why you would offer to go with me or why you always are so nice to me."

His arm encircles me. "I love you. I'm pretty fucking pissed right now, but I love you."

Shame burns my digestive track. "You should hate me."

"Nope. Not doing it." His hand moves gently on my back and once I've calmed he turns to look at me. "You need to call him."

All my muscles tense. "No. I'm not calling Alan. Leave it alone, Neil. I've made my decision."

Neil springs to his feet and exits the bathroom. A few minutes later he returns. Damn, he's carrying the cordless phone.

He holds it out to me. "Call him now, Chrissie. I'll stay

here with you while you do it, but it's not right to make this decision without talking to him. I would fucking hate it if you did that to me."

"I'm not calling," I repeat more forcefully and Neil continues to stands frozen holding out the phone. "Damn it. I've already called him. I've left a hundred messages. Alan won't call me back. He ended it. I can't tell him because he won't talk to me."

We stare at each other and I can tell that Neil's deeply engrossed in thought in the *guy ready to manage and fix shit* way. He sinks back down on the floor in front of me and something in how he looks at me makes my heart accelerate nervously.

"Does he know about us, Chrissie? That you were living with me while seeing him? Is that why he ended it?"

Damn. "Yes."

Neil turns on the phone. "Give me his number."

Fuck no! "What?"

"I'm calling him."

My eyes go wide. "Like hell you are. He won't talk to you. Why would he talk to you when he won't talk to me?"

Neil looks both amused and grim. "Oh, he'll talk to me, Chrissie. He won't be able to stop himself. It's a guy thing. I'm not going to explain it. He'll take the call even if it's just to tell me to fuck off."

Neil waits expectantly. I can tell he's not going to back down on this. "Fine." Reluctantly I rattle off Alan's number and Neil dials the phone. He stands up and moves away from me.

Seconds tick by in agonizing slowness as no less than

a dozen pictures of how dreadful this might go flash in my head. Then he clicks off the phone and tosses it on the counter. Frowning, I watch as Neil moves across the room and crouches down in front of me.

He brushes my cheek with his thumb. "He's disconnected the line. Is that the only number you have for him?"

My heart drops to my knees. It's the only means I've ever had to reach Alan, through the private answering service, and he has disconnected it. I struggle not to fall apart.

I nod.

"I'm sorry, Chrissie. What a prick." The tic in his cheek starts to work. "Fuck it, Chrissie. You don't need Alan Manzone. I'll stay here and be with you."

CHAPTER THREE

I sit on my bed and stare at the door. Even knowing Neil is waiting for me in the living room doesn't make this any less frightening or awful.

I stare at the phone sitting on my nightstand. I could call Linda Rowan. She'd know how to reach Alan. Or I could just call Brian Craig, Alan's manager. I've known Brian my entire life. Crap, I could even call Jack. Jack knows how to reach everyone. I could probably still call Alan before I do this...

No, Chrissie, no. Neil is wrong. It doesn't matter. Alan is just going to tell you to have the abortion, anyway.

I stare down at the stupid, fuzzy socks I'm wearing. I remember something about Rene saying her feet got cold during the procedure—so like Rene to complain about her feet and talk about absolutely nothing useful to help me mentally prepare for what getting an abortion will be like. I could definitely use some insight since she's the only girl I've ever known who has admitted to having an abortion— but gosh the socks look stupid peeking from between my tennis shoes and my sweatpants.

A knock on the door makes me jump and Neil lumbers in.

"You ready to go?" he asks quietly.

The tone of Neil's voice makes my heart ache.

41

Somehow I've dragged him into my abyss and between us there is a sense of shared misery. But it's not. It's not Neil's baby, this isn't Neil's problem, and this isn't Neil's misery. It's mine.

I nod, but my legs refuse my command and I continue to sit there, staring blankly at the phone.

Neil sinks down on the bed beside me. "Are you sure you want to do this?"

Oh crap, I don't want to rehash my decision again. For some reason, Neil doesn't want me to do this. He hasn't said it, but I can tell. He keeps asking me if I'm sure, as if any woman is really one-hundred percent sure about something like this.

My body tenses as he runs a hand through his tousled hair. It looks like he's been running his fingers through his hair all day trying to work through something he's been thinking about.

"I don't get you, Chrissie. You don't want to do this. I can tell. You don't have to if you don't want to. There are other choices."

Oh, why did he have to say it? I fight back another wave of tears.

"It's the right decision. I have to do it, Neil."

His mouth tightens and he shakes his head. "No, you don't." He sighs heavily. "Christ, we can get married. We can raise the baby if you want to. You can tell everyone it's mine. No one ever has to know it isn't ours."

My already roiling emotions start to twirl faster.

"God, Neil, I don't need to get married so I don't have to do this. I have plenty of money. Jack wouldn't think anything of me having a baby and not being married. That's not why I'm doing this."

His jaw stiffens. "Then can you explain to me why you are doing something you obviously don't want to?"

I stare down at my stupid, fuzzy socks. Trying to explain all this to Neil would be the worst kind of betrayal to Alan, and yet I don't think I can make Neil understand without telling him one of Alan's secrets. And he did just offered to marry me—he's such a good guy—Neil deserves the truth.

"Only a handful of people know this, Neil, but Alan had a little girl named Molly."

Neil's face shoots up, his eyes filled with confusion and surprise. "Molly?" He pauses, as if trying to make sense of something, and then his expression changes into disbelief. "You mean the song *Molly* is about his daughter not Ecstasy? It's not a song about drugs?"

"*Death takes us all. I want it. I want you*," I quote sadly. "That's not about addiction, Neil. It's about how Alan didn't want to live after his daughter died."

"Fuck." He stares at me. "What happened to her?"

No matter how I try to keep it away, that day in the barn when Alan told me about Molly rises vividly in my head. The way Alan looked. The expression in his eyes. I'm positive he wasn't even aware of what he let surface on his face that day as he calmly told me about Molly's death. But I can't forget it. It's haunted my every minute since I realized I was pregnant.

"She got sick and she died," I say simply. "It was a fucked-up situation. I can't have the baby and lie to him.

That would be unfair to him. Especially with what I know about Alan's history. And it would be unfair to you and to the child if I lied and said you were the father. I can't do that. Not to you and not to him."

Neil makes an obstinate shake of his head, and I can see that he thinks I'm wrong to care about Alan's feelings in all this.

"But what do *you* want to do, Chrissie? You've given me a hundred reasons why this is what you should do, but you haven't said a word about what you want."

"I don't know what I want."

"Then you shouldn't do this," Neil advises firmly.

I roll forward onto my feet and stand. "I don't want to talk about it anymore."

I head toward the door, stop and look back at Neil. Reluctantly, he stands and follows me out of the condo.

We are both quiet as we drive to the clinic. My insides are tight, knotted bands that feel like lead somehow jumping anxiously within me. Worse than anything I've ever felt.

I stare out the window, fighting not to look at Neil. Jeez, I can't believe he offered to marry me. Why would he do that? My exhaustion-dulled wits can't find the energy to try to figure that one out.

Neil finds a parking spot across the street from the building and I wait in my seat as he pulls the key from the ignition, climbs from the driver's side, and trots around the Volvo to get my door.

He takes my hand and I stare down at his fingers laced through mine as we slowly work our way through traffic to the other side of the street.

I don't know what I would do if Neil wasn't with me. It's so much harder than I imagined it would be. I don't know how Rene went through this twice, alone. She didn't tell me about either until after the procedure was done, and it hurt, really hurt, at the time that she didn't. I sort of get it now. I haven't told her about me.

Sadness moves across my jittery limbs. God, I don't think I could get through this if Neil wasn't willing to be here with me. I peek at him from the corner of my eye and my fingers tighten around his. I need Neil right now more than I have ever needed anyone. More than I've ever needed Alan. Or Jack. Or Rene.

As if he senses me watching him, Neil looks down at me. "It will be OK, Chrissie. I'll stay with you through it all. It's going to be OK."

I'm not sure which one of us he's trying to convince. Neil sounds worried and kind of despondent.

As we pass by the high stucco wall into the clinic parking lot, I wonder if that's how we look to people today: worried and despondent. Like a couple going through shit. Only this isn't our shit. It's mine and Alan's. Even if Alan doesn't know it and Neil has only stepped in as some kind of nice guy surrogate.

He drops my hand and pulls back the glass door into the waiting room. I step in, pausing to let my eyes adjust to the change of light, and my gaze does a quick scan of the room. Jeez, it's crowded, nearly every vinyl-covered metal chair is occupied, and there are a half a dozen girls working beyond the bulletproof safety glass. Bulletproof glass?

45

God, what am I doing here?

Neil's hand moves to my back, guiding me forward toward the counter. "You need to check in there," he says quietly.

I nod, wondering why Neil seems to know more about what I'm supposed to do than I do. Maybe he's been through this before. There is a lot about Neil's history with his fucked-up ex-girlfriend that I still don't know, but I've pretty much assumed that the parts he hasn't shared with me were really intense and grim.

I take from the check-in nurse the clipboard shoved at me beneath the safety glass separating us.

"Fill that out. Answer all the questions, front and back, and bring it back when you're done."

Her tone of voice is abrupt, matter-of-fact and efficient in this moment that is anything but matter-of-fact to me.

"There are two chairs over there," Neil says, and I follow him to the far side of the room and sink down beside him.

I stare down at the form, willing myself not to look back up at the other people here. Christ, it's bad enough knowing why I'm here. I sure as hell don't like knowing why *they're* here. Of course, everyone is not here for an…

I tap my pen against the clipboard. Jesus Christ, what kind of questions are these? They make me feel like a slut just reading them…*do you have safe sex?…what kind of birth control are you on?…how many sexual partners have you had?…how often do you have sex?…have you ever had an STD?*

Why do they want to know all this? I don't even want

to know this about myself. Cringing, I drag my eyes back up to the first line, not finding that one any easier to answer than the rest of the questions. *Name?*

I freeze, unable to write. Damn, I hadn't thought about that, putting my name on this form. A permanent record of the biggest Chrissie low point in my life. The pen hovers above the sheet and it feels like this becomes real, a forever part of me, the minute I put my name there.

Neil stares down at the clipboard, frowns, and leans into me. "What's wrong?"

I move my face close to his ear and whisper, "I don't want to tell them my name."

Neil exhales a breath, ragged and impatient. "Chrissie, medical records are private. No one can access them. It's no big deal. No one will ever find out about this unless you tell them. Fill out the form."

My lids go wide. "How do you know people can't find out about this? How do you know that?"

"I just do." He looks aggravated, and he runs a hand through his hair again. He waits for me to fill out the form, and when I don't, he exclaims, "Fine. Write 'Chrissie Stanton.' That way it won't matter if anyone ever sees it."

There's a touch of bite in his voice and it leaves me feeling like I've just had the wind knocked out of me and really shitty about having Neil holding my hand through this.

"I can't do that."

"Yes you can. I told you to. It doesn't matter. It's no big deal. Do it."

"It wouldn't be right."

Neil looks away, his jaw clenching slightly. "None of this is right, Chrissie. Just do it."

I flush. I'm not sure what just made him angry, but my emotions are too much of a jumbled mess for me to ask and I don't think I want to know.

I stare down and start to write. I can feel Neil watching me and I wonder if he's reading my answers… *sexual partners: two*…have there really only been two? And why does that feel like a lie when it's the truth? Oh crap, it is a lie. I forgot my one-night stand the August before I started seeing Neil. Does it matter that I lied?

The knots in my stomach grow tauter and I start to heavily check off boxes: no, no, no, no, no. I check *no* even on the questions I don't understand because there are a couple I *don't* understand. How lame is that? Twenty-two years old and not even able to understand all the questions on a women's health medical questionnaire. Where do people learn this stuff?

After I've been still for a while, Neil holds out his hand. "You done?"

I nod, and he takes the clipboard from me. I watch him amble to the counter and shove it under the partition.

He sits back down beside me, his body close but not touching, and I don't like the feel of his stoic remoteness. My leg starts to jiggle in that way it does when I'm trying to keep myself from freaking out. The wait is unbearable. I just want this over with…

"Miss Stanton?"

I look up to see a nurse standing in an open doorway, staring down at a clipboard. Neil goes to his feet.

He holds out his hand to me. "Chrissie. Come on."

My legs are weak and shaky, but somehow they manage to hold my weight. As I cross the room, Neil moves with me. I hadn't realized he was planning to go in with me. I thought he'd just wait in the lobby.

I stop at the door. "Neil, you don't have to do this."

His lips tighten and he nods, but he doesn't release my hand. He continues with me into the examination room.

Neil drops down in a chair on the far side of the room as the nurse makes a sharp tug to spread new sterile paper on the exam bed. She shoves a cup at me, orders me to pee in it, then to undress and put on a gown.

The door closes and I stare at Neil. I'm uncomfortable about having him here, even though he's seen me naked hundreds of times. Why is it different here? I organize the gown on the table so I can pull it on fast, and do a quick check at Neil—his eyes are unwaveringly staring out the window. I jerk off my sweatshirt, pull the gown in place, and then remove my other garments.

I hurry into the adjoining bathroom, pee in the darn cup, pass it through the tiny door in the wall to be tested by the technician, and rush back into the exam room to sit on the edge of the bed. I settle with a stirrup on either side of me, my heels banging into the metal over and over again. Feet hitting metal is the only sound in the room. Boom. Boom. Boom.

A fast knock on the door and the doctor walks in.

She gives me a brief smile. "Miss Stanton, I'm Doctor Leary. You are pregnant. Your last period was December 28th. Is that correct?" She looks at me. I nod and her eyes drop back to my chart. "I noticed you are requesting abortion services. I'll have to perform an exam today and then we can discuss your options."

She smiles in Neil's direction as if noticing him for the first time. "I see you brought your partner. It is always best to make these decision as a couple."

Neil's gaze shifts and he says nothing, but the tic starts twitching in his cheek again.

She pats my thigh. "Put your feet up in the stirrups and scooch down, dear."

Dr. Leary has an infinitely soothing manner, but I feel like I'm going to jump out of my skin anyway. I cover my face with my forearms since this is so embarrassing.

I cringe, wait and tightly close my eyes. God, I hate this...I feel her rummaging around down there... cold metal... pushes on my abdomen...fuck, a finger *there*...and a click of metal as something slips out of me. By the time she's done, every muscle in my body hurts from tension.

My gown is jerked down over my pelvis again. A tap on my thigh. "You can sit up now, Miss Stanton."

With a stethoscope she listens to my breathing, does a fast take of my pulse, then returns to her short spinning stool and wheels across to the desk.

Anxiously, I watch as she starts rotating that weird little menstrual calculator thingy they have. She quickly jots notes on my chart, and then whirls around to face me, shoving a stack of pamphlets at me.

"We can't do an abortion for you here, Miss Stanton. We're going to refer you to outpatient at the hospital. You should read those. I have an opening tomorrow morning.

I can do the procedure then. Is that what you want? Or would you rather speak with our counselors before you and your partner decide?"

She stares at me expectantly. *Why the hospital?*

"I don't understand. I thought I could take care of it today."

"You're in your second trimester. A different procedure. Perfectly safe. But we don't do D & E abortions here. The pamphlets will explain everything. I suggest you read them thoroughly. It will explain the entire procedure."

I can't catch hold of what she's just said…what does that mean?

I feel the displacement of air around me, and Neil's voice pulls me from my stupor. "How pregnant is my girlfriend?"

He's hovering near the table, alarmed and anxious.

"Close to fourteen weeks," Dr. Leary replies calmly.

Fourteen weeks? I frown up at him and I can tell we are both counting backward, trying to figure out when fourteen weeks ago was. Neil calculates conception faster. His posture changes, his jaw stiffening again. The math confirms that the baby isn't his.

He sinks back into his chair and I rapidly study his fast-changing expression. I'm not sure what I'm seeing flashing in his eyes. Relief or sadness…strange, but I can't tell.

"Chrissie is just beyond the cut-off for what we do here at the clinic," Dr. Leary says to Neil. She fixes her eyes back on me. "I promise you, it doesn't make the procedure less safe. It's just a different procedure."

I swallow down the lump in my throat. "Schedule it, please."

By the time I leave the clinic, I feel like someone has just dropped an anvil on me. I've got something inserted in my vagina to dilate me, a list of pre-op instructions, and Neil is carrying admission forms for the hospital in the morning.

Outside the clinic, I stop. I bend over, breathing in and out, trying not to vomit and trying not to cry.

"You don't have to do this, Chrissie," Neil says softly.

He looks sad. Achingly sad. Shit, and it's not even his baby. "I know. But I'm going to do this."

Neil folds me into his chest and holds me tightly up against him. He's talking but I can't catch the words and I don't want to. I don't want to think. Not one more thought until after this is through.

I bury my face against his chest to block out the world from my vision. Oh fuck, I've even screwed up getting an abortion.

~ ~ ~

I clutch the pillow tightly against my stomach, willing myself not to wake up. I don't really remember today clearly and I'm afraid that if I open my eyes I will suddenly remember everything *too* clearly. It's all just fragments and disconnected pictures and I want it to stay that way forever.

The snippets start to flash in my memory. The smell of the hospital. Jeez, why do they smell so bad? How cold and stark the room was. I don't know what I expected the hospital room to look like, I hadn't been in one before, but I hated how old and colorless it all was. Then something being injected into my IV and a mask with the gas coming over my face. Counting—yes, I remember counting, as Neil held my hand and spoke quietly to me. Then nothing. Merciful blackness.

The next clear moment is waking, and seeing Neil sitting in a chair near the bed, looking like a guy who's been run over by a truck. Then relief on his face, after noticing I was awake, mixing with a lot of other things that I didn't want to try to understand. Then the drive home and having Neil put me into my own bed. The feel of him sitting beside me, his long, tanned fingers lightly stroking my emotion-drained body. Then sleep. The absence of everything.

I lift up my head. Neil is sitting on the floor beside the bed, back against my nightstand, elbows on knees, face in hands.

"How long have you been sitting there?"

Neil looks up and his eyes slowly focus. "I don't know. Since you fell asleep." He turns to look at the clock on the stand behind him. "Four hours."

I manage to get myself into a sitting position. "You've just been watching me sleep for four hours?"

He shrugs. "Not watching you sleep. Thinking."

My eyes widen in surprise.

"Things were fucking intense today," he says and I cringe. I don't want to talk about today.

"I don't know how I'm ever going to repay you for all you did, Neil. I still can't believe you went with me. You're the best friend I've ever had."

His eyes lock on me, flashing and angry. "Fuck you,

Chrissie."

My cheeks flood with a burn and I watch as he rises and then reaches for my antibiotic on the table.

He pops off the cap. "You need to take one of these." He holds it out for me and grabs a bottle of water. He waits until I take my pill. "Are you in pain? The doctor said you could have ibuprofen if you need it. "

I shake my head and follow him with my eyes as he moves around the bed. He settles on the vacant spot beside me. A ragged, shuddering breath leaves his body.

"I hated watching you go through this today," he whispers and slowly pulls me close against him. "I fucking love you and you don't get it. I didn't stay to be here with you because I'm some fucking moronic nice-guy. I would have been out the door if it had been any girl but you. I stayed because I love you, Chrissie. And you don't even fucking get it."

The look in his eyes rends my heart. The room is so heavy with grimness. I want to pull away from Neil. I want to melt into him. I want not to hurt. I want him not to hurt. I want us to be all right.

"I'm sorry," he sighs. "You don't need more shit from me. Not now. Not today. I'm sorry."

The anguished look on Neil's face makes my numbness fade and too many things come tumbling back all at once.

How close to being perfect Neil and I are together. How much I love Alan. All the mistakes I've made, including this giant one from today—*and yes, it was a mistake and I didn't want to do it and I did it anyway*. How lost and alone

I feel. How afraid I am of the future since I don't really seem to be going anywhere. In a month I'm out of college. Shouldn't I be going somewhere? How unfair it is that I'm holding on to Neil for dear life, and how cruel my stupid *best friend* comment was.

Too much all at once. I lie against Neil, my emotion-drained limbs without sensation, and I don't know what to say. I brush at the tears dripping from my nose. "I'm sorry, Neil."

For some reason, my apology kicks up whatever is going on inside Neil. His jaw tightens more.

"I don't have to be in Seattle until the beginning of June. I'm staying in Berkeley until then," he says.

"No. I'm not letting you do that. I can't let you do that. I'm fine."

His green eyes look even more determined. "I'm staying."

The words clog in my throat, and my thoughts jumble in my head. I shouldn't let him stay in Berkeley, and I don't know how to tell him to go. I'm not even sure if I want to.

He closes his eyes and exhales. "It's done. Behind us. I'm not going anywhere. Don't tell me to. I won't listen. I wouldn't be able to work if I left before you were OK, Chrissie." A myriad of emotions crosses his face. "But I don't want to talk, not ever, about today. And don't you ever mention Alan Manzone to me again. Trust me, Chrissie. You don't want to fucking do that."

He looks at me and what's in his gaze is potent and leveling, so I just nod. I ease down until I'm tucked against his body and I wrap my arms around him. For the first time ever, it feels as if Neil needs to be held by me and something about that prompts me not to argue with him about staying in Berkeley.

I don't know why I do it. The voice inside my head is screaming at me not to. It's probably wrong. Another mistake. Everything inside me is in parts, dangling, and unclear. Nothing about my life makes sense to me anymore. But I do know I shouldn't let Neil stay and I sure as hell shouldn't let him love me.

Somehow, I've become my worst *me* with *him*.

CHAPTER FOUR

I exit the dimly lit lecture hall into the bright May sunlight to find Neil standing beneath the shade of a giant oak, calmly smoking.

I make my way down the steps and cross the grass to him. Neil stomps out his cigarette.

"How'd you do?" he asks.

"I finished the exam. Beyond that, no promises."

I make a silly face to maintain my surface expression of *no big deal* when I am anything but casual over having completed my last exam.

Neil drops a light kiss on my nose. "So how does it feel, Miss Parker"—his voice changes into a lousy Professor Lambert imitation—"to soon be graduating The University California Berkeley."

I shove my face upward into his. "The grades haven't posted yet, Professor Lambert. I could still disappoint you. And I could still fuck this one up."

Neil chuckles, his lips touching mine in a fast kiss. "Pessimist," he chides, then he takes a step back, grabbing my hand, as we walk off-campus in what I hope will be my last moments ever at The University California Berkeley.

A month ago I wouldn't have thought today would be possible. My world was crashing around me, and finishing school was something I believed wouldn't happen. But I've made it through my last final—I stare up at Neil as he loosely drapes an arm around my shoulder...*thanks to Neil*—and I am done, and will have successfully graduated from Cal in four years, in spite of the mess of my life I've made here.

"We're definitely going to have to work on getting you a more positive attitude, Chrissie." Neil's green eyes start to gleam. "It's a big deal that you finished school. I'm so proud of you. You should be proud. Especially with everything..." He breaks off, looking uncomfortable with himself, and then says, "It's a big deal to graduate Cal."

A slightly grim wash tempers the lines of his handsome features, and my insides shudder. Neil is thinking about April. I don't want to think about that day and I've definitely got bigger problems to deal with. Graduation means change, and I still don't know where I'm going after Berkeley.

"Are you hungry?" Neil asks.

"Sure, I could eat."

We cut across the grass and enter the food court area. Neil pulls back the door to our hippie vegan restaurant.

I stop. "Why do you always bring me here? Why don't we go get burgers or something? I've always wondered why we eat here since neither of us are vegan or vegetarian."

Neil's smile is boyish and sweet. "We leave Berkeley tomorrow and I want to eat here, Chrissie. It's where we had our first date four years ago."

Distress overwhelms me, and I fight to maintain my outward composure.

"I thought you said that wasn't a date."

Neil's eyes lock on mine. "It was to me."

I step rapidly ahead of him into the restaurant. My heart clenches even as the blood pumps faster through my veins. The way Neil looks at me is an overwhelming thing. I can see it in his eyes; he is in love me and he thinks we're going to be together again. But I'm not sure if I'm ready to try to make a go of it with Neil a second time, even though we've been really good together this past month. I probably shouldn't have let him move back into the bedroom. Oh well, it's not like we have sex, but even without the sex, things with Neil are as confusing as ever.

I just seem to be making more mess in my life. We live together, but we are *not* together. Same old, same old. That's our status and somehow it just sort of happened on its own. Easy and wrong. I never seem to be able to do the right thing with Neil. In my head I know what the right thing is. My mouth and my body refuse to cooperate.

Are we together again? It feels like we are, but I'm not sure. How can a girl not be sure about something like this?

Maybe it's just because he's such an incredible guy and it's impossible not to like him. And a girl would have to be dead not to get turned on by Neil.

I give him a fast once-over out of the corner of my eye, smiling at the way his gaze rapidly searches the case trying to find something he's willing to eat here. He is gorgeous in every way, inside and out.

I plant my arms on the top of the display case and try to decide what to order. Slim pickings. Not even sandwiches. There's hardly any food here.

"Do you know what you want, Chrissie?"

I shake my head. Nothing looks good.

Neil frowns at the sparse assortment and says, "Well, this might be a bust for our last date in Berkeley. There's not much of a selection today."

"We're shutting down early this afternoon," the waitress answers from her side of the counter. "Not much business with finals and students moving off campus this week."

"Yep, campus is pretty dead," Neil replies, continuing to stare into the cabinet. "OK, Chrissie, they've got vegan carrot cake, vegan brownie, and vegan…strudel?"

I roll my eyes. "That's apple popover not strudel."

He shakes his head. "Really? It doesn't look like it."

"She's right," the waitress announces.

"I was kind of in the mood for strudel." Neil rubs his chin with his long fingers. "Are you sure?"

The waitress laughs. "I'm sure."

"Crap." He frowns. "Carrot cake or brownie, Chrissie? I'm not really hot on either."

"Whatever you want is fine. Or we could just go somewhere else, Neil."

Neil looks up. "Not a chance. We're having our last coffee together in Berkeley here."

He leans in, lightly kisses me, and is smiling as he turns back to the clerk waiting for our order. The waitress's eyes widen and her expression changes, sparkly and astonished.

"I know you," she says in a stunned way.

Neil shrugs, dropping his gaze back toward the case. "You should. We've been coming in here four years. I think we want the carrot cake."

"No," she corrects with more enthusiasm. "I saw you at Sleep Train. You're that singer from Arctic Hole, aren't you? You're him. "

I bite my lower lip to keep from laughing. *Him*. There is something about the way she says that and Neil's reaction to it that is so amusing.

Then I note that Neil is not amused. He doesn't look up at the waitress and he gives every appearance of a guy who wants to drop through the floor.

The clerk frowns and I realize I am frowning too since calm, smiling Neil is anything but calm and smiling. He's pulsing with uneasiness.

The girl plants her crossed arms on the counter and stares down at Neil. "What? Don't you like being recognized? If you don't want to be famous why are you in a band?"

Neil shakes his head. "It's about the music. Nothing else. Recognize me. Don't recognize me. I don't really care, except today I'm kind of annoyed. I just want to have some coffee with my girlfriend."

She grabs some pastry tissue, and instead of being offended by Neil's comment, she nods approvingly. "That's why you're so cool. You don't give a shit about the hype. Your music is genius. Not like the shit they play on the radio."

"Thanks," Neil says, but his voice is clipped, strained.

"Are you in Berkeley for a concert or something? I'd really love to see you live again."

"Nope, just visiting home for a while," he says, and abruptly changes the conversation and orders two coffees and a slice of cake.

The girl sets our drinks on the counter. "I can't believe you live in Berkeley. My roommate is going to flip when I tell her you came in here today."

Neil reaches for his wallet, and the waitress waves him off when he goes to pay. After thanking her, Neil grabs our coffees while I take our cake and move quickly ahead of him to open the door.

We settle at a table on the patio and I rip open my packets of raw sugar. "It was kind of sweet that that girl recognized you and didn't make you pay. Why did you get all jumpy?"

Neil leans back in his chair. "I don't know. It makes me uncomfortable. I guess I'm not used to it yet. It's just weird, you know? Perfect strangers thinking they know you. People you don't know buying you shit. It's weird."

I stir my coffee. "How long has this been happening? People recognizing you on the street?"

Neil shrugs. "It doesn't happen very often. Four months maybe. Since the last album released."

"You have a song on the charts. It was bound to start happening. There are worst things than being recognized, Neil. It means people are starting to notice the music. It's a good thing."

"It's bullshit, Chrissie. Bullshit. You know that. Who gives a fuck if anyone knows who I am?"

"I do." I make a sweet pout across the table. "You've worked hard. I'm proud of *you*. And you better get used to it because the new album is amazing." I shake my head, stirring my coffee. "Boy, you looked awkward in there." I laugh. "But you are very cute when you are being shy and humble. Not at all like the conceited jerk I live with."

I'm smiling when I look back up at Neil, but my face falls and my heart stills. Why is he angry with me?

"Is that what we're doing? Living together? When I called you my girlfriend back there you got all tense and shit. And you still haven't told me if you're coming to Seattle with me."

My scalp prickles as heat covers my flesh. Oh shit, what made me say that last part—*jerk I live with*? Not smart, Chrissie. Not smart.

I focus on my fork as I cut into the slice of cake we're sharing. "I don't know what we're doing, Neil. I'm not there yet. And I can't think about Seattle yet."

Neil leans back in his chair, his eyes intense. "I leave tomorrow. You had better figure out what you want soon, Chrissie."

Oh God. How did we get from having coffee together to talking about *us* again? I'm not even close to having a reasonable response to that, but the thought of Neil leaving in the morning makes my insides collapse.

Tilting back his head, Neil finishes his coffee in one long swallow, then collects the trash from our table and throws it away.

He stands beside the table, and I don't rise.

Finally, he says, "We're good together, Chrissie. That should tell you everything you need to know about us. What more do you need from a guy?"

There's an edge of hurt to Neil's voice that cuts at my heart, and I stare down at my coffee.

"I don't know."

He crouches down until he's at eye level with me. "I love you. What more do you need to know?"

I look away, fixing my vision on a vacant space across the food court. I grow more rattled each time he says *I love you* to me and more panicked each time I think about him leaving. What a stupid contradiction of reactions. They make no sense. No wonder I can't figure out what I'm supposed to do about Neil and me.

He cups my face with his palms. "We're doing good, Chrissie. Don't fuck us up a second time over Alan Manzone. We're perfect together. You know it. Just let me love you."

His voice is breathy. Ragged. Intense.

The last thing I was prepared for was a plea from Neil not to end us delivered in front of our stupid, hippie vegan restaurant. Is that why he brought me here? To push me for a decision away from the condo, away from Rene?

I suddenly feel frazzled and disoriented. "Please, can we not do this now?"

He holds me against him, his body molding into me, his arms holding me close. It feels so good against his body. It would be easy to go with the flow and just be with Neil.

He whispers, "He will never need you the way I need you. He will never want you as I want you. He will never love you the way I love you. I don't care if you are in love with Alan. I'm in love with you. Don't go to Santa Barbara. Come to Seattle with me."

I feel his lips move along the side of my neck in light kisses and touches, and my body begins to ease into the contact, wanting it, even though I order myself not to.

It is too soon to think about trying again with Neil. Too soon to think about my life. Too soon to think about anything. April wasn't that long ago. I'm not over it yet, and there are too many parts of me trapped in the past, mourning and hurting.

"It's all happening too fast, Neil. I can't think. I need time."

"Fast? We've been together four years. Come to Seattle with me. Who says we've got to figure out everything today? Say fuck it to everything. Leave Berkeley and all the shit behind. I think it would be good for you to go out on the road with me for a while. You don't have to stay on tour with me. You can leave if it's not good. Just come with me. You don't have to decide anything. I just want you with me."

His impatience presses in on my already overly raw nerves. "I can't give you an answer. Not today."

Neil runs a hand through his hair, angry. "Fuck, Chrissie, I can't stay any longer and I don't want to leave without you. What are you going to do? Go back to Santa Barbara and wait around for some asshole who won't ever call you? Is that your plan?"

The earth falls away beneath me. *That was mean, Neil. So mean.*

"I don't have a plan," I say into Neil's acutely waiting silence.

After what seems like a monumental amount of time, he says, "You're coming to Seattle with me, Chrissie. You won't let me walk out that door without you. You just don't know it yet."

I frown, trying to process his words. He sounds so certain. But even I don't know yet what I'm going to do at that moment when life forces me to choose right or left; the moment we either part again or stay together.

"Don't force me to make decisions about us. I'm not there yet."

He brushes my tense cheek with his thumb. "Then don't make a decision. Don't make a plan. Don't think. Just come to Seattle with me, Chrissie."

He says it as if it's the easiest thing in the world. Don't think. Just come. Is life really that simple for Neil?

He straightens up and holds out his hand to me. "Come on. We should get home. You've still got packing to do."

I'm silent as we walk back to the condo. If Neil is irritated with me, it doesn't show. In fact he looks sort of happy. He's smiling, though there is nothing about our discussion that should make Neil smile. But then he rarely gets angry and his temper always cools fast. He can't stay angry. He's uncomfortable being hurtful. And even though he sometimes gives me a nudge here and there, he doesn't push hard, not like Alan. Neil is the exact opposite of Alan.

It's a short walk to the complex. In only a few minutes we're in the elevator, Neil leaning against one mirrored wall and me against another.

I slant a look at him and some of my anxiousness wanes. He doesn't seem the slightest bit distressed and doesn't have the look of someone who intends any more weighty discussions today. He's just sort of there, letting me be.

The doors open and he has my hand again. Outside our door, he fishes in his pocket, and removes his key chain. I can feel my eyes widen as I watch him unlock the door. I hadn't noticed before now that Neil still had a key to my place, that I had forgotten to ask for it back when we broke up in December. Strange, but I didn't even think of taking back my key.

Inside the condo I freeze. The condo looks like it's been hit by a hurricane. We were only gone for four hours and it doesn't even look like home anymore. Tall moving boxes sealed with black—or *pink?*—tape make it nearly impossible to get across the living room. In giant letters names have been written on the cardboard. *Rene. Rene. Rene. Chrissie...* shit, she started packing my things, too.

I rapidly notice the rest of the room. The pictures are gone from the walls. The books from the shelves. The CDs and albums. All the stupid clutter Rene and I accumulated in four years here, gone.

The music is blasting, and my anxious gaze floats through the room, but I don't see Rene. How the heck did she do this in four hours? Jeez, I knew we had to finish packing today, but I didn't expect it look like this and I definitely didn't expect it to plunge my emotions into free-fall again.

My brain can't keep up with what's happening here. Neil makes a low whistle, pulling me from my stupor. "Someone is eager to get out of Berkeley," he says, amused and jeering. He looks at some boxes, pausing at one with his name written on it. "She might have let us pack up our own shit, don't you think?"

"Rene? Are you here?" I call out.

The music switches off and Rene comes bouncing from the kitchen. She's dressed in short-short cutoff overalls and a tube top, her black hair pushed back from her face in a pink bandana. Perspiration speckles her rich olive skin.

She smiles, brushing at a wayward curl with a forearm. "I've packed all the kitchen things and marked them to go to LA for my new apartment, like you said I could." She stares down at something in her hand. "Do you want this or can I keep it?"

I maneuver through the boxes to see what she's looking at. It's a picture of the three of us our first Christmas after Neil moved in.

I hold out my hand, a lump rising in my throat. "No. I want to keep this."

Rene shakes her head and sighs. "I sort of like it. I was hoping you'd let me keep it." She stares at me expectantly, I stare back, and then she sets it next to an unsealed box. "Fine, you can have it." She taps two boxes. "These ones are yours, Chrissie. I haven't sealed and labeled them yet. You can finish putting your stuff in here. I haven't even started on your bedroom."

"Let's not have you packing our stuff from the bedroom," Neil says, sitting down on the couch.

Rene sticks out her tongue at him. "What's the matter? Afraid I might get all hot and bothered looking at your boxers?"

Neil laughs. "Nope. More afraid you might steal Josh

Moss's phone number from my address book."

Rene flushes, her eyes sparkly. "Asshole!" She crosses her arms. "So how is Josh?"

"Josh will be here tomorrow. He's driving back to Seattle with me." A teasing glint brightens Neil's eyes. "Might be your last chance with him, Rene."

She scrunches up her nose and shrugs. "Too bad my plane leaves at 6 a.m. Well, it's his loss."

Neil laughs and clicks on the TV. It's one of the only things in the room not disconnected or shoved into a box.

I finally find my voice. "I can't believe you packed my things without me. I don't even know what's in the boxes. I thought we were going to do this together. You didn't even wait for me."

Both Rene and Neil stare at me. *Shit! Why did that have to come out so loud and sound so irrational?*

Rene arches a brow. "My plane leaves early in the morning. We can't put it off any longer, Chrissie."

In the morning. I tense. For the first time it sinks in and holds the feel of realness that we are all leaving tomorrow, heading in different directions.

"Besides, it wouldn't be right to leave you having to do everything," she says.

She takes from her pocket a folded sheet of paper, shoves it at me, and sinks down on the arm of the sofa.

Her finger moves along the list as I read.

She says, "That's my address in LA. That's my new phone number. That's my new mobile number...thank you, Patty, for no longer being a cheap-ass mom and getting me a mobile phone. The boxes with the pink tape go to LA. And the boxes with the black tape go to Santa Barbara."

I nod. "That's easy enough to follow."

My head is swimming. After twelve years I will no longer be living with Rene. I've spent my entire life with her, neighbors in Hope Ranch, sharing a dorm room at boarding school, and now the condo in Berkeley. And poof, tomorrow we will be in different cities with different lives.

I move toward my bedroom. "I'll change and be right back to help you finish," I announce over my shoulder.

I close my bedroom door and sink down on the bed, trying to will the anxious churning of my stomach to stop. I'm frantic again and I don't want to be.

My eyes roam the confines of my bedroom and all the things I still have to do before the movers come tomorrow. Neil's junk is mingled everywhere with my own. It's strange how a guy's things can rest in your bedroom and you don't even notice them.

How could I not notice?

Neil's belongings are everywhere. A completely normal and comfortable thing. He may have moved out in December, but we have never totally pulled apart our lives, and staring at his possessions I'm shocked to realize it was because I didn't want to.

I held on to Neil even after I told him to go.

I'm not completely clear why I did that. I pick up his picture from my bedside table. I didn't even put this away. I kept it. Neil has never left me. Not for a moment. He's been with me every minute of these awful months since

December. How could I not see it before today?

"It's going to be all right, Chrissie."

Neil's quiet voice makes me turn. He is standing in my bedroom doorway watching me. *How long has he been watching? And why is he staring at me that way?* The expression in his eyes is compassionate; sad and hopeful at once.

"You're going to be OK," he adds quietly. "I'm going to be OK. If we stay together we will both be OK."

I nod, even though I don't know what I'm nodding about or what Neil means by *we will both be OK*. There is nothing for Neil to have be OK over. He's wonderful. Perfect. Emotionally together and not needy.

He settles on his knees on the floor beside the bed, his body between my legs. I stare at him and he has that look in his eyes, the one that is glorious but makes my heart contract.

He runs his hands up my thighs. "I'll help you with this when I get back."

"Where are you going?"

The edge in my voice surprises us both.

Neil's eyes widen, his thumb lightly brushing my cheek. "To get Chinese with Rene. I won't be long. That vegan carrot cake just didn't do it for me."

I laugh, a little sputter, rough. I lean forward and kiss his hair. "Didn't do it for me either."

Neil smiles. "What do you want?"

"I don't care. Surprise me."

I watch him leave the room and in a few minutes I hear the front door slam. I change into a pair of sweats and go back into the living room. I stare at the boxes and all the things still unpacked, not sure where to begin.

I sink onto my knees beside a bookshelf. All our silly photo albums are still there. Rene and I are crazy about making these albums. She probably left that, not knowing which ones she could take and which ones I wanted to keep. God, even Rene moving on is like a breakup, splitting our possession down to single photo albums representing both our lives.

I pull one out and look at it. Senior year at boarding school. I flip through the pages and then grab another. Freshman year at Cal. Each year of my life neatly pasted into a photo album. I grab another. Every picture is us together. Together or us with Neil. Stupid adventures we had together. Happy moments. Sad moments. Me and Neil. Rene and Neil. The three of us. Or just us.

I exhale heavily and stare at the room. I don't know what to take back to Santa Barbara, what to leave, and what to give to Rene. It is so much harder to figure this out than I thought it would be, and I can't find the will to pull things apart and tuck them away into boxes.

I've slowly carved out a life here. I never would have thought that possible when I started Cal, but now that it's time to take it apart that's exactly what it feels like. Like I'm disassembling my life. Maybe this is all that life is: an endless series of assembling a life only to take it apart later. I hope not. The endings are too hard for me.

I grab another scrapbook and slowly flip through the pages. The door opens and I look up. Jeez, Rene and Neil are already back from the food run.

Rene's eyes do a fast examination of the room as she

marches briskly toward the kitchen, Chinese cartons in hand. "It doesn't look like you've packed even one thing. Crap, Chrissie. We were gone an hour. You're not leaving everything for me to get done, are you?"

I flush. "Nope. Just trying to figure out how to split the photo albums. You've left me the hard decisions."

Rene pauses in the kitchen doorway and rolls her eyes at me. "Keep them. I don't care anymore. I just want this done so I can go to bed."

She sounds agitated and impatient, and her words hit me like a punch. She's so excited about the future, her new life, medical school, her new apartment, her new everything...*without me.*

I scoop up the scrapbooks and drop them into the box Rene said was mine.

"There. I've packed something. Happy now, Rene?"

She rolls her eyes and continues into the kitchen. I turn and find Neil watching me strangely.

"Come eat, Chrissie," he says quietly. "We'll finish this together after we eat."

That has the unpardonable power to make me feel like crying. Stupid. My emotions are so lame today. Without a word, I follow Neil into the kitchen. Rene is busily setting paper plates on the table since she's packed up absolutely everything in here she could take for her new apartment, and Neil is opening the cartons.

I drop heavily into my chair. Neil starts scooping chicken chow mein onto my plate and then settles at the table in his chair between mine and Rene.

There is a heavy tension in the room and I know that

the tension is me and I hate that.

I move my chopsticks in my food and don't really eat. "What would I do if I go to Seattle and on the road with you?" I ask softly.

Neil looks up and sits back in his chair. "I don't know. Whatever you want. Maybe just be with me. We'd be together, Chrissie. I haven't thought beyond that."

Rene's face snaps up from her plate. "What? What have I missed?"

I shake my head. "Nothing."

She frowns. "Are you moving to Seattle? Not Santa Barbara? Does Jack know? Why didn't you tell me?"

I shrug and say, "I haven't decided," and then drop my gaze to fix back on my plate.

"Would someone tell me what's going on here?" Rene demands, alarmed.

I feel the pressure of Neil's gaze and lift my chin, meeting the lush green of his eyes. "Nothing is going on, Rene. Stay out of it for once, for Christ's sake."

Rene's eyes widen and I don't like the way her expression changes. In a minute, Neil picks up his empty plate, dumps it in the trash and leaves the room.

My eyes follow him from the kitchen, then shift to Rene. Damn, she's staring at me in that way she has—*overly analytical and not pleased with Chrissie.*

Rene frowns. "Did he ask you to move to Seattle with him? Does he want to get back together with you?"

I ignore the question.

"God, you're an idiot," she hisses under her breath.

My temper flares. "What is that supposed to mean?"

Rene springs up from the table and starts to angrily scrape the food from the plate into the garbage disposal.

"You've been fucked up since you broke up with him. Neil is a great guy and you've done nothing but mess with him for four years," Rene hisses, shaking her head angrily. "I'm sick of watching it. I'm glad I'm out of here."

"You don't know what you're talking about."

She whirls from the sink to face me. "No? Well, here's what I do know. Even a guy as crazy over you as Neil is will get fed up eventually with your shit and walk away. Grow up, Chrissie. Learn to think about someone else for a change."

That was mean, so mean, Rene.

I am able to meet her stare for stare without flinching or crying, and I take a few more bites of my food and then toss what's left into the trashcan.

When I get into the living room, I find Neil rummaging through things and tossing them into boxes. I start packing up my shit, and occasionally peek at Neil. He doesn't say a word.

In the bedroom, he goes to his side of the closet and I go to mine. In less than an hour, I'm done. I undress, put on one of his t-shirts and climb into bed.

Neil is still packing up things from the drawers.

"I'm sorry I brought stuff up in front of Rene," I say. "It's a hard decision. I'm not messing with you. I hope you know that. I'm just not sure what I should do."

He doesn't look at me. "You'll do what you decide to do," is all he says, tossing the last of his junk into a box and then sealing it with packing tape.

He takes off his clothes, tosses them in a pile, and then climbs into bed. He turns off the light and settles back against his pillow. I become acutely aware of the space between our bodies.

I roll over on my pillow to face him. His eyes are open. He's awake.

"I don't want you pissed at me," I say.

His head does an aggravated flutter on the pillow. "I'm not pissed, Chrissie."

"Then why are you over there? You're practically on the edge of the bed."

"I'm just tired," he says, but then he moves his arm so I can rest my head on his shoulder.

He kisses the top of my head and closes his eyes. I stare up at him, the lines of his face, the messy arrangement of his chestnut waves. I lean upward. I kiss the underside of his chin.

He adjusts me against him. "Don't start anything unless you intend to follow through this time."

I flush. "What's that supposed to mean?"

His eyes open and the way he looks at me makes me tense. "You sleep cuddled against me. You touch me. You kiss me. You let me hold you. But you don't fuck me, Chrissie. I get it. But it doesn't help. I'm horny as hell."

I can feel the heat move from my cheeks to my neck. "I'm sorry."

His arms tighten around me. "It's OK. I get it. You couldn't after…" He breaks off, not going *there*. "I know it might take a while to get there mentally again. I just really miss being with you, Chrissie. I love you."

The way he effortlessly shares his heart makes me ashamed of how little of me I share with him. I don't know why I hold back. Neil is safe and loving and unselfish. The kindest guy I've ever known.

I kiss his chest. "I want to make love with you. I'm just kind of afraid to try."

"I know," he says, and his body turns a little more into me, holding me closer. He kisses my brow. "Don't be afraid. For once tell me everything you're thinking. We can think it through together."

Don't be afraid? He makes it sound so easy but it's not. Not for me and it never has been. There are times I feel like I'm possessed by my fear, paralyzed in my life, unable to manage anything because I am afraid.

"I want to go to Seattle. I'm afraid," I confess.

"I know, Chrissie."

He brushes the hair from my face and kisses my cheek.

"I don't know what I'm supposed to do with my life, Neil."

He kisses my mouth. Against my lips, he says, "I know. I don't know what I'm supposed to do with my life either. I don't think anyone knows for sure. I think we all just do."

His mouth lightly trails down my neck and I can feel him starting to work the t-shirt from my body. In a minute, I'm naked and lying staring up at Neil.

"You don't have to be afraid. Everything is going to be OK, Chrissie."

Neil stays balanced above me, reclined on a hip, his body angled. Those long fingers start to touch me everywhere. Up my arms very slowly, then my collarbone, to roam my breasts and then everywhere. He doesn't kiss me. He gently touches and stirs me until I am languid and aroused and he is fully erect.

I stare up at him. For the first time in many weeks, I want him. I want him now.

"Make love to me," I whisper.

He turns me in his arms until I'm straddling him and consumes my mouth in quiet, thrusting kisses, his tongue dancing and playing, fucking my mouth with the same unhurried glide as his fingers moving on my flesh.

I feel his erection between my legs, touching me *there*, but he keeps us separated. He lifts my hair and his lips are on my neck. A hand brushes feather-light up my back.

There is something different in me. I can feel something different in Neil. I am impatient inside and he is slow, achingly slow in this. He spreads me on the bed, his tongue running over my breasts and I can feel his fingers between my legs and then in me. As he cups my sex he teases me with the lightest of contact.

"I love you, Chrissie," he whispers, and I feel myself tighten and grow wet there.

I melt into his touch, wanting him hard and moving inside me, but he continues this controlled erotic play on my body and it is unlike Neil.

He has never made love to me this way. Not ever. A light kiss on my neck. A finger brushing my flesh. A kiss on my stomach. It is slow and tender and loving. I start to cry and I really don't know why. The tears roll down my cheeks and I can't stop them.

His lips tease my ear. I inhale a deep breath. "It's going to be OK, baby," he murmurs against my flesh.

A part of me aches even as all of me turns to mold into him. *Baby?* Why did he call me that? Neil has never called me *baby* before. Only one guy has ever called me that: Alan.

His tongue moves on my breast, circling my nipple before he takes it slowly into his mouth. I arch up into the play of his lips as his fingers move downward spreading me *there*.

He enters my body in achingly slow degrees. Inch by inch until he's buried all of his erection in me. He doesn't move. He holds his body still, breathing raggedly, kissing and touching me.

My senses swirl even as my emotions scatter with my thoughts. Why is he having sex with me this way? It's almost as if he thinks I can't take anything too passionate, too physical, too intense. Or maybe what I'm feeling is him, is his own reaction to all the shit I put him through with me. Maybe he's afraid to touch me. Maybe he's unsure he wants this, after having gone through *that* with me. I don't know what is happening here between us, but the quiet of his body is unnerving.

I realize the last month has changed us both. Death lingers in your flesh. It's metaphysically altering. It changes you.

Why didn't I remember this? I should have remembered that before I went to the clinic. I feel vacant inside, hollow. *Such a simple thing,* Rene said. Quick. No big deal. Life goes on.

Only it's not a simple thing. Death, in any form, changes you. And I definitely should have remembered that before I let Neil go with me to the clinic.

I start to cry harder. Everything around me, inside me, inside Neil, no longer feels familiar and I know it's my fault. I just want to feel good somehow, any way again. I need him to fuck me hard like he always does, physical without the emotional convolution. I want only to feel in my flesh. I don't want to think. I want not to hurt. I want my heart and mind to go mercifully blank and I want Neil to fuck me until I'm numb in my flesh.

I start to writhe beneath the tight cocoon of his body, my hips rising up in a frenzy, plunging him deeply within me as I devour his mouth with my kisses. His hands move and try to steady me. My nails cut into him as I run them up his back and bite his lower lip. I force him deep within me again. He fights it. I arch upward into him, rougher this time.

Over and over, until I feel the excitement build in his flesh, his muscles growing tauter, the skin across his face straining in the way it does when I've pushed him to come and he doesn't want to.

I wrap my arms and legs around him, and he starts raging in my body. The thrusts are gloriously painfully and I lay pliant beneath him, wanting it harder, deeper, always deeper. He is pounding in me in a way that numbs me.

"Oh fuck, Chrissie," he groans, pulsing within me as he spills into my flesh. He collapses against my body, sex-damp and quivering. And I don't know why, but I now know I'm going to leave Berkeley with Neil.

CHAPTER FIVE

We stand at the international departure gate at Oakland Airport. Rene clutches me against her in a firm and breezy hug.

"You stay sweet," she orders, tapping my chest with an index finger.

"You stay cute," I reply automatically, but our ritual banter hurts me today.

Her enormous brown eyes fix on me intently. "I'll be back from Costa Rica in a month." She makes a face. "That is if I can survive that long with my mother. I'll call when I get back. Make sure I have Neil's tour schedule. I want to see you both before I start medical school." She laughs, sparkly and excited. "I won't have time after."

I nod, trying hard not to break down here in the airport.

She pulls Neil against her. "You be good to her, jerk, or you're going to have to deal with me."

Inwardly I cringe, because it almost feels like I'm a baton being passed on in a relay race, as if by giving me over to Neil she can walk out of my life with a clear conscience. Christ, Rene, I'm a person not a thing.

I smile as Neil hugs her. She rushes toward the gate, pausing to do a swish with her hips and a *whoop*, her arms stretched above her head. "We survived University of

California Berkeley."

That was said loud enough to pierce the sound barrier. And then she disappears down the ramp, her laughter trailing behind her. I roll my eyes. Everything works for Rene. Almost every set of male eyes on the ramp lock on her to watch her go.

Once she's out of view, I turn to Neil and he gives me a gentle wraparound hug.

"Someday, Chrissie, you're going to have to explain to me why you're friends with Rene."

I laugh and peek up at him sheepishly. Neil knows exactly when and how to make me laugh. My emotions begin to settle and the anxiety of seeing Rene leave starts to fade.

"She's not that bad," I reply.

Neil shakes his head, but he's smiling. "OK. She sort of cares about you in her own warped way."

I rebuke him with my eyes, but I am not in the mood for a snappy comeback. I am silent as we walk from the airport terminal.

Neil opens my car door. "How much longer will it take you to be packed up and ready to go?"

I shrug. "Not long. I just want to leave a note for the management company so they know what to do when the movers arrive."

Neil leans against my open door. "High-rise condos. Management companies. Boy, you are definitely going to be slumming it in my place in Seattle. It's a good thing we're only going to be there a few days. You'd probably leave me if we stayed more than a week."

I roll my eyes and Neil leans in to kiss me, but I'm chaotic inside again. Seattle and the road. I don't know what I'm doing. Not really.

Neil sinks into the driver's seat of the Volvo and puts the key into the ignition. "Have you called Jack yet? Let him know about your change of plans?"

I stare out the window. "Nope."

"Why not?"

I shrug and look at Neil. "Just haven't. I'll do it when I get settled in Seattle."

Neil frowns and shakes his head, and I ignore his unspoken criticism.

As we pull into the condo parking lot, I spy Josh Moss leaning against a wall, smoking. We cross the parking lot and he straightens up, tossing his cigarette onto the pavement. He nods in Neil's direction and doesn't look at me.

"You ready to get on the road, man?" he says, giving Neil a one-arm, firm, fast hug.

"I've just got to grab our stuff," Neil says, rummaging in his pocket for the elevator key.

Josh frowns. "Our stuff?"

Neil shrugs. "Chrissie is going back to Seattle with me and out on the road."

Josh's gaze shifts to me and the way he's staring makes me uncomfortable. Josh has never liked me, not really, but it's never before felt like he hated me. What's changed? Why does he hate me?

The tic twitches in Neil's cheek. "You got a problem with Chrissie going out on the road with me?"

The sharpness of Neil's voice makes me jump. I stare at the guys wondering what this extremely tense moment is all about. The scene holds the feel of shit going on I don't know anything about.

Josh shakes his head. "No problem."

"Good. There better not be." Neil shoves the key into the wall panel, turns it, and calls the elevator.

The three of us are silent as we make the short ride to the top floor. The doors open and Neil grabs my hand, his fingers tight around mine, pulling me along with him out of the elevator ahead of Josh. I peek up at him from the corner of my eye, trying to read his abrupt change of mood. He's pissed off about something. What happened downstairs? I don't want to be a problem with the guys. I don't know why I should be, but it feels like I am.

I drop my purse on the table beside the door and kick off my flip-flops.

Neil points at my duffel and the small carry case next to it. "Is this all you're taking to Seattle?"

I nod, watching Josh sink onto the couch. I smile at Josh. "Do you want something to eat or drink before we hit the road?"

Stoic and reluctant, he shakes his head. I beat a fast retreat to the kitchen and write the instruction note to the management company and the movers.

When I return to the living room, the guys have already taken downstairs Neil's boxes of shit. I sit on my knees in the center of the living room, wondering if there is anything I should take other than the small collection of clothes and personal items I packed. I don't know how long I'm going to be gone or what I'm going to need. Oh well, I guess pretty much everything I own can go to storage in Santa Barbara to be dealt with later.

I stare at the condo, feeling teary again. It looks so stark, so unhappy without everyone's junk everywhere. A part of my life over. An ending, and perhaps it's time to make the ending complete.

I debate with myself and brush at a tear.

"Are you ready to go?" Neil asks.

I look up, startled to see him standing over me. He starts to collect my bags. I make a fast decision.

I point. "Take the duffel, but leave that one."

He sets down the small black bag, a quizzical arch to his brow. I smile.

"Go load my stuff," I say. "I'll be right behind you in a few minutes. I need to take care of one more thing."

Neil leans over, kissing me. "We've got to hit the road, Chrissie. Don't take all day."

"I won't. I'll be fast. I promise."

I watch Neil disappear through the front door and then I pull my black bag across the floor and unzip it. I rummage through my things, collecting the little tokens I kept from each time I went to Alan: room keys, his t-shirt, some little knickknack that caught my eye.

I fish out my journals, the ones with my Alan entries and then the photo of us holding each other as we sat on Alan's terrace our first spring together. That picture I cut from the newspaper before I left him in New York.

I jump to my feet and go to the moving box I haven't sealed yet. I take out the old cookie tin with his letters, lay my keepsakes of Alan carefully within, then I seal it with mover's tape. I bury it deep within the other things in the box, then I seal the box and write across the top *storage*.

I brush at my tears, and will my feet to follow Neil out the door. Downstairs I find him and Josh waiting by the van.

"You got everything you need, Chrissie?" Neil asks.

I smile, staring up at him and I can feel my eyes are sparkly and round. "I have everything I need."

He looks at me, a touch confused, and opens the door as he takes my bag from me. I fight to get breath in and out of me as Neil waits expectantly for me to climb in.

Neil drops a kiss on my lips and I climb into the passenger seat. An end of a life. The beginning of a new life. Another fast turn on the road and I am lost again.

CHAPTER SIX

Inside the van is so quiet it is nerve-racking. Neil hasn't spoken a word since we left Berkeley, there is a hovering feeling of conflict between him and Josh, and there isn't even music on since Josh is sitting on the mattress in the back, guitar in hand, working through whatever sound he is hearing in his head.

I stare out the window at the endless, ugly miles of road. Crap, who would have thought Northern California looked like *this*? The freeway between Sacramento and the Oregon border isn't really a freeway. It's more like two lanes cutting through nothingness where people drive fast.

I lean my cheek on the door, letting the air from the open window tease my hair as I watch Mount Shasta pass me by. Well, that's a little cool. It's kind of pretty, still covered with snow on the top in June. Ahead of me I start to see more trees. Giant trees. Redwood? Jeez, is the drive all the way to Seattle going look like this? Barren. Unpopulated. Boring. Why aren't there people here?

I shift in my seat until I'm facing Neil. "How long will it be until we reach Seattle?"

"Another 10 hours, if we drive all the way through."

My eyes widen. "Ten hours? You mean we've got 10 hours more of this?"

Neil laughs. "Ten hours if we want to make it to Seattle

tonight. What do you think being on the road is? It's road, Chrissie. Haven't you ever been to Northern California and Oregon?"

I crinkle up my nose. "Nope, I've lived a pretty deprived life."

Neil flicks on the turn signal and looks in the mirror, readying to change lanes. "Somehow I don't think deprived covers it." His eyes settle on me for a brief moment, serious, then back to the road. "Not having second thoughts are you?"

I shake my head. "Nope."

Neil smiles at me. "Good. This is just the drive to Seattle. When we go out on tour, the travel will be more comfortable, more interesting for you."

"Will it? I still don't know what you expect me to do here."

"Whatever you want. Anything. Nothing." He gives me a look that goes straight to my heart. "Just be with me."

He lapses back into silence and I study him. I still don't quite get why Neil wants me here, wants to drag me along in his life, back to Seattle and out on the road. I may have never been out on the road, but I do know a thing or two about musicians.

Most musicians wouldn't dream of taking their significant other out on tour with them. Shit gets crazy on the road. Men get crazy on the road. The girls get crazy on the road. It's a place to do anything, no regrets or explanations, where no one tells and everyone just parties. I'm far from a party girl and I'm not exactly a roll-with-it kind of girl either. I've heard stories about the road all my life. The last thing Neil should want is me along with him here. Especially if he loves me…nope, he shouldn't want me here.

I stare ahead at the road. *Stupid, Chrissie. Stupid. Neil loves you. That is the only thing about your life that's totally clear and why you left Berkeley with him. You may not know what you feel. You may not know what you are doing here. But you do know, it is a fact, that Neil loves you. No guy would go through the shit he went through with you if he didn't.*

I ease out of the passenger seat. "I'm going to grab a soda from the cooler. Do you want one?"

"No. I'm good, Chrissie."

As an afterthought, I drop a kiss on his cheek before I make my way to the back of the van. I sink onto my knees on the mattress that covers the floor, close to Josh, and I reach into the ice chest.

I pop open a diet coke, and sit with my back against the van wall. "What are you working on?"

Josh looks at me, impatient and irritated by the interruption. "Not shit now."

My cheeks cover with a burn. "Sorry. I'll get out of your way."

He runs a hand through his black hair. "No. Don't bother. I could use a break. I think I'll sit up front with Neil for a while."

I don't really want to sit on the floor in the back of the van, surrounded by luggage, boxes, instruments and surfboards, but I nod in an *it's OK with me* kind of way. Josh crawls past me and up to the front and I remain alone in the back, wondering what I'm supposed to do here. I can't even see the scenery since there aren't any windows, pitiful diversion though it was.

I zip open my black case, pull out a journal, then settle on my stomach, tapping the pen against my lip. I scrawl across the top of a fresh page the date and a notation— *Day One on the Road*—but when the words start to flow out of me, I'm not really writing about the road.

I'm writing about things dark and heavy in my heart, a forgotten snippet from another journal from years ago— *parts of me have been quieted, new parts of me stirred awake, parts of me I leave behind, and parts of me I take.* A part of me I don't want anymore. A part of me I'd hoped to leave behind in Berkeley.

~ ~ ~

I open my eyes and sit up in alarm. The van is still and empty and morning sunlight is streaming through the windshield. My journal and pen lie beside my pillow and someone, most probably Neil, pulled an unzipped sleeping bag over me.

Where the heck are we? Why is it so quiet? And how long have I been asleep in here?

I brush the tangled hair from my face and scooch on my knees to the door and slide it open. I stare. I'm surrounded by trees, dirt and nothing. A sound makes me lean out of the van.

"Morning," says Josh.

I frown. He's sitting on a redwood picnic table beside a small portable stove of some kind, with a pot I can only assume is coffee sitting on the flame.

I climb out of the van. "Where are we?"

"Harris Beach State Park, Oregon." Something on my face makes him laugh. "Haven't you ever been camping before?"

I shrug. "Nope. Haven't been to Oregon either."

He takes a sip of his coffee. "Get used to both. Neil loves camping and Neil loves the beach here. Decided last night not to push through to Seattle and cut over to the coast while I was asleep. I was as surprised as you when I woke up here."

I laugh and Josh gives a smile, albeit a small sort of reluctant one, but it's a smile. A definite improvement over yesterday.

I sink down to sit on the table next to him, and settle my feet on the bench. Through the thicket of trees encircling what I can now tell is a campsite, I can see the beach ahead.

He reaches for the pot on the stove. "Do you want some coffee?"

"I'd love some." After he hands me a cup I take in more details of my surroundings. Jeez, I've never been camping before. There has got to be a bathroom somewhere.

I feel the pressure of eyes on me and turn to find Josh studying me. Something in how he is looking at me makes my fingers tighten around my cup and my cheeks flush.

He says, "You fucked with my boy's head pretty good. He was a mess when he came back to Seattle in December. Did you know that? A fucking mess in Seattle. A fucking mess on the road. If all you're going to do is give him more shit why don't you bail on the tour before we head out on the road in Seattle?"

The color on my face turns into a burn. He looks away, staring out at the ocean, his jaw tense. I don't know what to say to that. A part of me is humiliated, a part of me pissed off because Josh has gotten more than a few things wrong, and a part sort of respects what a loyal friend he is to Neil—but it leaves me not knowing what to say, so I say nothing.

His eyes lock on me again. "Neil isn't like the rest of us assholes. He's a good guy. He never screwed around on you once. Not once in four years and I'd know it. Pussy gets shoved in his face 24/7 while we're on the road, and he doesn't fuck around. And then you mess with his head. You dump him just to prove you can or some other shitty rich-girl mind-fuck game. Then when he's got it together again, you take him back so you can fuck with his head again. Don't fucking do it. Leave him alone if that's your game here."

I'm breathing so heavily I'm nearly hyperventilating. I want to run as quickly and as far from Josh as I can, but *that* definitely deserves a response, and if I don't respond Josh is going to think he's right about everything and treat me worse on from here.

I stand up, meeting Josh's hostile, waiting gaze directly. "I didn't fuck with his head. We had problems. We fixed them. It's none of your business what we do. Stay out of it."

I meet him stare for stare.

Josh breaks off first, tossing his coffee onto the ground. "No problem. I just wanted to make sure you know where I stand here. The band is finally going somewhere. I don't want you to fuck up everything for everyone by fucking with him again."

I lift my chin. "That's not going to happen, Josh. Neil wants me here and I'm going on the road with him, whether you like it or not."

He shakes his head and looks away.

"Do you know where Neil is?"

He points at a path. "Down there you'll find Neil on the beach."

I toss Josh a stiff smile and head down the path toward the beach. I cut through brush and trees and then realize I could have taken the road here. It hugs the edge of the forest I'm cutting through. Jeez, what a prick Josh can be, sending me this way.

I walk down the road, into the parking lot that hugs the beach. The view is gorgeous, an unspoiled expanse of sand and an relenting, roiling current as the waves hit the shore and the giant rocks that rear from the water. The shoreline is practically deserted.

Shading my eyes with my hand, I search the beach for Neil. He is sitting in the sand, legs bent and arms around them, staring at the water. The image he makes is peaceful and intense at once, and brings sharply to my mind the way Jack sits and stares at the ocean, a quietness and a troubled air covering their flesh simultaneously.

I feel a sharp prick in my heart. Why do all the men in my life—Alan, Jack, Neil—have a deeply buried troubled soul that they will not share with me? What I am seeing is familiar to me, eerily so, and a touch disturbing.

For some reason, I hold back and simply watch Neil for

a while. He tosses a rock to skim across water, then he stills and stares. He is simmering with something internally, though the picture he makes to a casual observer would be one of contentment. But I can feel it and I am suddenly alarmed by it. Maybe he is regretting bringing me along with him to Seattle?

I plod through the sand until I'm near him and he gives me a smile over his shoulder. It's a lazy and content kind of look, deliberately so, and I'm not fooled by any of it.

I sink on my knees behind him, laying my cheek against his back.

"What are you thinking about?" I ask.

Neil shrugs. "Nothing. Just thinking. There won't be any quiet once we get back to Seattle and then on the road. No time to think."

No time to think. Sounds like heaven to me.

"Do you want to hear something silly?" I ask him and Neil makes a small laugh. "I've never been camping before. Does this count as camping?"

Neil laughs harder. "Sort of. God, you have been raised a completely deprived girl."

I look over his shoulder and make a face at him. "Pretty much. Why do you want a deprived girl?"

He kisses me lightly. "Because I love you."

My vision clouds from the power of emotion with which he says that.

"We're going to be OK, Chrissie," he whispers.

I place my lips on his back where my cheek had been. I don't know who Neil is trying to convince; himself or me?

"I know," I murmur. "We're both going to be OK."

He springs to his feet and holds out his hand to me. As we near Josh, I lean into Neil and whisper, "I'm going to hate that van before this is through. All you guys in there at once. With only Josh it's a nightmare."

Josh picks up the stove from the table. "Don't worry, Chrissie. We've already decided we're going to draw up straws each night to see who gets to share the bed with you."

Shit, he heard me.

Neil gives him a tap on the chest. "Don't fuck with my girlfriend." Josh laughs. Neil looks down at me. "We're doing ten months on the road opening for Scream. The US leg of their world tour. An arena tour, Chrissie. No van. Tour bus. Road crew. Everything."

My brows hitch up and my eyes widen. I knew things were going well for Neil, but I didn't know how well. And God, why didn't I ask him? I'm ashamed that in our month in Berkeley, I hadn't really asked him anything about the band or his life in Seattle. We'd been too consumed with my shit.

"Chrissie, we haven't done touring in the van for a year," Josh says, tossing the stove inside and then closing the cargo doors. "Neil just drives this thing because he fucking likes it. Don't think you're going to get him to get rid of it. He won't."

"Fuck you, Josh. I like the van. It was more fun when we toured in the van."

"The only one who liked the van was you, Neil," Josh counters. "I'm with Chrissie. I hate that fucking thing."

Neil laughs and opens the side door. "I'm going to get

95

an hour's sleep, Josh. Then we can head off on the road again."

I let Neil pull me up into the van with him and I notice how tired he looks. Maybe he didn't sleep last night. He settles on the mattress, pulling me into the tuck of his body.

He kisses my cheek. "Don't let me sleep more than an hour, Chrissie."

"OK."

I lie against him, wide awake, but in a couple of minutes Neil is sound asleep. In the quiet of the van everything suddenly feels different, inside me, inside him, and all around us. There is a strange sense that life is about to change in some unknown way for the both of us, and in the air there is that feeling of companionable sadness and despondent hope in me and in Neil.

A vision of him sitting on the beach rises in my head. I know where the deeply buried sadness within me comes from, each moment of my life that makes it an unrelenting part of me. But after nearly four years I don't know its source in Neil.

It should feel different, not good, when I touch him and feel what it is in *me* in *him* as well. Neil is still-water, in most moments of his life, an alluring at-peace soul, but for a moment I felt *me* in *him*.

I wish I understood what it is I'm feeling in him. I wish I understood why he loves me. I wish I understood why in this companionable sadness we sometimes share we always feel our best to me.

We feel good together. Right. Almost enough. But not quite.

It's not Neil's fault. He's a wonderful guy. It's me. I'm lost in a void. Going somewhere. Going nowhere. Having everything a girl *should* want. Having nothing completely fill me. Thinking of a whispering voice saying *Chrissie* as I let Neil hold me and sleep.

CHAPTER SEVEN

Something pulls me from sleep, and I slowly give myself over to waking, when I don't really want to. Our first five days in Seattle have been exhausting. We take off on tour in two days. If the grind is anything like this, I won't ever survive ten months on the road with Neil.

I'd forgotten the pace of life here, so different than in Berkeley. Neil and I are hardly ever alone. The days pass in long hours with the guys jamming in the rehearsal space or just hanging out in the apartment together. The nights are filled with parties and music. Life here exists in a never-ending torrent of creative fervor and camaraderie, a nocturnal existence of hungry musicians and artistic obsession. The center of the music world is in Seattle, and the entire city pulses from it.

I feel around in the bed for Neil. Gone. I look at the clock on the nightstand. 2 a.m. Why would Neil go out in the middle of the night? Why would he want to?

Every part of my body is limp. We went to bed early and fucked a long time. There has been something feral and frantic in both of us, a strange internal chaos that has been building and building since we arrived in Seattle. We were both crazy in our bodies last night and by the time we ended the fucking everything inside me was quieted for the first time in a very long time. Neil was passed out on his pillow the minute the sex ended.

Why isn't he here with me, still asleep? We fucked ourselves into quiet.

I sit up in bed and notice the light coming from the living room. I pick up my panties and Neil's shirt from the floor, pull them into place, and exit the bedroom.

My eyes widen. Neil is sitting on the sofa, fully dressed, lacing up those hideous black army surplus boots so popular up here.

"Where are you going?" I ask, crossing the room to him.

Neil shrugs and doesn't look up. "Just out for a walk. I'm kind of restless."

I become aware he is tense and agitated.

"Do you want me to dress and come with you?"

"You don't have to do that. I'd rather go out alone. I need to be alone sometimes, Chrissie."

Coldness prickles my cheeks from the edge in his voice and how he nearly snapped at me. I stare at him.

Neil closes his eyes and exhales slowly. "It's not you, Chrissie."

I sink down on the sofa beside him. "I didn't ask if it was me. Why were you so quick to say it wasn't?"

He shakes his head, brushing his messy chestnut waves back from his face, and then smiles. "Because I know how you think. You don't need to say it for me to know what you are thinking." He leans in and drops a fast kiss on my lips. "I won't be long. I'm just going to walk for a while."

"OK." My eyes follow him to the door, but this feels

strange to me and I don't know why.

At the door, Neil pauses. "Go back to sleep, Chrissie. I won't be long."

The door shuts and I sit, staring at it. That was odd. Really odd. But then, there has been a lot of oddness since we got to Seattle. Being in Seattle has always affected Neil strangely, he hasn't explained why to me, but I shouldn't be surprised by the brief flashes of *weird Neil* while we're here.

I try to dismiss my sense of unease. It is illogical and Neil would never do anything to me that should make him wanting to walk at night alone something I should be suspicious of. Neil is not a slip-out-to-cheat kind of guy. He'd be honest with me. He would confess. He wouldn't be able not to.

I consider going back to bed, and then sink deeper back into the sofa. I'm wide awake now. I click on the TV and turn the volume down low, since I'm not sure if Josh or Les Wilson are asleep in their bedrooms.

My gaze roams the mess and junk everywhere. It's a good thing I'd forgotten how awful this apartment was before I decided to join Neil here. Three guys living in a run-down flop house; that's what this place looks like. Still, it's kind of fun living with Neil in this hideous apartment. We are all sort of like a rowdy family here and there is a sense that something bordering on exciting is always happening.

I'm never bored here, and it is never quiet, too quiet, like it is in Jack's house.

The guys bicker. They laugh. They bullshit and tell

stories; stories about the road, stories about girls, stories about anything, and stories about nothing. They create music. They play music. They party. They fuck. Yep, that's pretty much guy world. Guy world, it seems, is the same everywhere.

I turn off the TV and move to the bookcase. Lots of pictures here. Some of them make me cringe. The guys with girls from the road. The guys performing. The guys misbehaving. Shit...I pick up a picture...I wonder if Les Wilson's girlfriend has seen this?

Lame, Chrissie, lame. She must have. There is no way to be in the living room and miss these darn photos. I set it back and continue to study the rest of the pictures. There's only one here I could give Neil shit over, him downing shooters from between some girl's tits at what looks like an after-party. But that's it. Just one. And since I don't know when it was taken, it could have been when we were broken up, so there isn't any point to giving him shit over this.

I smile as I stare at the photo, though I suppose I shouldn't be smiling. It's just he looks kind of shy even grabbing an alcohol shot with his lips from a girl's breasts.

After settling back down on the couch, I wrap a comforter around me. Life isn't bad here. It's not exactly good either. It's just different.

~~~

Hands gently shake me. My eyes fly open. Neil is standing above me and the room is filled with mid-morning light.

"Fuck, why'd you wait up for me?" he asks, a not fully concealed edge to his voice. "I told you not to."

I yawn and toss the blanket off me. "I didn't wait up. I fell asleep out here."

Neil starts walking to the bedroom. "I'm going to take a shower and go to bed. Let me sleep until dinnertime. We've got the sendoff on the road party tonight that Ernie put together and I'm really not in the mood for it. Let me sleep today."

The door shuts before I can answer him. Crap, what was that all about? Everything about him screams that he wants to be left alone, but I follow Neil to the bathroom anyway. He's already in the shower when I get there, clothes in the hamper and steam on the mirror.

I ease up to sit on the edge of the vanity counter. "Have you just been walking all this time?"

"Pretty much," is his abrupt response through the shower glass.

"Is anything wrong?"

"Nothing is wrong, Chrissie. Just because I do something without you doesn't mean there is something wrong."

My cheeks flush from that one. "Good to know. I'll try to remember that one." I say it deliberately silly and Neil laughs.

He opens the shower door and peeks out at me, his green eyes smiling. "I love you, Chrissie. Now go away and let me shower."

I laugh, tossing a towel at him. "Wouldn't you rather have me in the shower?" I ask, raising my eyebrows.

"Not today. Any day, all days, but not today."

The shower door closes. He starts to wash himself

there, and seeing him through the blurring glass of the door, touching himself *there,* lathering himself *there,* knowing what he's doing yet not seeing it clearly enough, gets me extremely hot.

I'm about to take off my shirt and panties when the water shuts off and the door opens. Neil grabs a towel, rubbing it across his head, then swiping his body before wrapping it around his hips.

I don't know why I ask it, but I do. "Where did you go last night?"

Neil looks up, startled. "I told you. For a walk."

"Until 10 in the morning, Neil? You expect me to buy that one?"

I don't know what he sees on my face, but he tosses the towel onto the counter and walks from the room.

"Fuck, Chrissie. Are you really going to start getting jealous now? After all I've been through with you, now is when you decide you can't trust me and start becoming jealous? Is that what you're telling me?"

Of course, the way he says it makes me sound stupid. I follow him to the bedroom and pause just inside the doorway. Neil is already in bed, lying on his back. He stares at me. I stare at him.

Neil starts to laugh, shaking his head at me. "Jeez, Chrissie, I can't believe you got jealous. But you are so cute when you get princess-ape-shit jealous."

He laughs harder and I glare at him. "I'm not jealous. I did not get anything close to princess-ape-shit jealous."

He turns onto his side, his cheek resting in his palms, his soft green eyes bright with humor. "Yes, you did. Admit it. You're jealous." His expression changes into *sweet Neil*. "I kind of like it. You being possessive and jealous for a change." Then comes a subtle darkening of his gaze, and I feel it *there*. "It's a fucking turn-on to see you be jealous over me for a change. Why don't you come back to bed for a while? You should probably sleep, too. We have a long night tonight."

"I don't want to because you're being a jerk and you won't answer me. Worse, you're making fun of me and I hate that."

That came out more peevish than I wanted it to, but it makes Neil's eyes gleam more. I wonder if I am starting to feel a touch possessive and jealous over him. He certainly thinks so and he's enjoying it.

Glaring at him, I sink down on the bed, sitting on my knees, close to him without touching him.

"You're such a conceited jerk," I murmur, tight-lipped. "Do you get jealous over me?"

He eases back against the pillow, hair pushed out of his face by his palm, his gaze serious and tender. "All the time."

I lie on my side, facing him. "Why didn't you ever tell me?"

His laughter is not of humor. It is more a rattling of exasperation. "How could you not fucking know that? I think of you all the time when we're not together. I get jealous when I don't know what you're doing. You're the first girl I've ever felt this way about."

My brows hitch upward in my forehead. "Really?"

He nods. It sounds like fluff, the kind of thing you say

to a girl to put to rest questions you don't want to answer, and yet Neil is never anything less than honest with me and in my center, in a sweetly warming way, it feels like the truth.

"You didn't feel that way about your ex?" I whisper cautiously, since it is territory we don't discuss very often.

His eyes lock on mine. "You are the only girl I've ever felt this way about."

Second surprise. Things were intense with his exgirlfriend. A lot of shitty history. Neil beat up Andy Despensa and put him in the hospital for fucking her. None of this makes sense, him claiming I'm the only girl he's ever been jealous over, but instinct tells me he's not lying.

I mold into his side, resting my head on his shoulder, and ease forward to kiss him on the chest. My hand starts gliding across his abdomen, then lower, lower.

Neil adjusts me against his side. "I'm tired, Chrissie. Let me sleep."

I brush him *there*. "You are also really hard, Neil."

A rough, frustrated laugh. "I always get hard when you touch me. Doesn't always mean I want sex."

I stroke him lightly and he groans. I peek up at him. "No?"

He looks down at me. "Why don't you kiss him," he whispers, "and put us both to sleep smiling?"

Oh yuck, not that again. Why do all guys want *that*? I continue the caresses, playing with his cock in fast little drive-bys, and he melts into my touch but nothing more. He doesn't move into me. He doesn't kiss me. He doesn't touch me. Unfortunately, every time I stroke his erection I get a little hotter and anxious in my flesh.

I stare down at it, running my hand up and down the length. I've never done it before. Crap, I don't even know how, but something in how Neil is luxuriating in me stroking him makes me kind of want to do it.

A first. Something sexually I haven't done first with Alan. Something that's just mine and Neil's. He twitches in my fingers and cautiously I take him in my mouth. His entire body jerks in surprise and he opens his eyes, watching as I run my lips up the length of him. I pause at the tip and his penis swells and pulses in my palm. I kiss it lightly and run my tongue around it. I watch the changing lines of his face and I can feel him tightening *there*.

I place my lips around him and his eyes close, his fingers coming to my hair. I suck harder. He groans. Then I tease him with my tongue and swallow him fully.

I still.

"Don't stop," he says through ragged breaths. I suck harder, flicking with my tongue, and his hips pulse in the rhythm of my motion.

I feel his fingers tighten in my hair, moving me up and down on him faster, then he guides my hand back to the length of him, wanting me to stroke and suck him. It's such a turn-on, the feeling of my power over Neil in this, his uncharacteristic selfishness, the way he is just taking what I'm giving and not offering a thing to relieve the ache in my body.

I suck harder, pushing him deeper.

"Chrissie…" He moans. "If you don't stop I'm going

to come in your mouth." But even as he says that, I feel his body flexing within my hands, his face tightening as he thrusts into my mouth.

He cries out, spilling into my mouth, his hand clutching my head there and I still. I don't know what to do with *it*. Do I spit it out? Before I can figure it out, I swallow on reflex. His hand drops away from me and my mouth leaves him. I kiss my way slowly up until I'm curled against him again. I kiss the underside of his jaw. It wasn't an act I thought I would enjoy, but I did. There is something in how Neil looks, his closed-eyed pleased expression that makes me feel really good about sharing this for the first time with him.

His eyes open and he kisses me. "I love you."

I'm a little embarrassed over having done that and more than a little pleased with how he looks like I did it well. I sink my teeth into my lower lip. "Are you both smiling now?"

Neil rolls his eyes, but his smile deepens. "Oh, definitely." He turns on his side into me and runs the tip of an index finger along the line of my cheek. "Why did you do that? You never want to give me a blow job."

I stare up at him. "Was it OK?"

He groans in pleasure. "Definitely OK. You can kiss him any time you want to."

I crinkle my nose at him. "Don't get carried away, Neil."

He kisses my shoulder. "I need sleep. Go to sleep."

I'm not tired, but I lie in the wrap of his body, listening to his breathing changes. I stare at his face, the softened features, the unkempt waves of hair. There are moments when we are together that I love Neil in a way that is sweetly painful.

I touch my lips against his chest. I wish I loved him in this sweetly painful way in more than just moments. I wish it were always. I'm not there yet, but the moments are good. They make me feel less anxious about this road I'm on with Neil. I try really hard to love him the way that I want to love him, but I only get moments here and there. But today it is enough.

~~~

Ernie Levine knows how to throw a party, I'll give him that.

I lean back against the bar on the far side of the room and stare into the club. The walls vibrate from the thundering music, loud chatter and laughter. The bodies are packed in to the point that the dance floor is suffocating.

Everyone is here. The Seattle bands who are famous and in town. The Seattle bands who are not famous. And the bands that are the buzz and in the process of breaking, like Arctic Hole. Blending with them are the famous, the *not*, the trendy and the weird. The strange mix of personalities that makes up the music industry everywhere, even in Seattle.

There is also quite a bit of press. More than I care for.

I take a sip of my drink. Ernie threw a nice publicity party for the guys, but it doesn't make me like him any better. He's just another opportunistic music industry insider, signing up bands, looting the creative talent in

Seattle, hoping to strike a big payday with another Nirvana or Pearl Jam. He doesn't know what the fuck the guys are about or how to manage them. No wonder it's taking the band so long to break.

My gaze shifts to Terry Moore. Ernie should have pressed the label for a better record producer than Terry. I could produce Neil and the band better.

I hear knuckles rapping against the wood bar behind me. I turn to look over my shoulder.

"Do you want another drink, Miss?"

I set down my glass. "Chardonnay."

I turn back around and my eyes fix on Neil. The band—Neil, Josh, Les Wilson, Nate Kassel, and Pat Larsen—are clustered together on sofas, the guys bizarrely looking exactly like they do killing time in the apartment. Only here they are surrounded by girls. Fawning, wooing girls, more than overtly making advances on the guys. Pat Larsen's girlfriend is furious and hovering over him, sitting on the arm of the couch, looking like she's going to kick in the face of the next girl who comes near him. The guys have been kissed, touched, pulled and propositioned more tonight that I've ever seen before. I quietly slipped out of the circle surrounding them after the first twenty minutes here.

I smile, though this probably shouldn't make me smile. Neil just looks so grossly uncomfortable being the center of the universe, surrounded and pulled on. It's so cute how frequently he looks at me to make sure he's not in trouble.

My gaze softens as it meets Neil's. I feel the smile in

his eyes in my center. He looks miserable. I know he wants me over there with him. I know he's worried that this is pissing me off, but I am not pissed. I just needed a breather from the damn thing.

Come here, Neil mouths.

I shake my head.

Not a chance, I mouth in his direction.

He gives me an exasperated look.

I toss him a pout.

Laughing, I turn back to the bar and grab my wine. I feel a light tap on my shoulder and look up to find that gross guy who has been staring at me all night, now next to me.

He leans forward. "Hi."

I smile stiffly in a perfect *rich-girl-not-interested* Rene kind of way and shift my gaze back to Neil. In a moment, the guy wanders off and I'm relieved, though I do feel badly over my rudeness. I've never felt comfortable with guys hitting on me. It's better to simply make them disappear quickly.

I down a hefty swallow of my wine. Crap, it's got to be after 2 a.m. When are things going to start shutting down here? We leave early in the morning on the road. A little alone time with Neil would be a really good thing since we're going to be trapped the majority of the time in a tour bus with the rest of the guys.

I toss down the remainder of my wine and set down the glass on the bar. *Maybe I'll just leave. I really want to get out of here...*

"How does it feel to know everyone here wants to

fuck him?"

Everyone here. Oh the wording, it could only belong to one person in Seattle. The surface of my skin begins to crawl. What the hell is he doing here? I turn and come face-to-face with Andy Despensa. *Shit.*

"I'm sure every girl here wants him. Neil is an incredible guy." I manage to say that in a way that conveys without saying it that Andy *isn't* an incredible guy.

His eyes bore into me. "He is an incredible guy. But you know that firsthand. Don't you?"

Something about his voice makes me want to vomit. His eyes shift to Neil. Fuck, what an asshole. I can't believe they used to be friends. Why would Neil hang around with a jerkoff like Andy Despensa? Even if they did grow up together in Santa Barbara, he would have made my list of *people in my life to lose quickly.*

"You stay away from me," I hiss. "There is nothing you could ever say that I would ever want to hear."

Andy arches a brow. "Are you sure about that, Chrissie? I think we should have a long talk someday."

It feels as though I've just been taunted and threatened at once. My cheeks redden against my will.

"Fuck you," I snap, and I move quickly from the bar and away from Andy.

As I make my way around the dance floor to Neil, I'm fuming inside and, oddly, somewhat internally messy simultaneously. God, what a weird reaction to being in close proximity to a *jerk.*

Maybe it's just knowing Andy's history with Neil. But Andy Despensa had a way of automatically stirring a reaction in me before I knew anything about him. Even that first night in '89, before Neil and I were a couple, when Andy had done nothing but watch us dance together at Peppers, I'd felt it this way, all at once, out of nowhere. Prickly skin. Shuddering emotions. A flashing, instinctive reaction in me.

I've never instantly disliked anyone the way I instantly disliked Andy.

I push my way through the circle surrounding the guys, and sit on the arm of the sofa, planting my feet on Neil's thigh. His fingers close around my feet and he smiles up at me.

The smile fades from his face. "What's wrong?"

I shake my head and before I can stop myself, I say, "Andy is over there. Who the hell let him into the party?"

Neil's eyes flash, alarmed. "Did he talk to you? Was he bugging you, Chrissie?"

Neil is halfway off the sofa before I realize what a stupid mistake it was to tell him about Andy. I spring to my feet and grab his arm.

"He's not bugging me. I just didn't want to be on the other side of the room with him."

"You're not lying to me are you, Chrissie? Because if he fucking did anything to upset you—"

"He didn't do anything," I interrupt quickly.

I stare up at him, then finally Neil starts to relax. I move into his body and kiss him on the jaw.

"Can we get out of here?" I whisper.

Neil brushes my lower lip with his thumb. "We can get out of here." In a low, husky voice he adds, "I am really ready to get out of here with you, Chrissie."

His mouth covers mine, and before I realize what he is doing, my body is eased up from the ground until my legs are wrapped around his waist and my arms around his neck. Neil is kissing me, deep, long and with full tongue, in a very *non-Neil* way.

At the exit the kiss breaks, and I look back over Neil's shoulder to find Andy Despensa staring at me. My insides go cold again. I didn't see it before this moment, but I suddenly know that I dislike Andy because *he* hates *me*.

CHAPTER EIGHT

Neil flattens me against the apartment door, his lower body grinding into me, his mouth punishing against mine. He's been on fire since we left the club, charged with restless adrenaline, and the urgency of his flesh has me boiling from head to toe. He's not usually like this…I feel him push his cock deeper into me…and I mold into him, moving my body *there* as I struggle to match the heated thrust of his tongue and the force of his kisses.

His mouth lifts, and his panting breath, face close to mine, drowns out my own rapid inhales and exhales. He continues to rub his cock into me as he rummages in his pocket for the apartment key.

"You have no idea how much tonight I've been thinking about fucking you," he whispers against my skin. His hand moves up my bare thigh, under my sundress, and his fingers start teasing me through my panties. "I love the fucking sundresses. I makes it so damn easy to fuck you wherever we are." His tongue flicks along my shoulder blade. "I stared at you all night, thinking I should take you in the bathroom and fuck you there."

He bites my neck and I arch upward into him. Whatever this is I feel in him, it is a freaking turn-on. Maybe he's just hot after hours of having tits shoved in his face and women kissing and brushing up against him everywhere. Maybe he's just hot over me. Jeez, who cares what this is? He is going to be *crazy Neil* in bed tonight and I am totally into *crazy Neil* in bed.

I wait breathy and excited as he fumblingly tries to unlock the door, and I stare up at his face, the tautness of his skin across his features. Then my brows pucker. I've seen him look this way before.

For some reason the image Neil makes reminds me of that night we shared in the hotel after he exploded over me speaking with Andy Despensa. Strange, but that night four years ago was exactly like this. Caveman Neil dragging me from the party. Rough, brutal, emotionally void sex. An odd, angry impatience to fuck me and a bludgeoning need to do it. Raging Neil and an endless night of hard fucking.

His mouth comes back to mine just as the door gives way behind me. We stumble through and my feet leave me, and only Neil's quick hands save me. He scoops me up into him, my legs encircle his body, his fingers dig into my backside beneath my dress, and we continue to frantically consume each other's flesh as he starts moving us toward the bedroom.

"Oh fuck," he groans.

My eyes fly open. All motion has stopped, and Neil is frozen in place, staring at something in the living room. Struggling to catch my breath, I peek over my shoulder and my limbs go as tense as Neil's are.

Oh shit! Jack!

He sets me quickly down on my feet. I jerk my clothing into place and turn.

"Hello," Jack says in a way that makes my cheeks

burn.

"Daddy, what are you doing here?" I ask and my dad's gaze sharpens.

Crap, that came out lame, but I'm still in shock over finding my dad *here* and it is not even worth trying to figure out how he got into the apartment to be waiting for me.

I force a smile to my lips.

Jack arches a brow. "You are my daughter. Where should I be?"

Oh crud, he is keyed up with worry over me. It would be so much better if he just got angry sometimes. But worry is the worst. I've worried him, yet again, only this time I didn't mean to do it. Shit!

Neil's eyes lock on me and I lower my gaze from his. Quietly, he whispers, "You never called Jack, did you?"

I sink my teeth into my lower lip. Great, now I have angry Neil to deal with later.

"Shit, Chrissie," he says under his breath and then Neil rakes his hair with his hand.

I finally find my words. "It would have been nice if you had let me know you were coming here, Daddy."

Jack shrugs. "It would have been nice to be able to talk to you about the decisions you're making in your life. I got home from the road, expecting to spend some time with my daughter. Found your boxes in the Santa Barbara house. What I didn't find was you, Chrissie. The condo complex confirmed you'd moved out without leaving a forwarding address for them..." Jack's blue eyes lock on me. "...or for me."

I change course. "How did you know where I am?"

"Rene," he says calmly, but he is fuming. "Unlike you,

she answers her mobile phone when I call her."

Damn you, Rene.

Trying not to look flustered, I reply, "I was going to call you, Daddy. Things have been crazy since we got to Seattle. But I wouldn't have left Seattle without calling you."

"No? You left Berkeley without calling me."

I flush. The room fills with a heavy, awkward silence. Neil quickly recovers from his stupor and crosses the room with his hand outstretched. "Hey, Jack, how are you doing?"

I watch as they shake hands.

"I'm doing OK, Neil," Jack replies graciously.

"Good to hear," Neil says, with a slight nod. He looks like he wants to drop through the floor.

"Been hearing good things about you," Jack says.

Neil shrugs. "Trying hard, Jack."

"It will come. It will come. Keep your head on straight. Ignore the hype. Don't do anything you don't want to do and stay focused on the music and it will come."

I stare at them, unable to believe my freaking ears. Did Jack really give one of his folksy motivational musician talks to Neil in the middle of his chastising me? Jeez—this keeps getting weirder and weirder.

I sink down on a chair and stare at my white Keds. *Freaking unbelievable.*

"Is there a twenty-four-hour diner or restaurant near here?" Jack asks Neil. "I'd like to take my daughter out to breakfast, if that's fine with you, Neil."

I roll my eyes. *I'm sitting right here. Why don't you ask me what I would like, Jack?*

"It's four in the morning, Daddy. I don't want breakfast."

His intense blue stare fixes on me in that way that screams *this is not debatable, Chrissie.*

"Hey, why don't I just get out of your way?" Neil suggests, grabbing his jacket from the floor. "I can take a walk and let you guys have some privacy."

Jack gives a slight smile. "Thanks. I'd appreciate that."

Neil's gaze shifts to me. "I'll be back soon."

I nod. *You had better be, Neil.*

Jack and I sit, both holding our tongues as we wait for Neil to leave. I stare off into space until the door clicks closed behind him. I slowly shift my gaze, expecting my dad to launch into whatever is on his mind that brought him here, but he doesn't. He just sits there, staring at me.

Jack couldn't make this any more awkward for me if he tried, and I'm a little irritated because I think he's deliberately doing that. Jeez, what do people do in such hideously awkward moments?

I ask, "Would you like some coffee, Daddy?"

"That would be nice, baby girl."

I stand up and hurriedly move toward the kitchen. I can feel the displacement of air behind me and know Jack is following me there. I focus on filling the pot with water, turning on the heat, grabbing a cup and then take the instant from the cupboard.

I put a level spoon into the mug. "We just have instant, Daddy. I'm sorry."

"Instant is fine."

I look over my shoulder to find Jack standing in the doorway and the way he's watching me nearly makes me cry. Now that Neil is gone, the worry is on Jack's face untempered.

"I'm sorry," I whisper. "I didn't mean to worry you."

"Well, you worried me." He pushes away from the doorframe and crosses the tiled floor to me. "What's going on, Chrissie? Something has been going on with you for months. Why won't you talk to me?"

He looks sad. Achingly sad and more than mildly concerned. Tears sting behind my eyelids.

I concentrate on pouring the boiling water into the cup. "There's nothing, Daddy."

"You haven't been home in months. You hardly ever call me and when you do talk to me, you are anxious to get off the phone quickly."

"I just finished my last semester at Cal. I wanted to focus on school. Make sure I graduate. It doesn't mean something is wrong. Why do you always overreact to everything?"

"I don't overreact. I'm pretty damn reasonable ninety-nine percent of the time. Don't try to change the subject. We're not talking about me. We're talking about you. Something is going on with you, Chrissie. Don't pretend that it's not."

I carefully carry the mugs into the living room, set them on the coffee table and then settle sitting on my knees, facing the sofa. Jack sinks down on the couch.

He stirs his coffee to cool it, and it looks like he's trying to figure out where to begin round two of this.

"So you're going out on the road with Neil?" he asks calmly.

Dammit, Rene, why did you have to tell Jack all my shit? There is no point in lying, so I don't bother.

"Yes. I am going out on tour with Neil. It sounded like a fun thing to do, and after school I could use a break from everything."

He stares at me, perplexed. "When did you start seeing Neil again?"

I flush, and it's so stupid that I feel guilty over not having shared *this* with Jack. "About a month ago."

"Why didn't you tell me?" Jack asks, and he looks hurt.

"I thought you liked Neil."

"I do. He's a good kid. That's not the issue here. The issue is what's happening in your life that you don't want me to know."

"Nothing!"

Jack crosses the room and sits on the floor close beside me. His fingers go to my chin and he turns my face so I have no choice but to look at him.

"Don't say everything is fine, when it's not. I'm not blind. I can see when something is going on with you. Let's talk it out, Chrissie, so I can stop worrying about you."

The earth falls away beneath me, taking my composure with it. I start to cry, and Jack takes me into his arms.

"It's OK, baby girl. It's OK."

I shake my head and say in a soggy voice, "I've made such a mess of my life. I'm a terrible person. Don't be angry. Please don't worry, Daddy."

He lays his cheek on my head. "You're my daughter. I've got to worry. Those are the rules. And your life isn't a mess. Nothing is ever that bad. And you are not a terrible person. You're an amazing girl."

I sniff, trying to keep my nose from dripping on his shirt. "I'm just sorting through some stuff, but definitely nothing that should get you all freaked out. I moved to Seattle with Neil. What's the big deal? We've been together for four years. You didn't need to come here."

"You moved to Seattle and didn't tell me," he counters.

I sit back and look up at Jack. "It was a good decision. I think the best thing for me. Neil is an incredible guy, the most amazing friend I've ever had. I couldn't have made it through the last month without him."

Jack's face tightens and his blue eyes sharpen alertly. "What do you mean not *make it through the last month*? What's happened in the last month? Did someone hurt you? Were you...?"

He can't say it, but I can tell by his face what he's thinking. He's wondering if I got mugged or worse. *Oh crap!* Why did I have to mention last month? I've kicked up Jack's worry about ten levels.

"It's not that bad..." The words die inside me as Jack's face grows more alarmed.

"Not that bad, huh?" He lets out a ragged breath, impatient and anxious. "What happened, Chrissie, that isn't *that bad*?" The way he says that makes me cringe. "I think it's time you talk to me."

Oh no, that was not a request. It was a warning that

Jack is not going to let this one go. He stares at me expectantly.

I drop my gaze. I can't believe I'm about to tell my dad about April. But if there is a way out other than just telling him everything, I don't see it.

"I had an abortion in April," I hear myself say, and my voice sounds far away, not even my own.

The room fills with crushing silence. I don't know which one of us is more shocked, me that I said it or Jack that he heard it.

Jack's expression is impossible to read. "Are you OK?"

My eyes widen to their fullest. "I'm fine," I say quickly to reassure him. "But I'm still a little overwhelmed by the experience. I didn't realize until after it was over how much I didn't want to do it."

Oh fuck, why did I confess that last part? I haven't even told that to Neil. Damn.

Jack's gaze grows more intense and probing. "Then why did you do it?"

That one I am not going to explain. Nothing could force me, not even the rabid concern I see in my dad's eyes, to tell him about Alan and me. Nope, that part of this mistake I'm not sharing.

"Was it Neil's?" Jack asks, his voice harsh and clipped.

"No. And Neil wouldn't have wanted me to have an abortion if it were his. He didn't think I should do it, but he respected my decision and was really cool through it all."

Jack nods, his mouth tightening in that way he has

when he is really hit emotionally by something. "I'm glad Neil was there for you." He looks away. "I'm glad you let someone be there for you. Christ, Chrissie, why didn't you tell me about this?"

I feel the tears burn behind my lids. "It was my mistake and I wanted to fix it on my own. And Neil was wonderful, Daddy. Really wonderful about everything. He took good care of me. I could never have finished the last month at Cal without him." I wipe at my nose and take in a shuddering breath. "After I'd done it, I realized I didn't want to. It's kind of messed with my head and I almost dropped out of school. But Neil wouldn't let me. He stayed in Berkeley with me until I got my shit together again. He let me talk, he listened and he really cares. He has been so supportive. It made me realize how stupid I was to break up with him."

Jack's brows lower into a frown. "If you didn't want to do it, why did you?"

"The guy wouldn't have wanted it. He dumped me and it didn't seem fair to make a decision all on my own that would impact us both for the rest of our lives."

Anger flashes in Jack's eyes. "He had a choice. His vote ended when he climbed into bed with you. After that, your body, your choice."

My face goes scarlet. I've never heard Jack so angry and I'm flooded with shame that I worried him because he's being the dad I've always known when I've let him be there for me: clear-headed, supportive, loving.

Jack places a light kiss on my cheek and brushes at my tears with his fingertips.

"I'm sorry, baby girl. I wish you had talked to me before you did anything. We could have talked it through together."

"Well, we're talking it through now," I say quietly.

"So the guy...what happened to him?"

Jack sounds angry again.

I shrug and fight back a new onslaught of tears. "We're over. I told you. He dumped me."

"Asshole," Jack says under his breath in nearly a growl. "I may be fifty now, Chrissie, but I can still kick his ass if you want me to."

I take a sip of my coffee, make a soggy laugh, and shake my head. Jeez—there is nothing here to make me laugh, but *that* one I didn't expect. "Don't bother. It's not worth it. He's out of my life for good."

Jack nods. "Good. I don't think I'd care for the guy. I hope that fucker never comes near you again."

He won't, Jack. Alan doesn't love me...

I cut off my thoughts and sigh heavily. "Being an adult is so much harder than I thought it would be. Why doesn't anyone tell you that? Every time I think I know where I'm going, the road changes. I'm so tired of the road always changing unexpectedly on me."

Jack gives me a sad and sympathetic smile. "The road always changes even when you think you're on a straight path. It does for everyone, Chrissie. Not just you. Try to remember it's about the journey, baby girl. It's not about where we're going. When the road changes it will bother you less if you always remember it's about the journey."

Typical Jack. Typical 60s mumbo jumbo. For some

reason it doesn't irritate me today. I'm actually sort of feeling better inside myself. Calmer. Less frantic.

"I don't know what to do with my life, Daddy."

"Welcome to the club, Chrissie. We are all in the same place and we're going to the same place no matter what we do with our lives. The best journeys I've had have been when I've not known where I'm going, on roads I've never expected."

I study my father. "How did you get over Mom?"

He looks at me, his face enigmatic. "Whoever said that I did? Just because Lena isn't here doesn't mean I'm not with her. Your mom doesn't have to be here for me to love her." He starts to pick up our mugs from the coffee table. "You can love anyone you want, Chrissie. Just don't forget that you still have to live."

I watch Jack move toward the kitchen. He says, "I'll just pop these in the microwave. They're cold. And you can go into the hallway and get Neil."

"Neil went for a walk. He's not in the hallway."

Jack laughs. "Oh, Chrissie, I saw the way he looked at you before he went through the door. The kid didn't get any farther than the hallway. I'm not happy about you going out on the road. I think you should come home. But you've got a good guy there, baby girl. Neil really cares about you. That I am not worried about."

~ ~ ~

We arrive at the load-up parking lot before the rest of the band. Neil holds up my suitcases in front of him. "Black one in the bus with you? Duffel in the cargo hold, Chrissie?"

"I think so. I don't think I'll need the junk in the duffel until we stop."

Neil tosses my duffel into the cargo bay, then turns to Jack. "Thanks for seeing us off."

"Thanks for letting me," Jacks says.

Jack stayed all morning in the apartment. It was nice he spent time with Neil and me. The three of us talked, really talked, and it was good. Even if it was filled with folksy advice from Jack to Neil about being out on the road, and at times a little awkward since it's obvious that me being with Neil means that I'm *with* Neil.

How lame is that? I'm an adult and it feel uncomfortable for my dad to know *officially* that I'm living with Neil. The pretense is gone with my dad, and it makes everything feel kind of different and not normal yet.

I struggle to contain my flashing thoughts. I definitely don't want to start turning in my head all the shit that went down at the apartment—*jeez, don't think about that one, Chrissie. What girl tells her father she's had an abortion?*—and completing the ritual of the tour bus departure is going to be strange enough. Why does this feel like I'm being sent off to summer camp?

I watch as my dad gives Neil a one-arm, halfway, guy-type hug, but before Jack pulls back he gives a couple of hard pats on Neil's back.

"You take care of my girl," Jack warns. "If you don't, you're going to hear from me."

"You mean there's more than what I've already heard from you this morning to hear from you?" Neil grimaces, but his eyes are sparkling.

Jack shakes his head, glaring. "A lot more. You had better have been listening earlier to every word."

Neil taps his head with an index finger. "Burned into my memory for life. Every word."

"Good," Jack says.

Neil smiles. "See ya, Jack."

"Don't be a fuck-up," Jack warns. "The road can only turns you into a fuck-up if you let it."

Neil nods. "I know. Besides, I'd have to deal with Chrissie and she is way worse than you."

Jack is laughing as he turns toward me. He rests his arms on my shoulder. "I'm going to miss you, baby girl."

I bite my lower lip to hold back the emotion. "I know, Daddy. I'm going to miss you, too."

His eyes fix on me, loving and intense. "Be careful. Stay smart. Things can get crazy. If it gets to be too crazy, come home."

"I will. It's going to be OK."

Jack nods. "Call me every stop, and fly home once in a while."

"I will, Daddy," I promise.

He puts a light kiss on my forehead, and sighs. "I never expected to be sending you off on tour. I never wanted you to be near any of this. Not ever."

I stare up at him, startled. *Is that why Jack never had me travel with him? He didn't want me near the music industry?* Most days I still can't make sense of my dad, but it's a nice thought, much kinder than the suspicions I used to have about why Jack never took me out on tour with him. So today I'm not going to try to figure out my dad.

The entire chemistry changes with the arrival of the rest of the band, and soon the guys are like a fast-talking, loud football huddle surrounding Jack. Everyone wants to talk to him—*everyone always wants to talk to Jack*—but today, it makes me a smidge wistful because I want him to be only my dad. Like he was in the apartment, sitting on the floor with Neil and me. Like he is when we are at home in Santa Barbara together.

The bus driver exits the bus and I have to forcibly keep from making a face. Oh dear. He does not look at all fun, and how the heck does he fit in the driver's seat? He must be nearly 6'5" and I'm sure 300lbs if he's anything.

"Listen up, dipshits," he says, silencing everyone. "I'm Markem. It's time to load up. It's time to go. Let's set some ground rules since we're going to be together for a long time. My bus, my rules. My job is to get you there on time. Your job is not to piss me off. Front of the bus: mine. Everywhere else on the bus: yours. And when I say cops, settle down, and you clean up whatever the fuck you're doing. Violate my rules, I set you on the side of the road. I don't give a fuck if we're in the middle of the desert. It's fine by me if you stay out there. It gives me one less asshole to babysit."

My gaze moves to Neil and he just rolls his eyes, but he looks like he's half-dying of humiliation and the other half like he wants to say something. I bite my lip not to laugh, but a chuckle escapes me anyway.

Markem looks in my direction and his eyes narrow. "Nobody told me anything about hauling a fifi. Whose fifi is she?"

This time I make a face. I can't help it. *Yuck, fifi?*

Jack cuts through the guys, extending his hand toward the bus driver. "Excuse me. I'm not one of the dipshits. People usually just call me Jack. And that girl is my daughter. She is not a fifi."

The driver's face goes through several alterations but it settles on a stunned expression. "Jesus Christ, Jackson Parker."

They shake hands. "No, just Jack."

Markem's eyes widen. "Are you shitting me? I'm hauling your daughter this tour? Why the fuck didn't anyone tell me?"

They turn in unison to face me, with Jack nodding his head. "Don't get pissed, Markem. No one told me until today she'd be on this tour. Kind of puts us in the same boat. And if any of the dipshits step out of line with her, I would appreciate it if you would kick the shit out of them."

God, Daddy! Can this get any more embarrassing?

"Will do, Mr. Parker," Markem assures him. "Will do."

Jack smiles. "Just Jack, please. I'll feel more confident that you'll kick the shit out of them if we're on a first-name basis."

Markem laughs. "Jack, then."

Jack and Markem launch into conversation while the guys disappear into the bus.

Neil crosses the concrete and drops a kiss on my cheek. "I'll leave you alone with Jack to finish saying goodbye."

"Thanks, Neil."

His gaze roams my face. "Are you OK? Not having second thoughts, are you?"

I'm having second thoughts, third, fourth…but I shake my head and smile. "No way. I want to be with you. You couldn't leave me behind if you try."

Once alone with my dad, I'm starting to feel internally messy. For some reason, this goodbye is particularly hard for me.

My dad gives me one last hug, and the way he is holding on to me feels almost like he doesn't want to let me go. He's never hugged me this way before.

I step back the minute his arms loosen. "I love you, Daddy."

"I love you too, Chrissy. Don't forget that."

I laugh and roll my eyes. "I won't."

I start making my way up the stairs and pause to take one last look at Jack, then step into the bus to see what the heck I've gotten myself into. The guys have already staked their own territory and are sprawled out comfortably.

My eyes widen in surprise. Well, this isn't as awful as I thought it would be. It's sort of comfortable inside even if it is less luxurious than I imagined it would be. A table with chairs. Small fridge and microwave and a cooking top. Long bench seats that convert for sleeping. A shower. A toilet. Yuck, I'm going to be sharing a bathroom with five guys, six if I count the driver. Storage cabinets, a TV, a sound system, and across the back of the bus a real bed built-in.

I spot my black bag on the bed and make my way to the back of the bus. I arrange the pillows into a pile and climb up to sit there. I guess this is where I'm supposed to hang, my own private space in guy world.

In a minute the doors close, Neil breaks off from his discussion with Josh and joins me. He sits with his back against the other wall, facing me.

"I'm really glad you're here with me," Neil says and he looks so happy that I joined him that I can feel it in my center.

"Me too."

"Fuck, I'm tired." Neil sighs, leaning his head back against the wall. "Jack sure can talk. I've never had anyone talk at me so much before. I'm exhausted."

I smile and pat the spot beside me. "Why don't you lie down? Why don't you sleep?"

He eases down beside me on his side and scooches me back into him. The ignition turns over with those loud rattling groans a diesel engine makes. There is the sensation of movement and we are leaving Seattle.

I pull back the blind and look out the back window. Jack is standing in the parking lot, watching me leave. Tears clog in my throat, because the way he is standing, the look on his face, reminds me of when I was a little girl and always had to watch him leave. Only now *he* watches *me*.

CHAPTER NINE

I tap my pen against my journal. *Day one on tour.* I want to write something, but it's been pretty dull. The guys have been sleeping since we pulled out of Seattle, and for three hours we have been stuck at the border.

I pull back the shades and peek out the window. Jeez, there are a lot of cars still ahead of us waiting to enter Canada. It should have only taken us a couple of hours to get to Vancouver, but we've been stuck in a long line of vehicles forever.

I scribble the heading *Things I hate about the road.* I glare at Les Wilson and write *guys who snore when they sleep.* A car behind us honks, like that's going to speed us up. *Border crossings.* I scrunch up my nose and try to ignore the odor. I'm not even going to try to figure out how the guys made it smell like a locker room in half a day. I hear the toilet flush. *Sharing a bathroom with six guys.*

The door opens and Markem's hulking frame contorts as he works his way out of the tiny closet that's supposed to be a lavatory.

He closes the door, catches me watching him, and smiles. "You doing all right, Miss Parker?"

"I'm doing great," I reply, fighting not to roll my eyes.

Miss Parker. Markem won't call me Chrissie no matter how many times I ask him to do it. From the second he learned I'm Jack's daughter, *fifi* went out the window and I am Miss Parker. The guys are still called *dipshit*, but ugh, I would almost prefer fifi because his extreme solicitous manner makes me feel like an outsider.

My gaze moves with him as he labors toward the front of the bus, making it shimmy with each step, and then he drops like a ton of bricks into the driver's seat.

Face it, Chrissie, you are an outsider. You always have been; in high school, at Cal, and now on the road. You will forever be the girl who doesn't fit in. Accept it, that's who you are. The only person happy you are here is Neil.

I shove my journal back into my bag, and settle on the pillow to watch him sleep. He's so cute when he sleeps. I feel a pleasant kind of tingle move through my body. Lightly, I kiss him. Nothing. Still sound asleep.

I close my eyes. I should probably take a nap. Our first day on the road, while a short hop on the highway, is still going to be a long day. There's a gig tonight. Neil is performing before a twenty-thousand-seat sold-out crowd at the BC Royale Stadium—that is, if we ever make it across the border.

I fidget and stare at the ceiling. Neil's hand is suddenly under my shirt, his fingers working their way beneath my bra.

I grab his wrist. "Stop it. Don't start anything we can't finish."

He leans up on an elbow, looking down at me, his fingers fluttering across my stomach. "You played with my body while I slept. It's only fair I get to play with yours."

I roll my eyes. "I kissed you. Once."

He lowers his face until his lips are in my hair near my ear. "One kiss, Chrissie, is a lot. We were interrupted last night."

My cheeks flood with color, but I don't stop him as his hand moves back to my breast. He brushes my nipple with his thumb. I feel myself tighten there.

"There's no privacy." I squirm against his touch and kisses.

The curtain is jerked closed, blocking view of the bed from the rest of the bus.

"You're crazy, Neil. I'm not doing it in a bus with five other guys six feet away."

Neil kisses my shoulder and then peeks up at me, determined.

"We should take advantage every time the guys are asleep on the bus. It may be the nicest place we find to have sex for the next ten months. I don't know who we will be sharing a room with and I don't know what kind of dives the promoter has put us in. I'm only the opening act. I've been on some really shitty, low-budget tours."

My brows lift. "You're opening for Scream on an arena tour. I thought it would be nice. You mean we may not even have our own room?"

Neil shrugs, but gives me a contrite look.

"Thanks for telling me ahead of time, Neil."

He nips playfully on my lower lip and then I feel his fingers trying to work open the clasp of my bra. I jerk away from him and sit, arms crossed.

Neil falls back against his pillow, exhales loudly, aggravated, and runs a hand through his hair.

"Don't be pissed at me, Chrissie. If the rooms are too awful I'll fix it."

I arch a brow. "Fix it, huh? How?"

"I don't know, but I will. I promise. Don't be pissed."

"I'm not pissed. I just wish you'd told me we might be sharing a room."

Neil pulls me down on top of him and holds me against his chest in spite of my protests. He starts kissing me again.

"You're not getting any, Neil."

His hands flatten on my butt, molding me against him. He moves against me *there*. His lips dance up my neck, feather light. Not fair. And even as I tell myself *no way* my body starts to rub against him.

The bus lurches forward and it feels like we're driving on the open road again. Neil stops touching and kissing me, and I frown at him, wondering why he stopped after getting me willing to screw him in the bus.

He takes in a ragged breath. "Fuck, you shouldn't have wasted time arguing with me. We'll be in Vancouver in a half an hour. Shit."

"You are so conceited, Neil. We don't need more than half an hour."

"Very funny." He groans. "Jeez, I've been horny as hell since Jack interrupted us last night and I really wanted to christen the bus."

I can feel my eyes opening to their fullest. "Oh. Christen the bus? That's what this is about. Jeez, guys are such jerks. What, is it a competition to see who christens the bus first? What other things do you guys christen on the road?"

He looks annoyed. "Nothing. I don't do the girls on the road. You know that, Chrissie. It's the best way to fuck up your life."

I ease off him and sit with my back against the far wall, facing him. I remember what Josh told me at the camp ground.

"Not ever?" I probe. "You've never had sex with a girl on the road?"

He's angry that I asked. "No. We've always been together when I've been on tour. I wouldn't cheat on you, Chrissie. I wouldn't do that to you."

I fight not to let the hurt show on my face from the unintended punch those words carry. I cheated on him and somehow he loves me. We're together again, but what I did still makes me feel awful. Neil has forgiven me. I need to learn to forgive myself.

I roll forward, crawl across the bed, kiss him on the cheek, and then lie against him.

"I'll try not to be a pain," I say.

Neil laughs. "That's not going to work, Chrissie. You're always a pain. And if this tour is as bad as the last one, you being a pain starts in about twenty minutes when we reach the hotel."

I make a pout. "I won't say a word. I won't complain. I promise."

Twenty minutes later, I hear the screeching of brakes against tires as the bus rolls slowly to a stop. Neil starts gathering our things.

"Have you been to Vancouver before?" he asks.

"Nope."

He looks surprised.

"I was a little disappointed we didn't have to use our passports," I say, following Neil to the exit on the bus. "That we could just cross through the border. I really wanted a stamp. Yours is full of stamps. I don't have any. It makes my passport look so pathetic."

Neil's brows crinkle. "You've never been out of the country?"

I shake my head.

"Not even Canada?" he asks.

"Nope. I've hardly been out of California."

He shakes his head and goes down the steps. Once at the bottom, he turns to offer me his hand.

We walk around the bus and my eyes fix on the hotel in surprise. Well, jeez, this doesn't look awful. A beautiful, high-rise hotel in an area of the city that looks upscale.

I give Neil a small shove. "You're such a jerk. Why do you like to mess with me all the time?"

"I wasn't messing with you, Chrissie."

I can feel Josh watching us.

"Bullshit," I counter. "All those stories about how tough it is when you are out on the road and how terrible everything is, they're crap, aren't they?"

"It wasn't crap. It's not crap." Neil rakes his hair with his hand. "Jeez, Chrissie, can we not do this?"

"I'm just saying it wasn't very nice of you in the bus to freak me out about how cruddy this is going to be. Sometimes when you're messing with me, it isn't funny."

He leans into me, and quietly says, "I just wanted to get laid. We haven't had sex in two days."

I make a face at him and Josh passes by us, rolling his eyes at Neil in way that lets me know he's heard every word of our argument and that he thinks I'm being a bitch.

I walk ahead of Neil into the hotel. At the front desk, I peek at him out of the corner of my eye. I struggle not to laugh. He has that *Chrissie is driving me nuts* look. Neil is adorable when he's aggravated.

We are quickly checked in and handed our keys.

Neil taps his knuckles on the counter to get Josh's attention. "We've got sound check in two hours."

"I'm going to hit the bar, get something to eat and drink. You coming?"

"Maybe later. But I don't think so," Neil says grimly.

Ah, nice touch, Neil. The Chrissie-is-giving-me-shit tone of voice.

I am silent in the elevator as we chug our way upward floor by floor.

"Would you like me to go out and get you something to eat?" he asks. "Or are you going to order room service?"

"I don't know yet."

"Do you want to come with me for sound check?"

"I don't know yet."

The elevator doors open. He shakes his head, runs a hand through his hair and waits for me to follow him into the hallway.

Inside our room, I drop my bag and I hear Neil securing the safety latch of the door. I kick off my flip-flops.

"How soon do you have to leave?" I ask.

"I've got about ninety minutes."

I pull off my shirt, unfasten my bra, let it fall to the floor, and then turn toward him. His expression changes as I unbutton my jeans and pull them off.

He makes a long, ragged exhale of breath, and then wags a finger at me. "God, you are a pain in the ass. You deliberately made me think the entire way up here you were pissed and we were going to the room to fight."

Naked, I step over to him. "No, I didn't. I let the guys think I was pissed. I hate it that they know all our shit all the time, and I didn't want them to know we came up here to fuck."

~~~

I'm pulled from sleep by the feel of Neil's arms at my sides and the touch of his lips. My eyes flutter open and I find him standing beside the bed, above me, a smile in his eyes.

"I've got to go, Chrissie."

I sit up and notice that he is dressed in knee-length army green shorts, flip-flops and an unspectacular t-shirt. The surfer boy from Santa Barbara, with his deep tan, the flecks of sun in his chestnut hair, and those lush emotion-bright green eyes. California Neil in Vancouver.

"Where do you think you're going? The beach?" I tease and he laughs.

"Very funny."

"Do you want me to get dressed and come with you?"

His expression changes and he looks uncomfortable. "Not today, Chrissie. First day on tour. I don't even have a set put together yet. I need to focus. I have no idea what I'm doing and I can't quite figure out how I got here. One day we're playing small venues, theaters, and the next we're opening on an arena tour. Twenty thousand people and they are not even our fans. I don't know what the fuck I'm doing, Chrissie."

My eyes widen in surprise. I didn't expect that. I've never heard Neil sound unsure of himself. It makes me feel more connected to him, a sense that he needs me a little bit, when it usually only feels like I need him. It's a nice feeling. Good. Really good.

I slip my arms around him and press my lips against his neck. "You got here, Neil, because you are incredible. The only problem you have, as far as I can tell, is that you still think you're on a Southern California beach."

Neil laughs. "Fuck, was that supposed to be motivational? That one is right up there with Jack's *don't be a fuck-up* speech."

I start to giggle even as I kiss lightly down his neck. I stop and smile at him. "Just be Neil and the crowd will love you."

He presses his lips against the flesh beneath my ear and the feel of him moves through me sweetly. A hand caresses my breast. I give him a gentle push away from me.

"Stop it and get out of here. You don't have time."

His eyes glow wickedly. "Wear something sexy tonight. You have no idea what it does to me when you let Rene dress you up in something sexy."

I throw a pillow at him. "I thought you thought the sundresses were sexy."

"Only because they're easy to get off you."

I throw another pillow and hit him in the face. He pulls something from his pocket and drops it on the nightstand.

"Your pass backstage. Don't forget it, Chrissie."

I pick it up, rolling my eyes. "I won't forget it." I turn it in my fingers. *Christian Parker. Band.* I frown. "Why did you tell them to put my full name on this? No one ever calls me Christian. Not even my dad."

Neil shrugs. "I don't know. I just did."

I turn it in my fingers.

Neil crosses the room.

"See ya, Neil."

"See ya, Chrissie."

The door closes, and I lie back on the bed and smile. Christian Parker. I kind of like that. Sort of a symbol of a new Chrissie. A new me. A new everything.

CHAPTER TEN

I climb out of the shower and grab a towel. I rub it briskly over my hair and then wrap it around my head. I take another towel, hastily drying myself as I cross to the vanity. Fuck, how could I have fallen back to sleep? I use my forearm to swipe at the steam on the mirror. *Good one, Chrissie. Good one.* You are already late, you steamed up the bathroom, and you don't have time for this.

I use the blow dryer, only to remove the dampness from my hair and not to style it. I rummage through my makeup bag. Mascara? Yep, a must. Foundation? No, not tonight. Maybe a little blush. Lip gloss. Necessity.

I stare at myself in the mirror to make sure in my hurry I didn't make any glaring mistakes with the eyeliner. OK, now time to dress.

In the bedroom, I sink to the floor beside my duffel. Crap, I'm way north of Southern California. What's the weather like up here? I pull out of my bag jeans, my Chucks, a tight black t-shirt, and Neil's old, ratty cardigan which I appropriated from him nine months ago.

I dress in record time and race back into the bathroom. I jerk the brush through my hair, flip it over to get the underside, toss my head back and spray. Thank God I have fluffy hair I can turn into a metal chick hairdo without effort. Makes me look sort of less nerdy.

I stand in front of the mirror and do a fast once-over. I look totally tacky, totally a mess, and totally *Seattle*. I'd look like a bum if not for the one-carat diamond earrings I always wear.

From my purse I grab the room key, some cash and a credit card. I take the backstage pass from the nightstand and hurry out the door, letting it slam behind me.

I take a taxi to the stadium. As I reach into my pocket for cash to pay, I realize how lame it was to take a cab. It would have been faster to walk. The traffic into the stadium parking lot was a nightmare. It couldn't have been more than a half mile walk and it took forty minutes by car, but shit I don't know Vancouver and I'm not about to wander around alone up here.

I shove the money at the driver and exit the backseat. I look at the crowd, and my face falls. Jeez, this is a madhouse. Scream is one of the hottest hard rock bands on tour, and they have a large and rowdy following, and they are everywhere.

I pause at the top of the garage entrance. I'm not even sure I can make it down the driveway to the underground security entrance. There are altogether too many people jostling against each other at the door.

Pushing through the crowd takes effort. Getting close to the security guard takes more effort, even though I'm standing there waving my pass in his face.

Finally, he looks at me. "You're in the wrong place," is all he says.

I have to fight not to make an *are you kidding* face at him. "I've got a pass. This is a security entrance. Let me in."

He nods to indicate deeper into the underground garage. "Band and crew entrance is down there."

"What difference does it make?"

He ignores me. I'm about to walk off when he grabs my wrist, jerks me behind him, and pushes me through the door.

Inside the stadium the concrete walls and floors vibrate from the activity. I feel like I'm suffocating in the packed, overly lit corridor, but I start making my way through overdressed women, underdressed men, and the diligently working road crew. More than a few guys check me out as I cut through the crowd, and I keep my eyes locked forward, watching nothing but the fast shifting path through the bodies.

I see an open door and look into a room. There's a guy sitting at a drum kit. I can tell by how the rest of the gathering huddles around him, nodding in time, that they are drummers, too. Two of them I recognize as famous—my favorite metal band drummer of all time, Lars, but the other one's name escapes me—and I don't know the guy with the sticks. It's not Arctic Hole's drummer, Nate Kassel, so it must be the drummer for Scream. But then maybe not. What do I know? I've never been a fan of the British metal band.

I work my way past more small rooms clustered with people. Intimate, private parties inside this one giant party that fills the stadium.

I spot a door with a sign, *Dressing Room A: Performer*, and I breathe a sigh of relief. It's a long walk down the tunnels and, if I'm near the dressing rooms, I'm near where Neil is most likely held up with the guys in the room where food and drink is set up.

I maneuver on, close to the wall, and find a second door marked *Dressing Room B*. I put my hand on the knob and then pause, wondering if I should knock. The room isn't labeled.

"They're not in there," exclaims an ear-piercingly loud voice and I whirl, coming face-to-face with an absolutely diminishing stare.

I frown. "Thank you, but you don't know who I'm looking for."

The girls laughs. "Every girl backstage is looking for the same thing. Guys in the band. It doesn't matter who you are looking for, sweetie, there is no one there."

I flush, since the way she says *sweetie* tells me a lot about what she's thinking about me.

She arches a brow. "Are you looking for the assholes or the Hardy Boys?"

"Excuse me?"

She gives me a sharp, once-over glance. "It doesn't really matter. None of them are going to be interested in you." She starts to laugh in a rude sort of way. "Who gave you the pass? Someone is playing a joke on you letting you backstage."

She shakes her head, touching her hair in a preening manner, and then fixes her intense stare down the corridor.

I'm submerged in a strange feeling of *déjà vu*. Oh, they don't look alike, not in any physical way, but this girl is the embodiment of Linda Rowan. Strikingly beautiful. Flirty, messy long red hair. Pierced and tattooed. Sexed up. Stylishly overdressed. Superiority and *I don't give a fuck* gushing from every pore. Nosy. All-knowing. Territorial. And rude.

Yep, she's with one of the members of Scream. She's someone in the band's wife or girlfriend. This is just like the day I met Linda Rowan.

"Do you know where I can find the guys in Arctic Hole?" I ask.

She arches a brow. "Aha. I know where everyone is. Always. I should have guessed you were looking for the Hardy Boys. Come with me, my little lost waif. I'll show you where they are. It won't help you. You won't get in with those guys. Honey, you won't get in with any guys, not even the crew. So save your effort, save your pride—" Her intense stare fixes on me. "Run before you screw up your life. You shouldn't be here."

I meet her stare for stare, and I don't know whether I want to tell her to *shove it*, or to laugh.

Before I can decide which to do, she takes me by the arm in a not-so-gentle hold, and tugs me along behind her. She marches down the corridor, shouting *get the fuck out of my way* with every step.

"By the way, my name is Nicole. Never Nicky. Never Nic. Nicole. Don't fuck it up."

Her voice somehow manages to be even louder that time since she didn't bother to look over her shoulder at me while she barked her warning.

I am pulled into a large room crowded with people. Against the walls are set-up bars and buffet tables, and everywhere there is chattering, laughing, drinking, eating humanity. Christ, it's as awful as I remember.

Nicole gives a husky laugh that tells me she's amused by me. "First time backstage at a concert?"

I arch a brow in my best imitation *you're fucking irritating me, get out of my face* Rene kind of way. "No." One word. Deliberately vague.

"Aha," she says, and before I get away from her, she sinks down on a sofa, pulling me with her. "If you're going to hang out with me you had better learn to play nicely."

Being threatened by Nicole is lackluster after dealing with Linda Rowan. Still, I'm ready to be done with this.

I stand up and glare down at her. "If you stay out of my face we'll get along fine. And don't ever call me a little waif again."

Nicole rolls her eyes. "Fuck, you need to grow thicker skin than that if that one got you pissed off. There is no need to run off." She seizes my wrist, dragging me down beside her again. "It's better to stick close to me, sweetie. You don't want to be alone here."

For a second it's like there is a crack in the wall of repelling hardness, and, startled, I realize she *is* trying to be nice in her own hideous way.

My body starts to relax.

Nicole sinks back into the cushions and smiles. "There now, we're friends." With a long, red manicured nail, she points into the room, her finger doing a little bob. "That's Vincent Delmo. He's mine. We've been together for nine years. And I see the Hardy Boys. Well, at least four of them."

I look in the direction of her finger. The guys are standing in a cluster, however, Neil is not with them. *Shit.*

"I should go find Neil." I start to rise and she stops me again.

Her smile deepens. "So you're looking for the cute one. The shy one. Good luck, sweetie. He hasn't been in here all night. I don't know where he hides, but he's somewhere. That one keeps to himself."

I feel myself make a small smile. "That sounds like Neil."

Her brows hitch upward. "Do you know him?"

"He's my boyfriend."

Her eyes widen in surprise. She starts laughing again in a rude, overly amused, humiliating kind of way. She's laughing so hard she's curled back against the pillows, eyes closed.

Her lids flutter wide, she looks at my face, and then makes a poor effort to stop laughing. "I'm sorry."

I try to keep all reaction from surfacing on my face, because even though I know I will never like this girl, I'm going to be trapped on the road with her for ten months and I don't need to make an enemy.

"I'm glad you find it amusing," is all I say.

Her laughter stops and she sits up. "I didn't mean to be rude. It's not you. You just hear such shit backstage. Too many bored people with nothing to do talking shit and making up nonsense."

What the heck does that mean? If that's supposed to clarify for me what's going on here, I didn't.

Her brown eyes bore into me. "Don't be pissed. Don't rush off. It's actually kind of sweet in a circuitous way."

"Excuse me. I've got to go."

Nicole leans forward, bringing her face too close to mine, and the strength of booze on her breath is overpowering.

"Neil is an interesting guy. It is the first time any of us have met him and he doesn't mix with anyone. He just kind of stays in his own zone. No one knows what to make of him. You wouldn't believe the things I've heard tonight." She laughs again, then puckers her lips, mildly contrite. "Well, never mind. It doesn't matter. Backstage gossip always turns out to be bullshit. Rule one on the road. Never believe a thing you hear. Always bullshit, but it gives everyone something to do and chatter about while we all sit around doing nothing."

OK, if that is supposed to make me feel better, she failed dismally. I stand up.

"I need to go."

I'm about to make my escape when an arm drops heavily around my shoulders and a large body blocks my path. "You going to introduce me to your new friend, love?"

The iconic Vincent Delmo is hovering over me. I don't know if the way he's holding me, too familiar and touchy-feely, is meant to intimidate or excite me. It does neither.

Nicole glares up at him and shrugs. "God, you are such a lecher. Get away from the girl."

Tension, serious tension between them. Vincent lifts my pass hanging from the canvas strap on my neck. His brows shoot up. "Christian Parker? Are you Jack's girl?"

Shit! He says that in a way that tells me they're friends, though I didn't know it and I find it hard to picture Jack hanging out with *him*. Vincent oozes ego-inflated jerk.

His stifling presence eases into a more respectful distance from me.

I smile stiffly and nod.

Nicole is suddenly overly alert. "Christian Parker? Really?"

"Yes," I say, clipped.

In a flash Nicole is laughing uproariously and I am so ready to be done with this, but Vincent Delmo won't release his hold on me and his body is blocking my exit route.

He glares down at his girlfriend. "Are you fucking drunk, Nicky? Stop messing with Jack's girl."

She stares up at her boyfriend. "I'm not laughing at her. I'm laughing at you, love. She used to be with Alan Manzone." More laughter. She's hugging her middle, practically in tears. "Do you know who she is with now?"

Vincent looks embarrassed and pissed. "No, but I'm sure you're not going to shut the fuck up until you tell me and the entire world."

"The kid," she says, excited and harshly gloating. "This is Neil Stanton's girlfriend, Vinny. The kid is fucking"—she can hardly get the words out—"Manny's toss-overs and you've been chirruping all night that you think he's gay."

She curls on the couch and surrenders to her laughter. My entire body is covered with a burn and I feel like I'm going to vomit. I don't know which is worse: hearing myself called *Manny's toss-overs* or having them spread such a ridiculous, vicious rumor about Neil our first day on tour with them.

She says, "Manny's toss-overs. Most definitely not gay, Vinny."

Vincent grabs Nicole's arm and jerks her from the couch. "Shut the fuck up. You've said enough. You're embarrassing us both."

"Go to hell," she screeches, struggling in his hold.

Vincent glances down at me. He looks sincerely apologetic. "I'm sorry, love. She's drunk. She's a mean drunk. Don't take her seriously. My apologies."

He starts dragging her out of the room and Nicole fights him the entire way, hitting his arm over and over again in a flurry of wayward fists.

I stare at the room, wishing I could drop through the floor since it's obvious by the stares that more than a few people heard them. *I want to die. That's all there is to it.*

I search the room trying to find a safe place or a friendly face. Why in the hell did I ever think joining Neil here would be a good thing? I'd forgotten how awful the music world can be, though I shouldn't have. And I can't believe that I did.

Oh no, I should have remember before I came here with Neil.

A flashing memory rises in my head of being trapped in Alan's bedroom, being forced to hear Kenny Jones say *he fucked her and dumped her thirty minutes ago.* The icky feeling runs across the surface of my flesh, just as it did that night in New York, bringing with it other things I'd forgotten as well.

When Alan and I weren't alone, it was awful. He was a different guy, the circle around him was dreadful, and shocking and hurtful moments jumped out at me from everywhere.

It is going to be the same here. Neil will be a different guy when we are not alone. Life on the tour will not exist without regular doses of heart-crushing and awful. I shouldn't have done this. I should have moved back to Santa Barbara. I should never have brought myself here.

I lift my chin, somehow managing composure, and work my way through the people to the tiny circle of Josh and the rest of the band. I internally contain a shudder, since they don't look very welcoming and they're not making the slightest effort to hide that they'd heard that ghastly scene.

I look at Josh. "Do you know where Neil is?"

He tosses down a sip of his drink. "He's where he is before every performance, Chrissie. Somewhere quiet where he can think."

"Can you tell me where?"

Josh glares at me. "Leave him the fuck alone. Don't run to him and dump your shit all over him. For one day can you not fuck with his head?"

My cheeks color like a burn. We stare at each other, but it's Josh who breaks off first, lowering his gaze to his drink.

"Go out the door and go left," Les says, surprising me. "Just keep walking. You'll see him eventually. He's sitting alone in one of the exit tunnels. That's where he usually goes to psych himself up for a performance."

"Thank you, Les," I say quietly, then head toward the door.

The hallway is less crowded and I can see that road crew has started clearing a path for the guys to get onstage. I peek into exit tunnels, and then ahead of me I see one of the security team standing in an archway and I know that is where Neil is.

I hold up my pass, but the sentry doesn't let me through. He says, "He doesn't want to be bothered."

I peek around his hulking form and beyond him I see Neil. He's sitting almost on the floor, crouched, back against the wall with hair tumbling forward. He's still, perfectly still, and he looks intensely quiet, a touch sad—though I don't know why he would be sad, tonight is a big night for him—and definitely nervous.

Maybe I shouldn't bother him. There is something about how he's sitting that screams he wants to be alone.

"Five minutes," blares a voice from the walkie-talkie.

The security guy looks in at Neil. "Five minutes, man."

Neil looks up and sees me. "It's OK. Let her through, Clive. That's my girlfriend, Chrissie."

Clive steps out of the way. I make my way down the concrete decline until I reach Neil. He doesn't move. He just sits there. I don't know what I'm seeing, what this is. But it makes my distress, that hideous scene with Nicky which made me want to run to the safety of Neil, seem instantly insignificant.

Josh's voice fills my head. *Don't run to him and dump your shit all over him.* I crouch down until we're at eye level and silently I reply, *I'm not going to, Josh. I love him. Why don't you get that and leave us alone?*

"Hi." Neil's voice is faint, nearly all breath. "I was wondering where you were."

"I was wondering where *you* were. What's going on?"

He shakes his head. "Just thinking."

He takes my body in his hands, turns me and then sets me with my back against him. He instantly surrounds me with his legs and arms, and I'm suddenly reminded of the night in his van when I confronted him and he told me his history with Andy Despensa. He feels just like he did then, as if he's filled with troubling stuff he doesn't want to share and is embarrassed over.

He lets out a long, shuddering breath and buries his lips in my hair. "I'm scared, Chrissie. I've never performed in front of such a large crowd. I don't want to fall on my ass. I don't want to do this."

His words don't surprise me, though I'm not exactly sure how to deal with this. This is new for me. Neil unsure, doubting himself.

"Then don't. We can fly home." I close my hands around his wrists, stretching out our arms and making a silly flapping motion. "Then you can surf. And I can do nothing. If you don't want to do this then don't."

A reluctant laugh fights its way out of his chest. Good. I've amused him.

"You can do nothing, rich-girl. I have to work."

"Then go out there. Work."

His laughter comes a touch less strained. He melts into me, his hands gently caressing my arms. "You are a pretty cool girl. Have I ever told you that? You're not blown away by any of this. You don't get impressed. Nothing will ever pull you into the hype. Wherever you are, you are always just Chrissie."

"I don't know if that's a good thing or bad thing being *just Chrissie*," I say in a silly, exaggerated way, and Neil relaxes into the wall, laughing.

He kisses my head. "A very good thing. You are the only thing real in my world right now. Don't change. Not ever."

"I won't." I turn in his arms until I can face him. I kiss him. "It's going to be fine. You're going to be great. I wouldn't be here if I didn't believe that."

"I love you, Chrissie."

I spring to my feet and pull him up by his hands.

"We're going to be OK, Neil."

He loops his arm around my shoulders and we walk toward the main corridor.

"You ready to do it?" Clive asks.

Neil nods and starts to leave, but we're held back by a tree-trunk-size arm.

"I've got to clear the hallway. Give me a minute, Neil."

Neil starts to laugh as Clive raises his walkie-talkie to his lips. He turns me to face him, holding me in a sloppy drape of his arms.

I frown. "What are you laughing at?"

He shakes his head and puts his nose against mine. "This. It's fucking nuts. I walked down the hall alone to get here. No one gave a shit about me."

I make a pout. "I give a shit about you."

He smiles. "Good. You're the only one that matters here."

A minute later we're being escorted down the main corridor, the guys about ten feet ahead of us. The sound from the arena is deafening and Neil is lumbering beside me, still looking like he doesn't want to go onstage. Excitement flutters start building inside me. I haven't seen Neil perform in anything but a small club. He's always gone out on the road without me.

The lights are shut off on the stage as we climb a short flight of metal stairs. Neil's held back again, and his fingers clutch my hand tightly. His fingers do flexing motions around mine. Squeeze. Squeeze. Squeeze. Then I feel the loss of contact and he is running on stage.

Clive points at an empty area just out of view of the audience. "You can stand here."

The stark corridor below is flooded with people and the side stage entrances fill up. There is a deafening assault of guitars. The lights switch on. I try to keep up with the action in front of me. A raspy, powerful voice, velvety and yet haunting and laced with despair. A voice I know.

I spot Neil center stage, hugging a microphone, hidden under his unruly hair, but he doesn't look at all like he did the last time I saw him perform. There is something supercharged about him, mesmerizing, coiled, and in control. It's a sharp contrast to the Neil I found in the exit tunnel. A sharp contrast to the Neil I expected to see now.

I stare at him, unable to see anything else. Center stage adores him, and my skin grows numb with roiling emotions. Their music is raw and fresh, powerfully intense. The band is amazing, and Neil doesn't hide beneath his hair on stage anymore. He is running wild, stirring the crowd into a frenzy. It didn't even take one song and he has them totally engaged and with him.

There are stories all over the place in the entertainment press about how Arctic Hole is about to be the next big thing out of Seattle. But those stories are wrong. Neil and the band are not breaking into stardom. Christ, how could I get so much wrong? Miss so much about what was going on in Neil's life? Simply not see? I was wrong about each and every thing I believed on the way to Seattle and then here.

Arctic Hole is not on the edge of breaking into stardom as a band. They've already broken, and it happened before today. Neil must have realized that. The guys know it. You can't miss something like this, not when you've worked so hard to make it happen.

Arctic Hole has already made it. There is not a single reason why Neil should want me here. Every door is going to fly open soon. Opportunity everywhere. Possibilities everywhere. Girls everywhere. Whatever he wants everywhere.

Another guy would have left me in Berkeley in the past. Neil should have done the same. Instead, he brought me with him and I am *in love* with him for the first time in our life together.

CHAPTER ELEVEN

The stage shudders from stomping feet throughout the stadium. Neil is on the last song of his set, and the stage's wings are packed with bodies to the point of being crushingly overfilled. People started pouring in from the tunnels when Neil climbed the rafters.

Jesus Christ, what possessed him to do that?

Still-water Neil hanging from twenty feet above the audience, somehow with the microphone still in hand and singing, and then dropping into the crowd beneath him. It was insane, and oddly exciting; his command of the stage, and I couldn't guess what he would do next. It moved the packed arena into something beyond frenzied. The crazier Neil gets the more they love him.

I should probably cut out now to the safety of the green room before the band breaks. With the way the stage sides are packed it is going to be madness to try to keep up with Neil once he comes off stage, but I want to watch this as long as I can. He's put on an amazing performance tonight.

The cluster around me starts fidgeting, alerting me that people are going to be in motion along the wings soon. Across the stage, security is already in place to cut a path for the band.

Pushing through the bodies, I slowly make my way

back to the green room. Crap. Delmo and Scream are still here, drinking, laughing, and doing their rituals to psych up for on stage.

I sink down on a sofa, really not wanting to be in here. Thankfully Nicole hasn't returned since Vincent shoved her from the room. Maybe I should go to Neil's dressing room because security will take the guys there first.

I'm about to leave when the atmosphere of the room shifts abruptly as Neil and the band return from the stage, sweating, exhausted and excited. Flash bulbs explode from all sides, but Neil is focused on the guys, a saturated towel hanging from his shoulders and still panting from the exertion of performing. They are laughing, talking, and oblivious to everything around.

Neil is oblivious even to me. I didn't expect that one, but it's definitely petty that it bothers me. He's got a lot going on, lots of people vying for his attention. It's stupid of me to be butt hurt that he didn't run to me first.

"You were fucking out of your mind tonight," Nate Kassel exclaims in an overly animated way unlike him.

"What the fuck made you climb the rafters?" Josh interjects heatedly.

Neil shrugs. "I don't know, man. I didn't think. I just did."

The stage manager comes in to give the two-minute warning for Scream. Delmo moves from his circle, pausing beside Neil. "Good show, kid, but if you keep that up you won't last a year on the road."

"Maybe you can't keep it up for a year, old man, but I can," Neil teases, earning an affectionate swat from

Vincent as laughter and heckles erupt around them.

I watch their faces move close together as Delmo launches into what looks like a keep-private kind of conversation with Neil. I wish I could hear their words, and anxiousness moves through my digestive tract. God, I hope Vincent isn't bringing up that hideous scene with Nicole. As Neil listens, surprise flashes on his face, followed by anger, then a *no big deal* kind of expression. Vincent pats Neil again on a bicep.

I wonder if I should continue to hang back or go to Neil. I don't know what to do. I don't know what they're talking about, but I definitely don't want to piss off the guys again by making the wrong move. Though that's probably hopeless. Pretty much everything I do ticks off Josh.

In front of me the crowd start to move, blocking Neil from view. Scream is exiting the green room for the stage and I wonder if Neil is going to want to watch from the wings, but I don't really want to.

Unexpectedly, Neil cuts through the bodies, takes my hand and pulls me to my feet. "Give us twenty minutes," he snaps to Josh.

Startled, I stare up at him as he practically drags me from the room.

"What's wrong?"

"I don't want to talk about it. Not now."

Fuck! What did Vincent Delmo say to Neil?

The tic in his cheek twitches the way it does when he's angry, and I feel something restless and pulsing inside him. Crap, I don't want him angry. Not tonight. I don't want to ruin this night for him. Or for me.

He takes me to the dressing room. He bolts the door, and I hang back, silent, as he crosses the room.

"I need to rinse off," he murmurs, not looking at me as he pulls off his dripping wet t-shirt and tosses it on the floor. At the doorway to the showers, he pauses and looks back at me. "The only person in the room I wanted to be with and you stayed away. Why, Chrissie?"

Crap. He sounds hurt as well as angry. I don't want to fight with him and I don't want to hurt him. Not anymore. Not ever again.

A knot rises in my throat. "I don't know. Everything happened too quickly in there. I thought it best to stay out of the way since you were deep in discussion with the guys."

His eyes rapidly search my face. "Don't leave. Don't move. I'll be only a minute."

I stand frozen on my spot, hardly in the room. I hear the showers turn on and sounds of him washing. The shower shuts off and Neil reappears, a towel draped low around his hips.

He lies down on a sofa. I bite my lip and his eyes darken. "Why are you staring at me that way?"

My breath catches. "I don't know."

He turns onto his side, his head resting in his palm. His gaze slowly moves down my body and then up. My heartbeat picks up and I am instantly hot everywhere.

"You haven't looked at me this way for a very long time." His voice is husky. "I've missed it, Chrissie."

Just like that the room is flooded with sexual tension.

Oh my. He's not pissed. He's totally turned on. I don't have the faintest idea what he is seeing in my eyes, but it's lit some kind of fire in Neil. My breathing alters and the soft muscles against my panties frantically start to pulse. Tingles move across my flesh.

"I love you," I whisper.

The color of his eyes darkens and there's a jolt through my veins.

"You've never done that before," he says quietly.

My brows hitch up. "What?"

"Saying *I love you* to me without me saying it first. That's the first time you've done that, Chrissie. Ever."

A hint of something I can't decipher mingles with my warmly liquid senses. "I love you, Neil."

The look in his eyes charges. The way he is looking at me takes my breath away. I have never had a guy look at me *this* way. Not even Alan. Never like this.

I stare back at him, panting and excited.

"You don't have a clue what you do to me, do you, Chrissie? How much I love you? What you are to me?"

The lines of his face tighten with desire and so much more. I want him. Here. Now.

"Why don't you show me?" I whisper.

He shakes his head. "No. Tonight you show me. Tonight you said *I love you* first. Please, Chrissie, make love to me."

I burn from head to toe, urgent to have sex with him even with the sharp bites of shame I can't repel nipping at my senses. The way Neil is looking me and his words say a lot about how unfair I was in how I loved him before, it tells me he knew it, and he stayed with me anyway. He's known all along that I never shared myself with him completely, and it doesn't matter, not to him. It is enough for him that I want to now.

Everything around us is changing, we feel different and new, and I want it so. And by the current moving between us I feel that what was inside me standing between us won't be there once we walk from this room.

My scattered senses are only vaguely aware of my movements toward the sofa and the removal of my clothes. Between kisses, I grab his towel and drop it to the floor. He is fully erect. He's out of his mind, burning hot, ready for me just like I'm ready for him.

I want him so badly I am not even conscious of the touches, the kisses or the moves that end up with me surrounding his body with my own and riding him. My breathing catches as I swallow his flesh, rush and claim him. I groan as he tilts his hips upward in the rhythm of my motion, filling me so deeply that my head begins to sway in pleasure. We are moving in an effortlessly perfect cadence. My lips on his lips. My hands on his body.

I have no idea what I'm doing. The command of my limbs is no longer my own, and we are gloriously one in the acts of our bodies. The feeling of him radiates through my limbs. His breathing is hard, matching mine, and his face is taut with anticipation and want. It feels so incredible, this frenzied exchange neither of us control.

I plant my hands on his shoulders and stop the motion of our bodies. His eyes open.

"I love you," I whisper against his lips. I take his

mouth in a deep, thorough kiss.

I gently roll my hips and continue, slowly increasing the pace with each swallowing of his flesh. His head rolls on the sofa and his eyes close. I watch him. I move my hips, slowing stroking up his flesh and then down. Over and over again. I kiss his jaw. I move my body. I kiss his brow. I move and touch him. I tighten around his cock, and his flesh quivers. I flick my tongue on the skin of his neck. My need is desperate and so is his and I am swept away by my love for him until I am nothing but frenzied movement, touches and kisses.

I watch him as I ride him and Neil is savoring this like a guy who has wanted this for a very long time.

~ ~ ~

We are sweaty and curled into each other, lying on the sofa. Neil is smoking and his expression says we are not moving from here any time soon. He told Josh to give him twenty minutes. We've been bolted in here two hours.

My eyes fix on the cases holding the band's change of clothing. I see everyone's personal shit everywhere. We left them sweaty and waiting on us in the green room. I bury my face against his chest, giggle, and then peek up at him.

"We have to get dressed, Neil. We can't stay in here forever. The guys might want to shower and change, don't you think?"

"Why not? We're alone. It's quiet. Perfect. Fuck them. They can go back to the hotel as is."

I sit up. "We've been in here a long time. I'm going to be totally embarrassed when we go out there. That is, if anyone is around."

Neil starts to laugh. His eyes are so bright they're gleaming.

I frown. "What's so funny?"

"You are." He eases up to put a kiss on my nose and then he stomps out his cigarette in the ashtray. His laughter intensifies.

I cross my arms and watch. "Are you going to explain why you're laughing?"

He stands up, pulling his fresh after-performance clothes from a case. He starts to dress. As if he can feel my expectant stare, he stops what he's doing and turns to look at me.

"Chrissie, everyone knows why we're in here. Why do you think no one has knocked on the door? I told Josh twenty minutes. It's guy code for leave me alone, I'm going to get laid."

My cheeks flood with color. Neil makes a mildly ruefully, extremely sweet expression.

"You are such a jerk at times, Neil."

I glare, throwing a sofa pillow at him, but I'm not angry and he can tell so this is pointless. He leans into me, kisses me fast, and then moves away quickly.

I lie back on the sofa, groaning. "It's so humiliating being girl in guy world." I glance up at him. "What else do you tell the guys about us?"

He shakes his head as he fastens his jeans. "Nothing. I don't talk about us."

I severely arch a brow. "You had better not."

"I don't and I won't." He grimaces. "Shit, Josh is right. I'm fucking whipped."

I throw a second pillow, harder this time. Neil deflects it and erupts into laughter again.

"*Whipped?* Yuck. I hate that word." My faces scrunches up. "Did Josh really say that to you?"

Neil nods and my grimace tightens even more.

"What did you say back to him?" I ask.

Neil shrugs and doesn't look up from lacing his boots.

"What did you say?" I press harder this time.

"I said *Yep, I am. Deal with it.*"

My expression softens and I can feel I'm smiling at him. *That was kind of sweet. You're forgiven, Neil, for your asshole friend Josh.*

I start to dress and I follow him with my gaze as he moves around the dressing room. He stops at the mirror and smooths his hair. He combs it with his fingers in a way that makes me think about how those fingers feel touching me.

I take someone's brush from a dressing table, and jockey with Neil for space in the mirror as I brush my hair.

"There's an after-party," he says. "Delmo is throwing it for the band. A welcome and kick-off for the tour kind of thing. I'm expected to go."

He says that in a way that tells me he doesn't want to.

I crinkle my nose. "Maybe I'll just go back to the hotel. I don't really want to spend any time I don't have to with Vincent Delmo."

Neil pauses what his doing, his gaze meeting my eyes in the mirror.

"What happened?"

Crap. Why did I say that?

I shrug. "Nothing. It's nothing. He's just not the kind of guy I'd want to hang out with."

"Nope, not buying it, Chrissie. Are you going to tell me what happened in the green room that I don't know about?"

Neil asks more forcefully this time. Oh crud. How did he know something happened in the green room? Is he fishing because I'm so terrible at hiding my thoughts or has someone already said something to him?

I drop the brush and fight to keep reaction from my face. If Neil doesn't know what went down with the Delmos, I don't want to ruin tonight by telling him the *Manny's toss-overs* comment or that *other* repulsive thing Nicole said.

"I don't like him," I say carefully. "He treats his girlfriend like shit. But then Nicole is a bitch. Not exactly a fun couple."

"Then we won't go."

I stare back at him in the mirror. "If you are expected to go, you have to go. Don't not go because of me."

He drops a kiss on my lips. "I'm not doing that party without you."

I roll my eyes. "That's not fair, Neil."

His arms slip around my waist, pulling me back against him. His lips start to lightly touch my neck.

"Come with me, Chrissie," he whispers into my ear before he softly nibbles on the flesh of my lobe.

I lean back into him. "That's not fair either." But I move into his touch, not away from it.

Against my back, I feel his chest shimmy with silent

laughter. "We'll stay fifteen minutes. We'll show up. Polite, but then we'll get the hell out of there."

I make a face at him.

"That's not polite."

Neil shakes his head. "Then we'll stay."

"I don't want to."

Shit. I'm doing it again. Being a pain. I can be so frustrating at times, but then again those are *difficult*, rude people.

I make an internally contained shudder.

"Fifteen minutes, then we're out of there."

It's clear he's not going to let me have my way in this. "Fine, Neil. Fine."

He takes my hand and starts guiding me toward the door. He unbolts it.

"He apologized, you know," Neil says quietly. "Vincent apologized to me before he went on stage. He's the headliner and I aint shit. But he manned up, wanted no hard feelings, and made sure things were cool between us. He's not that bad of a guy, Chrissie."

Crap.

He places a light kiss on my lips, his hands holding my face with his thumbs lightly stroking at the edges of my mouth.

"I don't give a shit what anyone says. Not about you. Not about me. And you're going to hear shit. Lots of shit, Chrissie. That's the road. Ignore it. Don't let it hurt you. Whatever you hear, be honest with me and we'll be OK. Don't let it hurt us."

I nod, but there is something in the way Neil's eyes fix

intensely on mine that makes me wonder if there is something he is worried I might hear.

CHAPTER TWELVE

I lie on my stomach on the cold stage floor, stare at my journal, and then write the date. *September 14th, 1993.* Have I really been on tour with Neil for three months?

I turn my head to look up at Neil sitting in the last row of the stadium. Sound check ended an hour ago and he's just been sitting there, staring off into space. But that's Neil. Only a stupid girl would try to change him at this point. Whatever this ritual is, it works for him. The performances only get more spectacular. The crowds larger. His fans nearly outnumber Scream's at every gig.

Still, I wonder what he thinks about while he sits there. I shake my head and focus back on my journal. I start to write. Blah. Not very good. I scribble a giant X through it. I flip through the pages, looking for something not dreadful, and stop. *Parts of me have been quieted, new parts of me stirred awake, parts of me I leave behind, and parts of me I take.*

I sit up, grabbing the Gibson acoustic guitar lying next me. I close my eyes and start to play. I pause to write in the journal. I play.

My concentration is shattered by the sound of boots stomping on metal steps. I stop playing and slap my journal closed just as Delmo and his entourage take over the stage.

"Nancy Drew, did anyone say you could fucking touch our stuff?" snaps Rex Dillard as he hovers above me, staring at the guitar.

I have to fight not to make a face at him. Why does he always have to give me such shit? Rex Dillard may be one of the world's greatest guitarist, but he's an absolute prick.

"Sod off," Delmo interjects before I can rally words to defend myself. "The girl can touch anything of mine she wants to."

He gives me a roguish smile and a wink. I roll my eyes and meet him stare for stare as he crosses the stage toward me.

"You're so obnoxious," I say, shaking my head at him. "If you stopped pretending to be an asshole, I might start to actually like you."

Vincent Delmo laughs, settling on the stage next to me. I bite back a smile. I do sort of like him, but I don't want him to know it. He's so conceited. But the rest of his unappealing traits, I figured out on my first week on tour, are all show for the fans. The obnoxious behavior. The parties. The women. The booze. Nonsense for the fans.

As far as I know, he hasn't stepped out once on Nicole, and we'd all know it, because it is impossible for that woman to say anything without everyone hearing it. And Vincent doesn't drink. That one was a shocker. He's a Twelver. That's how he knows Jack. That's how they became friends, another one of Jack's strange circle of twelve-step buddies.

Delmo is sort of OK, but Nicole and the rest of the band are dreadful. I can tell by how the guys are moving on stage that they are more than a little drunk, and their obnoxious behavior is not show. They're assholes. Total assholes every moment they are awake. But Delmo isn't. Neil was right. He's an OK guy.

He nods toward the back of the arena. "Is the kid all done here?"

I clip my pen to the cover of my journal. "They finished an hour ago."

Rex snatches the Gibson out of my lap. The rest of them are tuning instruments. I need to get out of here quickly.

I look up to where Neil is, wondering if I should wait or go to him. I don't really want to climb the stadium steps to the top. I resolve to wait.

Delmo's eyes fix on me. "I can't quite figure you and the Hardy boy out, Nancy Drew."

I ignore the comment as if I'm annoyed with it—Vincent was the one who first called me Nancy Drew, prompted for some reason by me always scribbling in my journal as I wait on Neil, and the wretched thing has stuck with the band—but I am not annoyed. It's amusing from him with his thick British accent and he doesn't mean any disrespect. It's just the way he talks. He hasn't a mean bone in his body.

He studies my face. "So is it serious with him, or do I have a chance?"

God, he's impossible. "I've already answered. Neil and me? Serious. You? No chance at all. Never."

"You break my heart, love. But it's probably for the best. Do you want to know what I think?"

"Not particularly."

"Ah, but I'm going to tell you," he announces.

I laugh in spite of my efforts not to and Delmo smiles.

"I don't understand these kids they keep putting on the road with me. More talent than they know what to do with, but they live like Quakers. They don't live the life. But that's a good thing. The kid is smarter than I was at his age. Keeps his feet planted on the ground and stays out of the mix."

"Neil doesn't buy into the hype. He never will. He's not that kind of guy. What you see is what you get with Neil."

"Smart." Vincent's expression changes and he looks almost wistful. "Here's the other thing, which you probably don't want to know. You and the kid have a good thing going on. You're the only two in this fucking madhouse who have it right. I have only one thing to say about that."

There is silence between us for a moment.

I arch a brow, since his long dramatic pauses are so irritating.

"Don't fuck it up," he says slowly.

He makes a face at me and I swat at him.

"Jerk. You've been talking to my dad again."

He explodes into laughter, lying back on the floor. His eyes open. "That one was for Neil. You're going to have to delivery it for me. I'm not climbing the fucking stadium steps to do it."

We both laugh.

"God, my dad is unbelievable," I murmur under my breath.

"Did I ever tell you he's the one that got me sober?

He still calls every month to check in on me. No matter where I am, I take a call from Jack. That's how it is, love, with your father. Oh, and I almost forgot to ask. Are you doing all right? Do you have everything you need?"

Oh yuck. Even more embarrassing. "Jeez, I can't believe Jack asked you to check up on me. I'm an adult. He still treats me like a little girl."

The way Delmo's gaze suddenly intensifies is strangely unnerving, sort of like Rene's scalpel-like examinations of me. Odd, but that's how it looks to me, though I don't know why it should.

"It wasn't Jack who asked me to make sure you were OK, love," he says quietly.

I try to ignore that one, since figuring out Delmo conversationally is impossible. "No?"

"No."

He stares at me and I grow agitated, but I don't know why. An odd sense of impending awfulness swirls in my stomach and it feels like wherever Delmo is going with the conversation isn't going to be good for me. Strange, but that's how I feel. An instinctive warning to walk away now. Maybe it's because of how oddly he is watching me.

More minutes of silence pass, with him lying there, studying my face. It looks almost like he's debating with himself over whether he should say something.

"Manny called last week," Vincent murmurs softly.

My heart drops to the floor and I fight to keep all reaction from my face, but my emotions are in full free-fall and everything is running frantically through me.

I shrug. "I didn't realize you were friends."

"We talk from time to time, but I wouldn't call us friends. He asked about you."

I lower my gaze and stare at my hands. *I don't want to know. I don't want to know.*

"It's not like Manny to take an interest in the rearview mirror." He pauses a moment. "He had quite a bit to say about you, love."

I cringe as the memory of how Alan and I parted refuses to stay put in the lockboxes. No, I definitely don't want to know this.

I force a smile. "I don't really care what Alan Manzone had to say. I would appreciate it if you didn't tell me."

"And I wouldn't tell you, love. Not even if you asked me. He was drunk out of his mind and rambling. Said more to me in that one phone call than he has the entire time I've known him. Probably a lot he doesn't remember and would regret if he did."

My face colors profusely. I can't stop it—*a lot he doesn't remember and would regret if he did.* Crap, Alan, after eight months why do you have to pop up and fuck with my life here? Things are finally going good with Neil and me. The way I want them. The way Neil deserves them to be.

I spring to my feet. "I'll get out of your way."

Vincent stares up at me. "Are you OK, Chrissie? I wasn't sure if I should tell you. I don't think I should have."

"I'm fine."

Only I'm not. I can feel it...*fuck...* Alan has turned me into a shaky, shadowy mess by simply asking about me, and Vincent Delmo can see it. *How awful is this?*

"When Neil comes down from there, will you tell him

I went back to the hotel? I'm tired. I probably won't be back for the show."

"Sure, love." He makes a face. "Consider me one giant answering service for the Parker family."

His voice is teasing, but it's a crappy joke, and it doesn't work to take the edge from my mood, instead nearly bringing me to tears. I can feel Vincent watching me as I rush off the stage.

~~~

I lie in bed, fighting with myself to stay focused on the TV, but it doesn't work. My gaze shifts to my mobile phone sitting beside me. Since I returned to the hotel, the urge has been overpowering to call Alan. Worse, I want to call him when I don't want to know what Alan said about me to Vincent Delmo, and paradoxically the desperation to know is bordering on obsessive.

Why did Alan inquire about me, after all this time? What did he say? What did he ask? Stupid. I shouldn't want to know. Not now. Not ever.

I should never have fallen in love with Alan. He's a like a cruel, unrelenting drug. Put a drug before a recovered addict and they'll crave it. Mention Alan to me and I become a mess. It doesn't matter how good my life is with Neil, how much I love him, how much he loves me; enter Alan and everything inside me sharply adjusts.

Fuck, why can't I shove him into a lockbox and leave him there? Why does he have such power over me? Is it because he was my first and my first love? That's what Rene says. Or is it because our history together is significant and there are parts of it that will always be part of me. Or is it him?

Fuck, I hear his name, I fall apart, and I am lost in the hold of him again. He is in my head. He is in my flesh. Even now. No matter what he does to me. No matter what I do. A stupid, drunken phone call with Delmo. Alan mentions me—*probably not even kindly,* I remind myself—I know I'm in his thoughts, and I am consumed by memories I don't want; the touch, the taste, the feel of him. And I want him.

It's fucking insane. Thank God I don't know how to reach Alan by phone. I don't doubt I would sink to a new Chrissie low and call him.

The hotel room door opens and I quickly drop my phone in my black case beside the bed. I don't want Neil to see me in our bed with my phone. I feel guilty, like I've cheated on Neil again, lying here all night staring at my mobile and trying to figure out how to call Alan.

Lame, Chrissie, lame.

I follow Neil with my gaze as he moves around the room, trying to read his mood. I shut off the TV and sit up in bed. The clock on the night table says 11 p.m. Neil didn't stay for the entire show. He cut out after his set. Not good, Chrissie. Not good.

He tosses off his jacket and sinks into a chair on the far side of the room. He starts to unlace his boots.

"Was the show good?" I ask cautiously.

He shakes his head. "I was off tonight. Flat. My routine out of whack. It didn't feel the same without you there. I couldn't get my rhythm."

He doesn't look up at me.

"I'm sure you were amazing."

He sits back in his chair, pulls his cigarettes from his pocket and lights one. "No. I kept thinking about you." His eyes lock on mine. "What's going on, Chrissie?"

Betraying color floods my cheeks.

"Nothing."

I say it too quickly, and something flashes in his eyes. I take in a deep breath. I need to reorganize. Neil is clearly fuming over something. The way he looks warns me to defuse whatever this is I'm seeing on his face quickly.

"I'm just tired, Neil. The road is so exhausting. I felt like I needed a night in. Didn't Vincent tell you I was tired and wouldn't be at the show tonight?"

Shit, that sounded overplayed and rambling.

He takes a long drag of his cigarette. "Yep, he told me."

He takes the bottle of JD from the table, unscrews the top and takes a long swallow. My brows hitch up, the gesture not like Neil. He hardly ever drinks. My internal distress kicks up another level.

"You're not to talk to Vincent Delmo without me ever again," he snaps unexpectedly and I jump.

I stare at him is disbelief. Did he actually just order me?

"I'll talk to whoever I want," I counter, hardly dismissive.

He takes another long swallow. The tic in his cheek twitches. "I saw you two together, huddled up in one of your chats. And then you ran off stage and didn't come back."

Oh crap, Delmo, did you babble to Neil about Alan? I can't tell what he knows, but I don't like his mood and I don't like this.

I lift my chin, a smidge haughty. "Don't tell me what to do, Neil. And when you get things wrong, you get them wrong. I didn't run off stage. I left because I was tired. I've been at every show for three months. Don't make a big deal out of me wanting a night alone for a change."

His eyes sharpen on my face.

"What did Vincent say to you, Chrissie? I thought we'd agreed. Whatever bullshit we hear on the road, we'd talk about it with each other. Not let it hurt us."

I school my features into a deliberate *you're being ridiculous* kind of expression. The pressure of his gaze doesn't lift, and I look away into a vacant spot in the room.

"He didn't say anything, Neil," I say with gritted teeth. "He gave me his usual shit. Told me the story about Jack getting him sober. *Again.* Like I'm not tired of hearing about that one. And he told me he thought we had a good thing going on together. That's all. Nothing."

Long minutes of silence pass and it doesn't feel like either of us has moved, but I can feel something building in Neil.

There's a loud crash in the room. It takes a moment for my mind to catch up, and I stare in disbelief at the booze stain on the wall and the broken glass on the floor. Jesus Christ, did Neil just throw a bottle against the wall? Neil?

I stare up at him with painfully wide and disbelieving eyes. "I can't believe you did that!"

Neil stands, his posture furious, and as close to out of control as I've ever seen him. "And I can't believe you're lying to me."

Fear shoots through my veins. My body freezes. I stare up at him. "I'm not lying. Why would I lie about this?"

He shakes his head at me, then puts his hands over his face, his fingertips squeezing into his skull. "You fucking drive me crazy."

A flash burn covers my skin. How could he say that to me? He drops back into the chair.

"The second things get good between us, you fuck with *us*," he says, his voice nearly a ragged growl. "I should never have brought you on tour with me. It was a mistake. You don't know how to stay out of the shit. You always fuck up everything the second it gets good."

I don't know what has Neil so irrational, but I am not staying here any longer.

"Then I'll leave," I hiss and scramble off the bed.

I start grabbing my stuff and shoving it into my duffel. I can feel Neil watching me, but he doesn't move from the chair or try to stop me. How did everything get so wrong so quickly?

"I'm out of here," I snap. "You won't have to worry about me driving you crazy. Or fucking us up. Or anything about me. You have fucked us up big time all on your own, Neil."

I jerk angrily at the zipper and close my duffel. I spring to my feet, snatching my black bag from beside the bed, and then I go to the bathroom. With a swipe I dump my things from the counter into the bag.

I go back into the room and stand in the middle, shaking, frantically searching for something to change into, then I realize I've packed all my clothes.

Fuck, fuck, fuck.

The tears start to give way and I don't want them to. I don't want him to see me cry. I just want to get out of here with some shred of pride intact.

I drop to my knees by my duffel, unzip it, and rummage inside for something to wear. As I dress, I catch a glimpse of Neil in the wall mirror above the desk.

My heart contracts. Totally together, always calm Neil looks in complete emotional disarray. I don't know why. I definitely shouldn't care. After that *you drive me crazy* comment only a pathetic girl would worry about what's happening with him.

I collect my bags, do a fast glance around the room to make sure I haven't forgotten anything, and turn toward the door.

Neil looks at me. "Where are you going?"

I bite my lip. I don't need to answer him. "The airport," I say stiffly.

I hear a ragged exhale of breath.

"It's the middle of the fucking night, Chrissie."

I fumble with the chain and stupid latch thingy on the door. "What? People don't fly at night? If there isn't a flight home tonight I'll sleep there until morning. I'm not staying here. Not with you."

No response. I look over my shoulder at him. His jaw is clenched and he's shaking his head as if to keep himself calm. He's just going to let me walk away and despite all the rotten things he said, I hate that he's letting me. And doubly so, I hate that icky feeling of having lived this before.

Why do all the men in my life let me go? I walk away and they let me. I start to hyperventilate. I'm thinking of Alan again and I don't want to. About how different my life would be if he hadn't let me walk out the door in Malibu.

I struggle not to let my emotions give way as I pull back the door. The knob is ripped from my hand with a slam of wood, I'm turned around in a dizzying spin, and Neil has me trapped between him and the exit, his hands planted on either side of me. His body is shaking.

His face hovers above me, only an inch from mine. Startled, I smell the booze on his breath. He's been drinking tonight. Heavily. Not just the JD in the room. More.

"Don't go, Chrissie."

"I'm not staying." I'm proud of how my voice sounds. Calm. In control. Rational.

He leans in to kiss me and I twist away.

"I'm not letting you go." He eases back from me, blinking. "You're not leaving."

My emotions sharply adjust. Damn him. I can't push out my words so I stay still, not backing down, but not fighting to get away.

"I've had a miserable night worrying about you, Chrissie. Worrying about us."

I don't want to. I tilt my head so I can see his face. It's almost like he's frightened and fear pulses through him. It feels strange. Neil feels strange, and yet I suddenly don't know what I should do, if I should leave or stay.

"I think I should go, Neil."

"No. Not this way. Not how we are now," he pleads, raking a hand through his hair. "I want to know what Vincent said to you. I want to know we're OK."

I can barely breathe, and it is probably stupid, completely vain, but right now it feels like if I walk out that door he won't be all right.

"It doesn't matter what Delmo said," I whisper. "That's not why I want to go. You scared me tonight. I've never seen you like this. What is happening to you?"

His eyes widened in pain and almost tortured reluctance. "I have a lot going on. I didn't mean to scare you. I'd never hurt you. You are everything to me, Chrissie. We matter to me. More than you will ever know," he admits after a long while.

"Then tell me why you exploded tonight."

"You left without a word to me. I've called you fifty times this afternoon. You didn't answer the phone. You didn't want to talk to me and I thought..." He cuts himself off, impatient and frustrated.

"I took a bath. I went to dinner. I slept. I didn't answer the phone. It didn't mean anything, Neil."

"I can't do this, I can't make my life work without you, Chrissie. If you leave, everything falls apart."

My scattered thoughts can't begin to form a response to that. This is too much emotion. Too much intensity from Neil. I don't want to fight, I don't want to leave, and I don't want to stay.

My legs give way and I slide down, my back against the door, until I'm sitting on the floor. He sinks down on his knees in front of me. I can see how exhausted he is. How distraught he is over everything that's happened tonight.

"I don't want to argue anymore," I whisper.

"I don't either." He swallows.

He inhales sharply and closes his eyes. The way he looks makes me want to curl into him, hold him, even after our horrible fight and his awful words.

"I just want to be with you," he says. "Be happy with you and love you."

I can't stop myself. Slowly I put my arms around him and ease him into me, his face against my shoulder and my fingers lightly caressing the back of his neck.

"We're OK, Neil."

He looks up at me. "Are we? I can tell when something is going on with you. I felt it when I stepped into the room. You wanted to tell me we were over and that you were leaving."

Oh God. Is that possible? That after a stupid comment from Delmo about Alan that I wanted to end it with Neil? Is that how I've been feeling all afternoon? Why I have been internally messy?

I'm not sure and that scares the hell out of me. Could I be that terrible and pathetic of a person?

Neil's gaze is raging and intense. "Tell me the truth, Chrissie. If we don't talk, if we're not honest, the bullshit on the road will tear us apart. What did Vincent say to you that made you think about ending us?"

I lower my gaze. "He told me that Alan called him and wanted to know if I was OK."

Heavy silence fills the room. I stare up at him. A visible shudder rolls down his arms.

"Are you telling me the truth, Chrissie?"

I can't find my words, so I nod.

We stare at each other, exhausted and emotionally drained. Slowly, the tension melts out of Neil, and it is strange, very strange, but he looks almost relieved.

CHAPTER THIRTEEN

I push Neil off me and give him a playful kick with my leg. "Would you stop already? If this is you being contrite, you suck at it. It's irritating."

Neil gives me a sweet, half-pouting smile. "I'm not sure that I'm forgiven."

I catch out of the corner of my eye Josh giving me the *God, what a bitch* look. I shudder internally. It's awful how the guys know everything that happens in our life. Six hours on a bus with no privacy, and Neil being overly attentive, carrying an expression like a wounded puppy, still unsure and still worried. Josh blames me for the crap that went down last night at the hotel. He doesn't say it. He doesn't have to. I can see it in how he looks at me.

Crap, I wish Neil would go and sit at the table with Josh and ignore me like he usually does when Josh wants to work.

I lean into Neil, my lips close to his ear. "You were forgiven this morning," I whisper with heavy meaning.

His fingers play at the buttons of my shirt. "I want to be forgiven again."

Color rises to my cheeks because I can tell he's thinking about how we were in bed. We should fight more often, though I don't really want to, but Neil is very good at makeup sex.

I push at him. "Go away. It's not happening. Not here. Haven't you figured that one out by now?"

Neil slowly lowers his face to mine. His lips move gently at first, then the kiss deepens and deepens as his thumb teases my nipple through my shirt.

I'm breathless when he pulls back.

"No?" he cajoles.

I shake my head. "No."

He lies back on his pillow and makes an aggravated sigh. He look at me. "Are you sure?"

I roll my eyes, but I feel laughter bubbling inside me. "Positive. Stop asking. I'm not doing it."

He rolls off the bed, ambles down the bus, and sinks into a chair beside Josh.

Minutes later they are focused on trying to create lyrics for Josh's new song. Neil is leaning forward in his chair, his head bobbing, his eyes closed, and there is no music except for whatever he is hearing in his head.

From horny to working in the blink of an eye. Jeez, why are musicians so weird? One minute I am everything and the next forgotten.

God, he's impossible to live with.

I watch them for a few minutes. I grab my journal and sink lower onto the bed. I chew on the tip of my pen and stare at the blank page. *Do I write about our fight?* Some parts of it are still bothering me. I frown. Everything is good between us again. That ugly scene in the room shouldn't be nipping at my subconscious still.

Maybe I'm not completely over the fight. Maybe Neil senses it and that's why he keeps trying to make love to me.

Guys think everything can be fixed by sex.

Do we have something that needs fixing? Stupid, Chrissie, stupid. You are being hyper-analytical again. Let it go. It was a fight. Nothing more. Things are good with Neil today.

The mattress moves and I lift my nose out of my journal to watch Nate Kassel stretch out on Neil's pillow beside me.

I arch a brow. "Excuse me? Did I invite you here? Front of the bus: Markem's. Back of the bus: Chrissie's. Middle of the bus: dipshits'."

Nate laughs and grabs off the blanket the journal I finally completely filled yesterday. He starts thumbing through pages.

"You write fucking incredible lyrics."

I roll my eyes. Why does every guy think I write song lyrics in my journal?

I hold out my hand. "Did I say you could read that?" I ask.

He turns a page. "No. But I always do when you and Neil sneak off the bus to do *whatever* you two do. I like reading your journals. They're kind of interesting. Sometimes a little twisted. But the words are good. And I don't want to watch porno flicks with Les and Pat. I'd rather hang with you."

I crinkle my nose and make a *you're disgusting* face. "Thanks a lot. I really don't need to know when they're watch their fuck films."

He looks at me, amused. "It's not exactly a mystery, Chrissie. When the VCR's running, it's fuck film time."

"Why are guys such pigs?"

Nate shrugs and starts rummaging through Neil's bag. "Boredom. We're only pigs when we're bored."

"Then Josh is bored 24/7."

"Josh is not that bad. Stop giving him shit. He doesn't hate you. He just gets easily pissed off by the wrong things because he's so tight with Neil. Besides, who cares about Josh? The rest of us like you, Chrissie. You're a pretty OK girl. If we had to have a band chick this tour, we're glad it's you."

"Yuck. *Band chick?* I'm not a band chick. Don't call me that."

"Suit yourself. Band chick is not a pejorative."

I relax against my pillow and watch him as he continues violating Neil's privacy by taking the shit out of his bag. I should tell him to stop, I don't even go through Neil's stuff, but I don't say anything.

It's better to roll with this and it's nice that Nate told me that the guys like me. They're pretty cool guys. They give me crap, but I bet if someone disrespected me they'd defend me before I could say *Hardy Boys*.

It's like having three big brothers, though Josh is more like the oppressive, disapproving uncle always in my face about something.

Nate pulls a bottle of JD out of the case. He holds it up in Neil's direction. "Hey, man, can I drink this or do you plan to throw it at the side of the bus later?"

Nate starts to laugh, and I give him a hard smack in his chest. *How the hell do they always know everything? And why do they have to be so rude and let me know it?*

"Asshole," I exclaim.

"Don't worry. Neil didn't even hear me."

He unscrews the top. He takes a long swallow, offers me the bottle, and when I shake my head, he takes another gulp. He sits there for a while, staring at me, searching my face.

"What was all that shit about last night?" he asks.

I flush. "Nothing. It's private. No big deal." Then frustration forces me to ask. "How do you guys know everything that happens with us the second it happens?"

He takes another drink. "Nicole. She was in her room last night. Heard every word. Said Neil was throwing things. Came to my room, pounded on my door. And trust me, I didn't want to be interrupted last night. But she ordered me to go break it up before someone sent for the cops and if Neil put so much as a finger on you, that I had better kick his ass or Vincent would. And that I should be smart and not leave it to Delmo to take care of."

I groan, burying my face in my hands. "Fuck. It's so humiliating on the road. As if Neil would hit me. As if he'd hit anyone."

He reclines on his side and arches a brow. "You mean other than Andy? That one still doesn't make sense to me. Neil is a total pacifist and he fucked up Andy good. Anyway, you guys were quiet when I got to your room, so I didn't knock—you're welcome, by the way—and I figured Nicole got it wrong and everything was cool."

I stare at him, hard. "Everything is cool. Nicole definitely got it wrong."

"I didn't think he would step out of line with you, but

my boy was acting weird last night. Edgy. Going off on everyone."

I don't want to think about the events of last night, so I ignore that comment and resolve to focus on my journal. Nate watches me expectantly, takes a sip from the bottle and then starts reading my most personal thoughts again.

We lie together quietly for a while. Nate has been in an unusually talkative mood. I debate with myself whether to ask.

I look over at him. "Why does Josh dislike me so much? Is it just that guy loyalty thing because I broke up with Neil for a while? Or is it something else?"

"Something else." He turns a page.

I stare at him, impatiently. "Well?"

"I don't want to get in the middle of it."

"Too late. You already put yourself in the middle of it with the *he doesn't really hate you* comment. You shouldn't have told me that if you didn't want me to ask you to explain."

"Shit. That's totally fucked-up logic. I'm not in the middle of anything."

I ease over to lie on my side and stare. Nate breathes in, he breathes out, and then he finally turns to face me.

"Don't fucking repeat this," he warns. "It will just cause shit. It will just blow up."

My eyes widen. "I won't. I promise."

"He thinks you fuck up everything we're trying to do by just you being here. You don't serve a purpose. You're not doing anything. You're not working. You write fucking great words no one will ever hear. You don't even know

192

why the fuck you're on the road with us. But everything is different because you're here and it drives Josh up a wall. Get it?"

I frown. "No."

He looks agitated. "Everything is different with you here."

"What's different?"

"For one thing our press. You get more press than everyone in the band combined, even Neil. You are fucking famous for being famous. It's really starting to be a problem with Josh."

I sit up, alarmed. "What are you talking about?"

He shakes his head. "Don't play dumb, Chrissie. I know you don't go to the meet and greets, and I know you haven't been at the press ops, but you must read the press clipping files Neil gets every morning."

Press clipping file? "No. I don't read them. Neil doesn't read them. He doesn't want either of us to read the press. He says reading your own press fucks with your head. I don't look at the newspapers. Not ever."

"You've got to be kidding me," he counters harshly.

"No. Not kidding you. Why do you say it that way?"

Nate frowns. "Neil hasn't mentioned how the press ops go?"

I shake my head. "No. Why would he?"

"Because every fucking time we sit down with the press, the first question Neil gets is about you. They never ask the rest of the band anything. First question, you can fucking bet on it every time, is something about Chrissie."

I'm stunned. Oh no, this can't be true. He's messing

with me. *Good one, Nate. Ha, ha, ha.*

I settle back against my pillow. "You're so full of crap. Why do all you guys like to mess with me? It's not funny."

"Fine. I'm full of crap, but that's why Josh is always pissed off at you and working really hard to get Neil to boot you off the road. He's fed up with the tabloid Chrissie frenzy. He thinks it interferes with what the band is about and what we're trying to do."

It is too absurd. *Chrissie frenzy.* I'm still not sure if I should believe him.

He studies my face for a moment. "It must suck. Being famous for being famous. That must really suck for you."

"I'm not famous for being famous. I'm not anything. I'm not even a band chick. If I were I'd be screwing all of you."

His fingers flutter on my stomach. "If you're interested in becoming the official band girl we can fix that now. Neil's going to be tied up for a while."

I shove him hard, nearly knocking him off the bed. "Not a chance. Jeez, you're obnoxious."

Nate laughs and I smile.

He tosses my journal at Neil and it lands at his feet. "Why don't you use those lyrics? They're probably better than anything you're thinking up."

Josh glares at him, but Neil picks up the journal and starts to read.

Nate settles comfortably on the bed, and closes his eyes. "I'm going to sleep for a while, Chrissie."

In a few minutes he's sound asleep beside me. I stare

out the back window at the passing scenery. I wonder where we are. It's beautiful here. Who would have thought the United States was so large, so much of it unoccupied by people, and every state different and yet oddly the same at once?

I grab my journal and start to write, then Nate begins to snore. *Crap.* I crawl over him and leave the bed. I stop next to Neil and drop a kiss on his head.

"Do you know where we are?" I ask.

Neil opens his eyes and looks up. "Sorry. I haven't been paying attention."

I shift my questioning gaze to Josh. He ignores me. I move to the front of the bus and sink down until I'm sitting on the floor, my back against the dash console.

Markem glances down at me. "Did I say you could sit there, Miss Parker?"

"Nope, you didn't but then I didn't ask. Where are we?"

"South Carolina."

"Do we have enough time to stop for a while? It's pretty here and I could use some fresh air."

He checks the clock. He nods. "For you we can stop. For them, no."

I laugh. "You don't really mean that. You like the guys. I can tell."

He shakes his head and doesn't say anything, but I can see he has something on his mind he'd like to say. It must be impolite. Markem is never impolite with me so that would be the only reason he's not speaking what he's thinking.

I pull myself up. Josh follows my movements with his gaze in a rude manner and, just to piss him off, I sink down on Neil's lap.

Neil frowns. "You OK?"

I curl into his chest. "I'm good. But I'm tired of listening to Nate snore."

Neil laughs.

"We're stopping," I whisper in his ear.

"Oh, thank you. I am very ready to stop."

I blush and do an anxious peek at Josh, and I can tell by his expression he's annoyed with me.

I feel Neil's fingers move in my hair and close my eyes. His touches get more stirring and he starts kissing me on the neck. I wasn't thinking about sex when I asked Markem to stop, but everything is suddenly lit inside me.

The bus screeches to a standstill on the side of the road, and everyone stumbles out, anxious for a bit of space from each other.

We scatter in our customary pairings. Neil pulls me by the hand in one direction. Josh and Les take off in the opposite direction with their guitars, to get high and jam together. Pat and Nate hover near the bus, as if they're worried it will leave without them, tossing a football. And Markem stands at the edge of the road just smoking and staring.

Halfway across the field, Neil lifts me up to carry me, and we are kissing and touching all the way through the meadow of tall grass and wild flowers. We are both impatient in our bodies, out of nowhere. The pulse in Neil's neck beats fiercely against my lips as I kiss him there.

I make a soft bite then run my tongue down his skin. He groans. My muscles clench *there* in anticipation of making love with Neil in the grass, feeling the wind touching my skin between the play of his fingers, feeling as if there is nothing on this earth but us. Lost in each other in a rural idyll where nothing can hurt either of us.

He continues into the trees at the edge, through thick green foliage and dense arching tree branches. The world is utterly tranquil and quiet here. And yet the vivid colors, so much richer than the colors in California, remind me of another meadow.

A whisper of sadness starts to move through me as my thoughts drift to another time, a time when I was not a girl who would fuck in the grass. Though I wanted to. I burned to. I burned for *him.*

"Hey, what's wrong?"

I look up to find Neil studying me.

I shake my head and smile. "Not a thing."

We step out from beneath the trees into more field. He stops, setting me on my feet, and between kisses he undresses, spreads out his shirt as a makeshift blanket, and then removes my panties from beneath my dress, kissing his way down my legs until they are discarded.

He lies down and pulls me on top of him. Desire thick and pulsing dances through my flesh. He grabs my hips and fills me quickly. I groan and arch my back. Slowly he withdraws and then sinks into me. The tempo builds, harder and faster.

I open my eyes to find him watching my face. I watch him watch me and it makes my blood boil through my veins. But my passion-claimed senses haze my vision and the colors of him—deep tanned skin, chestnut hair with golden sun-flecks, lush green eyes—blur into the rich colors of the meadow. I close my eyes and behind my lids there is only black.

I savor the feel of callused fingertips touching my skin, my muscles tightening *there* around him, and I change the rhythm of our bodies until it is quick and rough and I can feel nothing beyond my own flesh.

We come apart together, and I explode around him, my whimpers the only sound on the air. I collapse into him until my head is cradled against his chest and we are both struggling to breathe.

"I love you," Neil whispers.

"I love you, too." I kiss his chest and then snuggle back into him.

Neil trails his fingers up and down my back. He is quiet for a long time.

"I want us to get married," he says.

The languidness leaves my flesh in a jolt.

I lift my face from his chest. "Neil, we just got back together again four months ago. I'm not ready to think about marrying you. I'm not ready to think about spending the rest of my life with anyone."

"We've been together four years, Chrissie. We are already spending our life together."

"I know. But I can't say yes. Not today."

I see something on his face, a fleeting emotion that is quickly lost behind the usual arrangement of his features.

"Then explain it to me, Chrissie. Because I don't know

why you're saying no."

I pull out of his arms, hunt in the grass for my panties, put them on, and then sit on my knees beside him.

"I'm not saying no," I whisper. "I'm saying not yet. There is a difference."

He's angry now.

"That's a bullshit line guys give girls, Chrissie, when they don't want to marry them."

I blink at him rapidly, my entire face burning. He moves away from me, stands, and starts to grab his clothing from the ground.

"Neil, don't be pissed."

He shakes his head. "I'm not pissed, Chrissie. I just don't get you sometimes."

I can feel him watching me.

"Can you answer me one question, Chrissie?"

I don't look at him. I nod.

He sinks down in front of me, crouching at eye level, and lifts my face until I'm looking at him.

"Why do you not want to marry me?"

Shit. Why that question? I don't know how to answer that because I don't know the answer myself. Neil is a great guy. He loves me and I love him. I don't know why I panic every time he asks me to marry him, even back in Berkeley when I used to pretend I thought he was joking. I knew he wasn't. His proposals made me internally messy.

I shake my head. "I don't know, Neil."

He studies my face for a long time, almost like he's searching for something, doesn't find it, and then the anger leaves his body.

I frown, not sure what to make of that. He kisses my forehead. "I love you."

I nod. "I know."

"We're getting married. Someday. You'll say yes."

I nod, but I know that I shouldn't, that it's wrong, because I don't have the slightest idea why I say *no* or if I'll ever *yes*.

He stands and offers me his hand. "Come on. We should get back."

I let him guide me through the meadow, but my limbs suddenly feel too weak and heavy. We are quiet on the way back to the bus, and once everyone is loaded up, I move away from Neil to sit back on the bed.

I pull out a journal just for something to do. I grab my pen. My thoughts drifted back to The Farm. I start to write.

I wish I had made love with Alan in the grass during our spring. I wish I could let go of the past. I wish I could move forward. I wish I understood why I love Neil, and yet the thought of marrying him terrifies me.

I stare at the words on the paper, realizing I'd written my thoughts when I didn't intend to. I tear out the sheet and rip it into tiny pieces. I scrunch it into a ball and shove it deep into my backpack.

I wish I understood me.

CHAPTER FOURTEEN

Neil sits on the edge of the bed, watching me pack.

"I don't want you to go, Chrissie."

The way he says that tells me he's worried that my leaving is about more than wanting to go home to see Jack.

"We've been on the road six months," I explain for what has got to be the tenth time. "I haven't been home once. It's my birthday. I've got to go home, Neil. Jack will get disappointed if I don't."

"If you wait a few weeks, there is a break in the schedule. We can go to Santa Barbara together."

"My birthday is Saturday. I'm not changing my plans."

I focus on neatly folding my clothes and tucking them into the bag to avoid meeting Neil's unwavering stare.

Everything feels strained and awkward between us. Neil is definitely overreacting to my wanting to go home for a few days. But then, we've been off since he asked me to marry him. I know it hurt him that I didn't say yes, but I'm not ready for marriage, and he should be willing to wait until I am.

I zip closed my bag and sink back to sit on my heels. God, I wish he'd stop looking at me that way.

"I'll only be gone two weeks." Then, deliberately silly, I add, "Unless after having me gone Josh has convinced you not to want me back."

Neil chuckles softly, reluctant humor at best. "Not a chance. I'm going to miss you every day you're gone."

I walk on my knees across the carpet to him until I'm between his legs. I rub my hands atop his thighs. "You better miss me at night, too, or you're going to have pissed-off Chrissie when I return."

His laughter erupts in a more lighthearted way. He leans in and starts kissing me on my neck. "I will definitely miss you at night. Will you miss me?"

"Every second. I've gotten kind of used to having you around."

He eases back, touching his nose to my nose. "Me too."

I make a face. "I need to finish packing or I'll miss my plane."

I spring to my feet and go to the bathroom to collect my toiletries.

"Are you seeing Rene while you're there?" I hear Neil ask from the bedroom.

I pop back into the room. "I don't know yet. I called her to let her know I'd be in Santa Barbara, but she sort of blew me off and didn't commit to anything. So I don't know if I'll see her."

He rolls his eyes in that *Rene's a bitch* kind of way. "What do you plan to do there for two weeks?"

"Go the beach every day. Get some sun. Hang out with Jack. *Not* be on a bus with the guys. Maybe sleep an entire day and night."

"You make me jealous."

"You should be. Santa Barbara sounds like heaven to

me these days."

His eyes cloud over again, troubled. *Crap, why did I say that?*

I change the subject quickly. "I'm going to see your mom while I'm there. And your cousin Mia, too."

"I know. They told me. My mom is really excited about spending time with you. It meant a lot to her that you made a point to call her and set up something."

I smile. "I like your mom."

"You like my family enough to become a Stanton?"

Oh damn.

"Definitely your strongest pro on the pros and cons list, Neil," I taunt. "Your musical genius and sexiness rank only second and third. Family number one."

He laughs and I search the room to see if I've forgotten anything. I feel frazzled and disoriented.

I sigh. "I think I've got everything."

Neil stands and gently pulls me up against him. He buries his lips in my hair. "I'll call you every night."

"You had better call me every morning, too."

"I want to go with you to the airport," he says.

"Nope. I want to say goodbye here."

~ ~ ~

I stare out the airplane window as we make a wide circle over the ocean and then start to descend. I didn't realize how much I'd missed home until I could see Santa Barbara through the glass; the foothills, the mountains, the beaches, the clusters of track homes, and even the palm trees. It all looks so marvelous to me.

I feel a series of bumps, landing gear touching earth,

and then I hear the loud whoosh of the rapid slowing of the plane on the short runways we have here.

Everyone starts moving even though the flight attendant hasn't opened the doors. I climb from my first-class seat and take my small black bag from the overhead bin.

Light floods the cabin, and I step out onto the metal steps, feeling the California sunshine warm my cheeks even in mid-November and smelling the sweetness of clean ocean air.

I make my way across the tar-stained, uneven concrete of the tarmac and step into the courtyard outside the terminal.

Surprise jolts through my limbs as I spot Jack waiting on a bench. It is the first time he hasn't stayed with the car when picking me up at the airport. Tears mist my eyes.

Jack comes to me and takes me in a sloppy bear hug. "I've missed you, baby girl. I'm so glad you're home."

"Me too, Daddy. I've really missed you. But you better stop hugging me or I'll start crying right here."

"Go ahead and cry, baby girl. It's nice to know you're glad to see me."

He holds me as if he doesn't want to let me go, and I realize he's spent a lot of time worrying about me the past six months. He saw me off in Seattle. He didn't want me to go on the road with Neil, and the memory of how he'd stood there watching me leave vividly fills my head.

He holds my face with his palms. "You look great. Are you doing OK, Chrissie?"

I nod, smiling up at him. "I'm good. Neil's good. He

told me to say hi for him and to tell you he's sorry he couldn't be here."

Jack places a light kiss on my cheek, then takes my black case. "Let's find your suitcase so we can get you out of the airport."

We wait in the baggage claim area for only a few minutes. Jack grabs my duffel from the cart, and we head out to the front drop-off loop.

He opens my door. "Anything special you want to do while you're home?"

"Just stay home," I say and he smiles at me as I climb into my seat.

I watch as he tosses my bags in the back, then settles in the driver's seat.

I frown. "New car?"

Jack starts driving from the airport. "New car. The lease was up on the Volvo. I swapped it out for this. I wasn't sure what you wanted."

I laugh. "I'm old enough to get my own cars, Daddy."

"Not a chance. I like taking care of my girl."

I settle more into my seat. It feels really good, better than any other time before, to be home. I don't know why, but it feels incredible today.

I roll down the window and let the air tease my hair as we drive past the beach and turn onto the freeway.

I feel Jack's gaze on me.

"Happy to be home?"

I turn from the window. "Ecstatic."

Jack laughs. "The road can do that. Nothing makes home look better than the road."

I smile, but I'm not sure if that's what I'm feeling, relief to be off the road, or even if that's why this feels so good to be here. There's been a quietness in me that I didn't expect since I left Neil at the hotel.

Strange. It makes no sense to be feeling this way. I've just left him alone on tour, where every night is filled with hundreds of girls panting after him, hot for his boxers. I should feel anxious not peaceful. Guys lie for guys. He could do anything he wanted while I'm gone and no one would ever tell me.

I should be suspicious. Paranoid. Jealous. Those feelings would be logical. Not this odd sense of almost relief to be taking a break from each other.

What a strange girl I am. My internal processes rarely ever are normal. Like my reaction to the marriage proposal. I feel myself getting emotionally messy all over again, and push the memory from my mind.

"What's weighing so heavily on your mind, baby girl?" Jack asks, startling me. "Something tells me you didn't come home just to be with me for your birthday. Something is bothering you, Chrissie."

I shrug and stare out the window. I surprise myself by saying, "Neil asked me to marry him."

Jack smiles. "Not exactly a shocker. Neil's twenty-eight. Things are starting to take off for him. He knows what he wants."

A long moment of quiet passes that feels as if Jack is waiting for me to tell him what my answer was. "What did you say?" he asks, finally.

We drive beneath the high black metal arch into Hope

Ranch. I didn't plan on discussing this with Jack, I don't know why I am, but we're nearly home so I can escape this conversation quickly if it grows too uncomfortable.

"I said maybe," I answer softly.

"Oh," Jack replies heavily.

I arch a brow. "What is that supposed mean? *Oh?*"

Jack makes a quiet, sort of sympathetic laugh. "Maybe doesn't mean maybe in this situation. Maybe is *no*. How'd Neil take that?"

Crap, that's exactly what Neil said. Is there some guy code book somewhere in this world that all men get? My maybe meant maybe. I don't know what I want yet.

"He was hurt, but you know Neil. He got over it fast. And everything is fine."

"So why did you say no?" Jack asks, and I can tell that's far from a simple question. He wants to know if there is something he should be concerned about between Neil and me.

I shake my head. "Because I'm not sure. Not ready yet or even sure if marriage is the right thing for me."

Jack makes an approving nod. "Then keep saying maybe, baby girl. It has to be the right thing for both of you for it to be a good thing for either of you."

I frown. "How do you know, Daddy, when it's right? Everything with Neil is really good. I just don't know if it's right."

Jack laughs. "You'll know when you know. Don't worry about it. When something is *right* it isn't something you can miss."

I study my dad for a moment. I've always wanted to

know this and have never asked, but we just rummaged around in my personal life, so shouldn't it be fair for me to rummage in his?

"Why haven't you remarried?" I ask.

Jack's eyes remain forward on the road, but there is a strange look on his face.

"I almost did. Once," he says quietly.

Holy shit. I wasn't expecting that one. How could he have a relationship serious enough to contemplate marriage without me ever knowing about it?

My eyes widen to their fullest and I turn in my seat until I'm directly facing him.

"Who? When? How? What happened?"

Jack gives me an amused look.

"I'm not answering all that. And you don't need to know the details. It didn't work out."

"Why didn't it work out?"

He shakes his head, exasperated with me giving him more questions.

"It doesn't matter why. I've had a good life, Chrissie. No one gets everything that they want. Having enough is a pretty damn fine thing. I have enough."

I watch him as we pull into the driveway, and suddenly I remember that day when Maria told me about Jack's *long-term lady friend*. I wonder if the *long-term lady friend* is the woman Jack wanted to marry, if he still loves her, and if I will ever meet her.

He hops from the car and moves quickly to get my bag. For once it looks like he's running from one of our father/daughter chats.

I climb from the car, shaking my head. Why doesn't Jack share the details of his personal life with me the way he expects me to share mine with him?

He opens the front door for me, smiling as he waits for me to enter. Conversation over. Well, maybe we've both talked enough serious shit for one day.

Jack goes in one direction to put my suitcases in my room and I make my way through the rooms, poking my head in here and there, looking for Maria. I pause at the entry to the family room.

Maria is sitting on the couch, folding laundry and watching her Spanish soap opera. Well, it's noon. Even my coming home today doesn't change her routine. Her eyes are fixed on the set, and she doesn't even notice I'm here.

"Well, this is anticlimactic," I say. "Not even a hello."

Maria whirls on the sofa, and her round matronly face brightens with excitement.

"Chica. You are home. ¿Cómo está mi niña?"

Mi niña. My girl. Warmth moves through my veins. I feel really home, finally; I've now heard *mi niña* from Maria. I'm home.

"I've missed you, Maria." I drop down on the couch beside her and she quickly pulls me into her arms. "I'm so glad to see you."

She lays a palm on my cheek. "I am glad to see you, Chrissie. You look good. Everything going well for you?"

I nod, sinking down to sit cuddled up against her. "I'm doing great."

She nods in a serious way, as if the important matters have been taken care of, and then starts folding the laundry again. I bite back my laughter.

"¿Tu novio no está aquí?"

I stare at her and frown. Nope, can't translate that one.

"What does *novio* mean?"

Maria arches a brow. "Ah, you forget your Spanish, Chrissie. You have been from home too long. It means fiancé. Boyfriend." She stares at me with wide eyes and makes a funny face. "Neil."

I laugh. "I don't hear a lot of Spanish these days. I'm surrounded by surfer boys and Brits."

"So where is Neil?" she asks, in that nosy mother sort of way.

"Working. He wanted to come with me, but he couldn't. He told me to ask if you would make enchiladas to take back to him. We can't get good Mexican food on the east coast."

"I like him." She nods, takes a fast peek at the action on the TV, and then glances back at me. "He is a good boy. Remind me, Chrissie. I'll make tamales just for him. You can take those back. They'll travel better."

My brows hitch up as I pull back from her. "Tamales, huh? You don't even make tamales for me when I ask for them. Jeez, you are such a pushover for a cute guy."

Maria gives me a stern look, but her cheeks flush a tad. "You are so full of it."

I smile. "I'm glad you like Neil. I couldn't date him if you didn't."

She rolls her eyes. "Chrissie does what Chrissie wants to do."

"I'm not that bad."

Maria tilts her head to the side and gives me *the look*.

"Maria! Stop it. You're going to hurt my feelings and I haven't been home five minutes."

She pats the sofa beside her. "Sit down. Watch our program with me, and help me finish my work."

I grab a towel from the basket. We sit together, eyes glued on the set, neatly stacking folded laundry on the coffee table. I come home and Maria puts me to work. Some things never change.

Maria shuts off the set, stands up, grabs the empty laundry basket from the couch and puts the piles of towels in it.

She points. "Carry that for me, Chrissie. I need to put it away."

My eyes widen in surprise. She's never asked me to do anything except help her fold, but then she's not as young as she used to be.

I follow her down the back hallway to the linen closet, holding the basket until she's emptied it again.

"Put it on the floor and come to my room with me," she orders.

I set down the basket and follow her. When I enter her bedroom she is rummaging through her armoire. She turns back to face me and my heart drops to the floor.

"I did not keep this from you, chica. It came last week. I did not know how to send it to you, but I kept it because I knew you were coming home."

She sets the envelope in my trembling hands and tears burn behind my lids. There is no return address, but I don't need one to know who it is from. I recognize the handwriting with an instant jab to my heart.

I stare at it. Ten months. A single letter. Alan wouldn't return a phone call, but he sent this. I get a single letter ten months later, probably just a briefly penned note to tell me to *buzz off* since I pathetically called him repeatedly after we first broke up.

I can't feel my arms. I can't feel my legs. I can't breathe. I desperately want to open it. *No, Chrissie, no. Be smart.*

I shove it back at Maria. "Rip it up. Throw it away. And if he sends more don't give them to me."

I leave the room before Maria can answer me and rush down the hallway to my bedroom. I shut the door behind me and stand in the middle of the room, staring, trying to figure out if I should run back in there for Alan's letter.

Do I retrieve it before Maria can destroy it? Or is it better never to read it?

I breathe in. I breathe out. Slowly I become aware that the trembling in me has stopped. I'm surprised by how quickly it left me. I've never before driven away the *Alan internally messy* so quickly. I feel myself easing into comfortable order again. It's a new feeling, really good, and I know with a certainty that not reading his letter was the best thing for me.

OK, Alan panic attack over. But new panic is here to replace it.

What the hell do I do alone in Santa Barbara for two weeks? Rene's not here. Neil's not here. I don't have any friends, not really. There's Jack. But I can't exactly hang exclusively with my dad all day. How pathetic that would be.

Shit, Chrissie, why didn't you think of this before you came home? I'm never more alone than when I am in Santa Barbara, which is so bizarre because this is home.

I drop to my knees beside my suitcase and rummage through my clothes for my bathing suit. I quickly change, grab a towel, shove some things into a small carry tote, and head for the beach.

Sun. I'll lie in the sun. Sun makes everything less awful.

I cut across the lawn to the steps built into the cliffs. I look in both directions. No one. Perfect. Not even Jack.

I trot down the steps and settle in a lush spot not littered with driftwood and seaweed. After spreading out my towel, I lie down on my stomach.

My mobile phone rings and I tense, wondering if it's Neil and if this is how the two weeks apart are going to be, him calling me endlessly.

Then I chide myself for the snotty thought as I search in my bag for the phone, and I admit that I'm already kind of missing him. *Not kind of, Chrissie. You do miss Neil.*

Less than a day apart from him and I really miss him. I didn't expect that. Nor did I expect it to be a surprisingly nice feeling. It's so unlike me, but I've had two uncharacteristic nice feelings in a single day: not completely melting down over Alan and missing Neil.

I flip my phone open and hold it to my ear. "Hello?"

"Chrissie, I'm not bothering you, am I?"

Michelle Stanton. A smile covers my face because Neil's mother is such a sweetheart and I'm more than a little thrilled that she called.

I sit up. "You're not bothering me. I'm just lying out on the beach."

"You take calls on the beach?"

She laughs and I shake my head. She makes that sound like the strangest thing in the world to her.

"Where I go, my mobile goes. You raised a worrier, Michelle. If Neil can't reach me by phone he starts to call nonstop."

She sighs.

"Yes, that boy is a worrier. Always has been. I haven't the first clue why he's that way. I think Neil was just born a worrier. But it's sort of sweet that he cares so much that it's important to him to talk to you, isn't it?"

I've never looked at it that way before. "Very sweet." I curl around the phone, hugging my knees. "So what's up? You didn't call just to discuss Neil."

She laughs. "No. A smart mother stays out of their children's relationships. We're supposed to have lunch tomorrow. Remember?"

"Of course I remember. Where do you want to meet up?"

A long pause. "I'm not really sure I'd know any restaurants you'd like, dear."

I bite back my laughter, but the *any restaurants you'd like, dear* makes my smile grow. "I'm pretty much good with anywhere."

"I think Mia is going to join us. Perhaps we should let Mia pick where we go."

This time I can't hold back my laughter. *So she doesn't know where Neil gets his worrying? Oh, Michelle, he gets it from you, and all we're trying to do is figure out a place to eat.*

"Why don't we all meet at your house tomorrow at noon?" I offer, surprising myself. "I'll drive. We can just figure it out after I get there."

"Perfect." She sounds relieved. "See ya tomorrow, Chrissie."

"See ya, Michelle."

See ya. Something else Neil got from his mother. I toss my phone onto my bag and lie on my back, shading my eyes with an arm.

Funny, but I never noticed before how much like his mother Neil is. His at times extreme worrying over nothing. That's Michelle. *See ya.* That's Michelle. How considerate and understanding he is. Michelle. He's just like his mother.

I crinkle up my nose. I wonder if I'm just like Jack. Nope, not going to go there. I wish I could remember my mother better. I wish I knew if I was like Lena. But I don't remember her well so I won't ever know if I'm like her or more like Jack.

I roll back onto my stomach, almost decide to go sleep, then I reach for my mobile phone. Four hours in Santa Barbara and Neil hasn't called yet. It surprises me.

I grab the phone and punch in the numbers for his mobile.

Ring. Ring. Ring.

"Chrissie," is whispered into the receiver.

I laugh, and everything inside me starts to warm. "God, you sound like such a pervert when you say my name that way. It isn't the least bit sexy, Neil."

His laughter sounds rough, a touch gravelly. "I'm not trying to be sexy. My voice is shit today."

I make a pout, even though he can't see it through the phone. "Sorry. You didn't call me after I landed. I was wondering if you forgot about me."

"Nope. That's not going to happen, not ever."

I smile. "Well, I don't want to wear out your voice. You sound awful today. I'll let you go."

"No." This word is spoken on just a breath.

"No?"

"I know you hate the sappy shit, but I really do miss you. I really do wish you were here."

"I miss you, too." How quickly I say that surprises me.

"I hate the road without you, Chrissie."

"I'll be back soon."

"Have fun in Santa Barbara. I didn't mean to be such a downer before you left. I get why you went home. Everyone needs time alone to think. You always run home when you need to think. Think about us getting married, will you?"

Shit. How did he know that was partly the reason I left?

I change the subject. "Do you think I'm like my dad?"

His laughter comes loudly and more gravelly. "Shit, Chrissie, you're exactly like Jack."

I scrunch up my face. "Really?"

"Yep." A few minutes of quiet, and then he says, "You're both pains in the ass."

I burst out laughing. I don't want to laugh, but Neil is probably right.

"I love you anyway, baby," he whispers into the

phone.

"I love you, even though you're exactly like your mother," I taunt.

"What the hell is that supposed to mean?"

Laughing, I click off the phone.

~~~

I park in the Stantons' driveway and sit in the car, staring at the house.

I love this house. A small, lively blue bungalow with white shutters and a pretty porch crowded with plants and furnishings. It's the kind of place I imagine when you have to imagine *home* in a story and the author doesn't help you by providing a description. The iconic Americana image of home, California-style, crowded with a loud, rowdy, outdoors-loving family.

Yep, that's the Stantons. Even if Neil does like to say he was raised in the 6-6-6, which pisses me off because his family is wonderful and should never be compared to the *satanic*, but I know that isn't how he means it. It's just Santa Barbara code for the rougher neighborhoods on the eastside—six blocks from the beach, six blocks from State Street, and six blocks from school—the 6-6-6.

I crinkle my nose, I definitely don't like that, and pull my keys from the ignition. I climb from the car, hurry up the walkway, and then pull back the black iron security screen and knock on the door.

Lots of sound comes from inside, then the door is jerked wide and Mia Stanton, her pretty face bright with excited welcoming, closes in on me as she grabs me in a fast, exuberant hug.

"Chrissie. I'm so happy you're home."

I pull back smiling. "I'm happy, too. It's great to see you, Mia."

She makes a motion with her arm. "Come on in. Michelle is still getting ready." She leans into me, whispering, "She's changed her clothes three times. She's driving me crazy. So wants to make a good impression on our—and I quote—'first girls' day out with my future daughter-in-law.'"

I grimace. *Oh shit, Neil, why did you tell your mother you asked me to marry you? Fudge.*

Mia reads my face without effort and grimaces in sympathy. "I shouldn't have said that, should I? Now I've made everything all awkward and shit. I'm sorry, Chrissie. We tell each other everything. It's just the way large families are, and Neil couldn't have asked you to marry him without finding out if Michelle approved. They're really tight. And we know you said *no*. But Michelle is an eternal optimist."

By the time her rambling chatter finishes I want to drop through the floor. *Jeez, this is awful. Lunch is going to be a nightmare.*

Mia crinkles her nostrils. "That didn't help, did it?"

I laugh. "No."

She gives me a one-arm, wraparound hug. "Don't worry. It will all be fine. Lunch will be fine. Let me go get Aunt Michelle."

I watch Mia disappear down the hall and I sink to sit on a sofa. My leg starts jiggling and I try to will it to stop, but I can't.

A few minutes later, Mia returns with Michelle, and the way Neil's mother smiles at me puts my unease instantly at rest. There is nothing but welcome on her face. If she resents me turning down her son's proposal it doesn't show, and the way she smiles is so like Neil's I feel a little twinge of missing him again. He doesn't look like his mother—she is blond-haired and brown-eyed—but their smiles are the same.

I stand up before they reach the sofa.

"I'm so glad you wanted to do this, dear," she says, leaning in to hug me. She stops and hold up one hand. "It is OK that I hug you, isn't it? Or would it be weird? I never know what's correct nowadays."

I laugh, wondering how I could have ever thought Michelle would make today awkward for me. "Of course. If you don't hug me you'll hurt my feelings and make me think you don't like me."

"Then I better hug you quickly, because I adore you, Chrissie."

She gives me a breezy embrace, but steps back from me quickly. She looks around the living room.

"I think we're ready to go," she announces dramatically, and I stifle a laugh.

We go out the front door and pile into my car.

I put the key into the ignition. "Where does everyone want to go?"

Michelle turns slightly toward me from the passenger seat. "Well, it's your birthday. This lunch is sort of your day. You should pick where we go, Chrissie."

I smile. "Michelle, my birthday isn't until tomorrow."

She smiles back. "But I won't see you tomorrow so today is your birthday for me."

My cheeks warm. The way she says that makes me feel really good, special. "OK. I know just the place."

Two hours later we're sitting on the upstairs patio of a restaurant on the pier. It's a brilliantly sunny day, and there are people everywhere, walking on the beach and along the waterfront.

I curl in my chair, my flip-flops discarded under the table, my heals balancing on the edge of the seat with my legs bent in front of me, listening to Mia and Michelle's endless chatting. The Stantons sure can talk a lot.

I smile and take a sip of my wine. I haven't been to this restaurant since I came here with Neil on our first date-date. It didn't occur to me until the hostess directed us to a table that the last time I was here was with Neil.

God, how awkward that was. We hardly spoke to each other. But the night definitely ended amazingly. The memories warm my cheeks and send emotion pulsing through me.

Michelle shifts her gaze to me. "What are you thinking about, dear? You look lost in your thoughts."

I shake my head, blushing and embarrassed. "Nothing."

Mia crinkles her nose. "She's thinking about Neil."

The color darkens on my cheeks and Michelle laughs. "They drive us crazy when they are around, but the second we're without them they are all we think about. So not fair. Men don't think about anything."

We all laugh.

Michelle straightens in her chair. "I almost forgot. I have a present for you for your birthday. Is it OK if I give it to you now since I won't see you tomorrow?"

"You didn't have to get me anything, Michelle."

"Of course I got you something. You're important to Neil. That makes you important to all of us. I couldn't *not* get you a birthday present. You're part of the family."

"Why don't you come tomorrow, Michelle? Bring Robert and the girls, and give me my present then. It's just going to be my dad and me barbecuing on the patio."

Her eyes grow huge. "No. I wouldn't know what to say. What to do."

I stare at her, confused, but Mia starts laughing uproariously. "Jeez, Michelle, he's just Chrissie's dad."

Michelle blushes and Mia shakes her head.

"Michelle has the worst kind of crush on Jack, Chrissie," Mia explains, trying to contain her laughter and doing a terrible job of it.

"Stop it," Michelle warns, but she's blushing and smiling. She looks at me. "Your dad is incredible." The color on her cheeks darkens. "I saw him on the beach once and almost fainted. He's just so freaking gorgeous. He is so hot."

Mia and I look at each other and we both go *yuck*.

"Too much information, Michelle. I don't think Chrissie appreciates hearing how hot her dad is."

Michelle's blush darkens. "Anyway. No, I'm not going to horn in on your birthday and I'd rather give you your gift today."

She reaches into her tote and lays a box on the table.

A slight hint of worry appears on her pretty face.

"You are probably going to think this is lame. I didn't know what to buy you. What you'd like. What you would need. So I made this for you, Chrissie."

She sets a beautifully wrapped box on my side of the table. I stare at her, feeling my eyes mist.

"I would never think anything you gave me is lame," I assure her firmly. "I'm blown away that you made me something."

She sighs. "I figured with being on the road with Neil, you wouldn't have time to do something like this. My daughters seem to really like having them, so I thought you might want one."

I'm touched beyond words, and more than a little curious. I open the card and am blown away again. The entire family signed it and penned a little note. I start to laugh. Neil's dad signed his name *Officer Robert*. By the time I've finished reading it all my cheeks hurt from smiling.

I tuck the card neatly back into the envelope. Beneath Michelle's alert and anxious stare I carefully unwrap the present. I pull back the tissue and my eyes widen.

I finger the cover. "You made me a scrapbook."

Michelle nods, scooting her chair over close to me. "I started saving pictures from the newspapers the first day, and I thought you might like them. A little keepsake of your time traveling with Neil. Life goes by fast. It's good to have things to remember it by."

I lift it from the box, and it feels heavy, filled. We don't look at the papers, ever, and I haven't a clue what's in here. But Michelle and Mia look excited, so I open the cover.

Oh my God. The first picture is Neil and me in the exit tunnel when he didn't want to go out on stage. I'm sitting between his legs, smiling at him, and he's hidden beneath all that hair. Jeez, I didn't even realize someone had caught a picture of us. That there had been press anywhere near.

I start turning pages. Me and Neil on stage together during a sound check. Me and Neil arriving at an arena for a performance. Me and Neil holding each other. It goes on and on.

Jeez, Nate wasn't messing with me. *Chrissie tabloid frenzy. Famous for being famous.* The photos. The captions. The tabloids like to create sensational romance to splatter in print, and they have definitely done that with us. No wonder Josh hates me. Some of it borders on ridiculous.

All this was going on around me and I never knew it. Moments of my life caught and barely remembered. Then the flash of distress gives way as my heart starts to melt. It is an overwhelming thing to see us in a picture. The way Neil looks at me. The way I look at him. I finger a photo. I didn't know that this is the way my eyes look when I look at him. That *this* is the way we look at each other.

All my emotions run heatedly through my veins.

"Thank you," I whisper. "I love it."

"You guys look so happy together," Michelle says, a touch emotionally. "Really beautiful. I never thought my son would ever love anyone the way he loves you."

I nod.

Mia does a shudder. "Michelle, we are not getting all mushy here today. Please, you're embarrassing Chrissie."

I look up. "She's not embarrassing me." I shift my

gaze to Michelle. "This is the nicest present anyone has ever given me."

Michelle beams, pats my hand, and sits back. "Well, I just thought you might like something."

I hold it against my chest. "I definitely like it, Michelle."

~ ~ ~

I sit on a patio chaise watching the sunset with Jack.

Jack glances over at me. "Did you have a nice birthday, baby girl?"

"Wonderful, Daddy. It wouldn't be a birthday without barbecuing with you on the patio."

"I'm surprised you didn't invite anyone over."

I reach for my ice tea, hiding my smile behind my glass. Jack still doesn't get it; I'm a loner like him.

"Nope, Daddy. You and me. That's how we roll."

He takes my hand. "I love you, Chrissie."

"I love you too, Daddy."

Jack sighs. "So why don't you tell me what you've been thinking about all afternoon?"

Jeez, is it so obvious?

I scrunch up my face. "Would you be disappointed if I left Monday instead of staying the full two weeks?"

Jack laughs. "A little disappointed. But not surprised."

I flush. "I love being home, but I'm kind of missing Neil."

"Definitely not surprised."

I stare out at the spreading shades of orange, pink and purple swirling in the sky above the Pacific.

"Did they have guidance counselors when you were in

high school, Daddy?"

Jack shakes his head. "That was like a thousand years ago. I don't remember. Why do you ask?"

"We had this one we had to see every month through our senior year to help us plan our future. Every time I went there, she asked me *Chrissie, what do you plan to do with your life?* It used to annoy the hell out of me."

Jack rolls his eyes. "What did you say?"

"I don't want to be anything. I want to meet a nice guy, get married, maybe have some kids. Just be and be happy."

"That sounds like a plan to me."

I make a face. "Mrs. Lowell didn't think so. She said that wasn't a plan. She made me feel like a slacker. Like I was a loser for not wanting to be something more."

"She's wrong," Jack says firmly. "I wished you told me this story back then. I would have spoken to her. We all figure out things in our own time. Our own pace. She shouldn't have made you feel that way."

I struggle to keep my emotions from surfacing. "It doesn't matter. After I told her I didn't want to be anything, she never called me to her office again."

His eyes sharpen on my face. "What's stirred this up, Chrissie? Why are you thinking about this?"

I shrug. "Nothing. It's just I'm twenty-three years old today. Everyone I know is doing something. I'm not in school. I don't have a job. I'm not trying to be anything and I still don't have a plan for my life."

"I'm fifty, baby girl, and I don't have a plan either."

He laughs and I give him a playful swat.

"That's such crap, Daddy."

Jack's smile deepens. "No it's not. I don't worry about where I've been or where I'm going. I worry about where I am."

Where I am? I'm sitting with my dad on the patio watching the sunset on my birthday. Nice, but not what I want.

"I'm going to leave Monday."

Jack nods, doesn't say a word, but I can see that he's thinking about something serious. His expression tells me it's the type of thing he will never share with me.

It's such a distinct look on his face. An expression of wistfulness and other things. I wonder what he's thinking of when he looks the way he does now.

The sky slowly darkens.

I yawn. "I think I'm going to go to bed, Daddy."

Jack looks amused. "So early?"

"Yep."

"You are less fun than I am," Jack teases.

I give him a light kiss on the cheek. "That goes without saying."

I grab my ice tea from the table and plod across the patio to the French doors. I step into the kitchen, startle and drop my glass to the floor.

White roses surrounded by dozens of red, in a vase tied with violet ribbon, sit on the center island. Alan sent me roses for my birthday.

Dammit, Maria, why didn't you throw them away?

I tell myself not to, but I do it anyway. Shaking, I lift the card from the vase and open it. Not the words I expected. Not *Happy Birthday*. But two words all the same.

Call me. And a phone number.

How did Alan even know I would be here?

I scoop up the flowers and toss them in the trash. Then I reach in and remove the card. I shouldn't keep it. I should burn it. But I tuck it into my address book anyway.

CHAPTER FIFTEEN

I rush from the airport with my bag, go to the first taxi at the pick-up line, and climb in.

"The Omni Hotel, please," I say.

I rummage through my purse for my mobile phone. I punch in Neil's number and wait. Ring. Ring. Ring. Crap, voice mail.

"Why are you not answering?" I say with an aggravated growl. "Call me back. I'm in Indianapolis. I don't know what room we're in. If you want me, you had better tell me where, soon. Or I might go back to Santa Barbara. And for a guy who claimed to be really happy that I was coming back early, you are..."

Beep. Damn, cut off by voice mail.

I settle back against the seat and stare out the window at passing scenery. Jeez, who would have thought I'd be so excited about being in the Midwest? It's kind of an interesting city. Really flat compared to California. Tall buildings even here in Indiana. Big freeways. Lots of people. Urban America looks the same everywhere. Urban yucky.

My phone rings and I smile. I flip it open and put it against my ear.

"You are in such freaking trouble," I say into the receiver. "You better have a good excuse for not calling me back earlier. That's all I have to say."

Silence. Shit, maybe Neil thinks I'm serious about being pissed.

"Don't hang up the phone, Chrissie."

The earth falls away beneath me and everything inside me goes numb. *Alan.* I say the first thought I can string together. "How did you get this number?"

"It wasn't difficult. Vincent gave it to me."

Fuck. Why did you do that, Delmo?

My head spins. "I don't want to talk to you."

I can hear him breathing through the receiver. Shit, why did that have to sound so little-girl pathetic? *Fuck, Chrissie. Pull yourself together.*

"I know you don't want to talk to me. I wouldn't want to talk to me either, love. But don't hang up. It doesn't matter what happened between us. I will always care about you, Chrissie. I didn't want to make this call, any more than you wanted me to, but we need to talk some things out, love. Please, don't hang up."

We need to talk some things out?

Every muscle in my body shakes from panic. Oh God, it can't be about *that.* How could Alan possibly know about April? Only three people on this earth know. Me. Neil. And Jack.

My trembling fingers tighten around the phone. "I have nothing to say to you. There is nothing you could say at this point I would want to hear."

"Please. Five minutes, Chrissie, and I'll never bother you again. You have my word."

My face scrunches up as I battle to fight back my tears.

Never bother you again. I feel my heart still because for a foolish half-second I thought Alan called to beg me to take him back and to tell me he still loves me.

"I sent you a letter. Did you read it?" he asks, his voice strangely intense, serious.

"No." I gather every scrap of my shredded composure and make myself do what I should have done when I first heard his voice. "I didn't read it. I don't want to talk to you. There is nothing between us worth talking about. Don't contact me again. Just leave me alone, Alan."

I click off the phone and toss it away from me. Why did Alan have to call today? Since boarding the plane in Santa Barbara, everything has felt really good inside me, like I finally know where I am going in my life, and now nothing feels certain. Neil. The past. The present. Nothing.

Shit, why did he call me? Crap, why do I care? I stare at the phone. *Don't call him back, Chrissie. Whatever it is Alan wants, you are not interested.*

I breathe in. Breathe out. Don't think about Alan. Keep him in the lockbox where he belongs. Think about why you are in Indy. Why you wanted to return early. What you've been thinking about since you left Neil five days ago in Memphis.

Think of Neil. Nothing else. Think of Neil. What was it Jack said? *I think about where I am. Not the past. Not the future.* Well, Chrissie, you're in Indianapolis. Think about why you are here.

A measure of calm has returned by the time the taxi pulls into the circular driveway in front of the hotel and a sharply dressed valet rushes forward to open my door. I take cash from the pocket in my purse to pay, and before I climb out of the car, my bag is sitting on the curb with an attendant in wait.

"Are you checking in, Miss?" he asks.

"No, I already have a room." I hold up my index finger. "One second. I just need to call and find out where."

I dial my phone again and wait. I stare into the lobby. The hotel is packed with people from the tour like it always is everywhere we stayed, but I don't see anyone I am friendly with. Definitely none of the guys from the band are loitering in the lobby.

I cover my ear not pressed against the receiver with my hand to block out the noise. Ring. Ring. Ring. Fucking voice mail again.

I snap it shut and enter the hotel, cutting my way through the people toward the front desk. Crap, there is a line at check-in. I don't want to wait in line just to get a room number.

I drop my arms on the marble countertop, smile and stare at a clerk. After trying to ignore me several minutes, he comes over to the spot across the counter from me.

"How may I help you?" he asks in that snotty way clerks do in the better hotels.

"I don't know what room I'm in."

Jeez, that sounded lame.

"Name?"

"Stanton."

"Do you have ID, Miss?"

"Yes, I have ID." I drop my purse on the counter. I

pull out my wallet. "Oh crap. My license says Parker. But the Stanton room is my room. Get it?"

Now the way he's looking at me is just plain insulting. "Hold on."

He grabs the phone and dials.

"Mr. Stanton, there is a Miss Parker at the desk..." His voice trails off and he nods for a while. Then, "OK. I'll send her up."

I exhale slowly, but internally I'm really annoyed because if Neil is in the room why didn't he answer his fucking mobile?

I'm emotionally messy by the time I climb into the elevator, and I don't want to be. I wanted this to be a perfect first day back with Neil. I definitely hoped Indy would be a special kind of day, sort of like a new beginning for us. Me being less frustrating and indecisive. The both of us more clear on where we're going together. I'm not ready to say *yes, I'll marry you*, but I'm seriously considering it and I want Neil to know that. I think it will make him happy.

Well, that's what I'd hoped when I boarded a plane seven hours ago in Santa Barbara, but the Alan phone call has knocked me out of whack. Then the Neil phone calls— or rather *non-phone calls*—have started to make me feel anxious, though I don't know why and I know they probably shouldn't.

We exit the elevator, and the floor with the bank of rooms for the guys is noisier than usual. Crap, Delmo must be on the same floor with us again. There are people everywhere, girls everywhere, things I don't want to see everywhere, doors open, small parties within this giant party. Give them an extra day on the hop and this is what guys do with it.

I glance into a room as I pass, and I really wish I hadn't. I know that Les Wilson is a freaking man-whore, but I don't like to see it because I know I'm going to be hanging out with his girlfriend again someday. Jeez, how will I ever be able to look Veronica in the eyes again after this tour?

The music, the activity, the loudness is intense, and I take more interest in the open doors I pass. *Stupid, Chrissie, stupid. Neil isn't a partier. He's a loner like you. Stop checking out the action all around you and trying to catch him doing God knows what.*

The bellhop drops my bag outside a door and hands me a key.

"Here you are, Miss Parker."

What the heck? All that, the phone call from the desk, the escort to the upper floor, just to give me a key and then walk away. *My bag. You could carry my bag inside.*

I stare at the door. Now I'm pissed. I was already edgy before I exited the elevator into this madness, but something about this has my nerve-tips prickling. What's up with the ignored phone calls and Neil having me escorted up here?

Really, Neil, escorted?

I struggle to get the key in the lock, turn the knob, shove open the door, then hold it with my leg and drag my bags in. I let the door slam behind me. I look up.

Oh my. My eyes widen. My gaze slowly moves around

the room and everything inside me turns to hot, roiling liquid.

My eyes lock with Neil's.

"Welcome back," he whispers.

I suck in a breath. The room is bathed in soft candlelight. The candles are everywhere, on every table and on every surface, dozens of them. And Neil is lying in the center of the bed, reclined on a hip, facing me and gloriously naked, every inch of him fully exposed, in an inviting posture waiting for me. His cheek rests in his palm and his messy waves frame his face, and the look in his eyes takes my breath away.

I start to take in other details of the room. The champagne on the night table next to a neatly arranged plate of Oreo cookies and strawberries. I laugh. What kind of guy remembers your weird food preference? Crap, there is even a cake and an elegantly wrapped present beside it.

I don't know what to say. *This* I did not expect.

"You took an early flight," Neil remarks into my silence. "We only got into Indy an hour ago. It didn't leave me a lot of time to work with."

Understanding comes to me in rich waves, making me acutely aware of why I love him. "You ignored my calls on purpose. You slowed me down getting to the room on purpose, so you could do all this."

"Happy birthday, Chrissie."

Moisture blurs my vision. "It is now, Neil."

~ ~ ~

I lie naked in the wrap of Neil's arms, quiet and sexually spent. The sex only ended because I think we're both exhausted, but we've been kissing and touching ever since. Five days apart. Too long. If there had been a shred of doubt he missed me or that he'd cheated on me while I was gone, it would have died the first time we made love.

I feel drained, or I would be working toward sex again in this quiet after our passion. We have had nothing but mind-blowing sex for hours. Neil has been on fire tonight. I was on fire tonight. I didn't expect that when I stepped into the room.

Everything changes. It changes quickly. This time it has changed in a good way.

"I can't believe you did all this," I whisper and then touch my lips to his forearm.

"You came back early. I wanted it to be special for you."

I turn in his arms and stare at him with what I'm sure is lust-sparkling eyes. "Oh, definitely special. This night goes into the record books."

Neil laughs.

I look at him. "If we were to get married, how would it work?"

He eases up to stare directly into my face and the passion haze leaves his gaze. "I don't know, Chrissie. How does marriage work for anyone?"

"That's not what I mean."

He settles back against the pillow, draping me across his chest and holding me in the circle of his arms. He starts stroking my back in a gentle, soothing way.

"Why don't you tell me what you mean, Chrissie? Things work better when I don't try to figure out what you are asking."

God, I feel stupid. "Very funny. Ha. Ha."

His eyes grow serious. "I'm not messing with you. I want to know what you're thinking and it does work better when I don't try to figure it out and just let you tell me."

I take a moment to organize my thoughts and worries.

"I don't want to stay with you on the road," I whisper. "I'll travel until we have kids, but after that I'm done. I want lots of kids, Neil. That is the only thing I've ever been certain of. I want kids."

He starts plucking hairs from my face and brushing them back. "Then you won't travel with me if we have kids and I won't ask you to."

I bite my lower lip. "I want to have a family. That is the most important thing to me. More than anything else, that's what I want."

He takes my face in his palms. "So do I, Chrissie. I want it with you."

We are both quiet, pensive for a while. I'm sprawled on his chest, Neil gently caressing my back.

"Are you saying yes?" Neil asks.

I lift my chin to look at him. "I'm not saying maybe anymore, Neil. I'm saying someday instead."

CHAPTER SIXTEEN

April 1994

I slouched down on my lounger, curling on my side and hugging the cushion for dear life. I haven't enough strength to manage even a slightly presentable posture.

Fuck it, who cares here?

Nicole laughs. "You're too young to be so tired."

I frown. "It's four in the morning. It's perfectly normal to be tired."

"Not here, love."

I stare out across the pool on the rooftop patio. It's packed with people laughing, drinking, and celebrating. Last show on the road done, a packed house at the LA Forum. Everyone tore it up on stage. God, Neil was incredible, even though when we arrived in California yesterday he looked like a limp dog on his last leg.

We slept fifteen hours straight, but when he woke, Neil was supercharged, amped and ready to go crazy on stage. Last hop. They all are letting loose tonight. The party started the second we returned to the hotel after the concert.

I stare. "I don't know how they all keep going. I wanted bed two hours ago."

"Testosterone." Nicole's eyes fix on Neil, surrounded

by people and still going strong. Her expression changes and is mildly wistful. "If I had that kid I'd want my bed, too."

I blush and Nicole laughs.

Her gaze shifts to Delmo and she makes a face. "Regrettably, I have that. I'm staying on the roof until they boot me out of here."

I laugh faintly. "You're impossible. You and Delmo deserve each other."

"That we do."

My eyelids start to drift. Nicole's laughter causes me to open them again.

She smiles. "We survived ten months on the road with Vinny and all we got is this lousy party and cheap booze on the roof of the West Hollywood Hilton. Damn man loves this place. Loves the nostalgia. Personally, I think it's so he can slip away at night, party and partake of the scenery."

I roll my eyes "He does not. Vincent wouldn't do that to you. You can't mess with me any longer. The man adores you. You adore him. Bicker. Bicker. Absolutely nonsense."

She scrunches up her nose. "Sad, but true." Her gaze shifts to me. "So where do you and the kid go now?"

I shrug. "I don't know." And I don't, and it doesn't bother me in the least. The tour is over, and I'm starting a new road with Neil. I don't know what it is, but we're doing it together and that's enough.

Nicole studies my face and her relentlessly bitchy expression softens. "I can tell you one thing, Delmo is glad he's not following the kid on stage anymore. The kid just keeps growing and growing each show. He's on his way." She grimaces. "Unfortunately, wherever you go it's going to look like this."

I laugh. "I hope not."

She gives me a sympathetic smile.

I push the wayward hairs from my face and my gaze locks on Delmo cutting through the party toward us.

He sinks down behind me on the chaise without asking, his legs on either side of me, and surrounds me in a sloppy hug complete with overly wet smacking kiss on my cheek.

He rocks us side to side. "Nancy Drew, I'm going to miss you."

I try to wiggle out of his hold and then stop. "Don't tell anyone I said this. They're all too drunk to remember if they hear me, and if you repeat it, I'll call you a liar, but I'm going to miss you, too."

Vincent laughs. "You break my heart, love, but I love you anyway."

He settles back against the cushion, taking me with him.

"Ah, will you look at this. We're too fucking old for this, Nicky."

"Speak for yourself, old man," she taunts.

I laugh.

Vincent's face appears over my shoulder. "You're not going to have to miss me long, Chrissie. You'll get to see me again Saturday, and I have another shot at convincing you to run away with me. But if you reject me again, it will be back to missing me because we're off to Europe next."

My eyes widen, surprised. "You're going to Jack's party?"

"Of course. Take a phone call from Jack anywhere you are. If Jack sends you an invite to the annual foundation fundraiser, you put on your best clothes and grab your checkbook. That's how it is with your dad, love. We're going to Santa Barbara."

I smile, then droop and close my eyes again.

"Hey, asshole, that's my girlfriend." I hear Neil's voice booming from across the party. I open my eyes to find him staring but smiling. "Let her go."

Out of my peripheral vision I see Vincent bobbing a thumb toward Nicole. "Take my girlfriend, mate, and we can call it even."

As exhausted as I am, I laugh and manage to avoid Nicole's clumsy swat at Vincent's chest. Jeez, I shouldn't be attempting laughter and I start drifting into sleep.

"Let's go, Chrissie."

When I open my eyes, Neil is standing beside the chaise, staring down at me.

I nod and then frown. "I don't think I can walk. I'm exhausted."

Neil scoops me out of Delmo's clutches and soon I'm held against his chest, legs and arms wrapped around him, my cheek resting on his shoulder.

He carries me into the hallway toward the elevator.

"We don't have to be in Santa Barbara for two days," he says, struggling to hit the call button with his elbow. "Nate wants to go La Jolla. Hang out. Surf for a day. What do you think of that?"

My head moves limply on his shoulder. "I don't care."

He steps into the elevator and maneuvers again to hit the number for our floor. He starts trailing light kisses across my face.

He laughs. "You're a mess, Chrissie. Are you drunk? You're not even being a pain tonight."

I adjust to look at him. "Nope. Not drunk. Don't want to be a pain. I sort of like you tonight."

His kiss moves lightly and stirringly against my lips. "Do you love me tonight?" He starts kissing my neck. "Why don't you do all those incredible things to me you do when you're feeling loving."

I roll my eyes. "Not a chance. If you wanted that you shouldn't have held me hostage at that party for four hours. You missed it. That feeling is gone. Be happy I still like you."

He makes a slight, upside down smile. "No?"

I lay my cheek back against him. "No."

"That was definitely decisive. I don't know if I like decisive Chrissie yet."

I laugh weakly. I can tell by his voice he's frowning and only half-joking.

We make the short walk from the elevator to the room. Somehow Neil manages to continue to hold me and get the door open.

He sets me on the bed, and moves around the room, undressing. My half-closed eyes stay glued on him. Naked, he returns to the bed, eases me over on my back and starts undressing me.

"I don't want sex," I whisper. "I want sleep."

He settles on the bed close to me, kissing me everywhere, touching me everywhere, and the tingling starts and my muscles pulse *there*. He moves his body until he is hovering above me, arms on each side of me, his kisses roaming from my breast to my belly and then lower. I feel warm breath and then his lips there and the feel of him shoots through me.

My head starts to sway on the bed and my body without command pushes in to the play of his tongue and fingers. He nips on my thigh and lifts his head.

"Do you want me to let you sleep?" he whispers.

I stare down at him. "You better not."

His mouth closes over me. I arch my back and melt into the expert flow of his tongue and fingers and breaths. I come apart quickly against his face, and I'm still pulsing and panting when he enters me. He moves in me, deep and hard and fast. He doesn't hold back, he pounds until he comes, and he collapses against me.

"You are never too tired for sex if I kiss you there first. It works the same way with me, Chrissie. Maybe you should try it again someday."

"Someday," I promise softly.

He's laughing as I fall asleep.

~~~

I swat at tickling on my cheek and open my eyes to a room filled with painful light.

Neil's face closes in on me. He kisses my hair.

"I'm having breakfast with Ernie. I should be back in a couple hours."

I try to focus my eyes on the clock. "Jeez, it's only ten a.m. What kind of manager gets you out of bed this early the day after a concert?"

"A manager catching a plane to the east coast in three hours." He kisses me on the lips this time. "I ordered you an omelet and some coffee. Eat. Dress. Pack. I want to take off as soon as I get back. I don't want go to La Jolla with Nate. Think about where you want to go. I'm horny as hell. Take me away someplace where we can be alone and in bed for two days."

"We could just stay here. Not move for three days. How does that sound?"

He makes a *maybe* kind of face. Then his expression changes, sweetly serious. "I want to do something you want to do. Figure out what you want and I'm all yours."

Hmmm, possibilities. I snuggle deeper into the blankets. The door closes. I try to go back to sleep and I can't.

I roll onto my back and stare at the ceiling. *Figure out what I want.* My mind is a blank. More travel doesn't sound appealing. We could just drive to Santa Barbara early. That would be nice. Yep, I'd like that.

Reluctantly, I toss aside the blankets and get up. I take a fast shower, pull on a sundress, and am just putting on the finishing touches of my makeup when there is a knock on the door.

Breakfast. I hurry to unbolt and let in room service.

"Omelet and coffee?" the guy asks, reading off the ticket.

"Yep. Put it over there on the table by the window,

please."

He sets down my tray, lifts off the metal cover, and places the *LA Times* beside my plate. I smile as I sign the ticket and show him from the room.

I drop down into the chair, grab a fork and pick at my meal as I open the paper. *Thank you, Neil, for remembering the newspaper. I've almost got Michelle's scrapbook complete.* The guys were incredible last night. There has got to be photos somewhere in the *Times* today. I start flipping through pages. Flip. Flip. Flip. Ah, Delmo. I study the photo for a while—what a ham. Why does he like to look so mean?—and then I scan the rest of the page.

Ah, us. Even better. The caption makes me smile. I go to my black case and pull out the small canvas zip bag with my scissors and paste. I neatly cut the photo from the paper, trim it, and then secure it on the last page. Done. Ten months on tour. History complete.

I finish my breakfast, and start packing up. Clothes. Check. Toiletries from bathroom. Check. Neil can deal with his junk here. I see the scrapbook on the table and put it back in the duffel. I grab my scissors and paste, and as I start to tuck them away, I note the edge of a news clipping saved from last week.

I still haven't written about this in my journal. I couldn't do it. Not when it happened. I take my notebook from the black bag and reach for a pen.

I pull out the news clipping from the canvas bag and stare at it. I still get misty-eyed when I read the story headline *Kurt Cobain Dead Twenty-Seven*. I print today's date on the top of a page and start to write:

It is strange how someone's life can touch your own from a distance. I didn't know Kurt well. We crossed paths in Seattle, nothing more, but he was the subject of the silly bet Neil and I made the first night we met. It sure rattled the guys, in that way the sudden unexpected loss of someone like yourself can only stir.

I'll never forget how Neil looked when he got back to the hotel after learning of Kurt's death. Sad, confused, angry and overwhelmed.

We sat for a long time silent, and then Neil said, "I love you, Chrissie. More than you know. Sometimes you are all that gets me through. Don't let me fuck up everything we have."

There was something in his voice I'll never forget. I don't know what it was, but I've never heard Neil sound that way before.

I was alone when I opened the paper to find the write-up on Kurt's death. Too many lockboxes inside me broke open at once. My brother. My mother. Then Alan.

I looked at the headline—twenty-seven—and my memories dragged me back to New York and Alan in the parking garage, and Alan's voice whispered through my memory: "The great ones die at twenty-seven. Hendrix. Joplin. If we are both around after we're twenty-seven, we'll both know what we are."

I reached for my mobile phone and Alan's number on the card that I still carry for some reason. I stared at the phone for an hour. Something in me wanted to talk to Alan that day.

The news made me think of him. Our crazy spring. Us in the parking garage. And I felt ashamed about the way I spoke to him the last time we talked. The mean little girl in me, kicking him away because I was afraid. I regretted not talking to him. I regretted how I felt that day. I still wonder why he called, what he wanted.

I stared at the phone, wanting to call. We are connected. No matter how we ended, there are parts of me only Alan will understand. And there are parts of Alan only I will understand. But I didn't call. Too much had happened. He hurt me. I hurt him. We both hurt each other too much the last time. It was better for us both that I didn't call. It would have only unsealed old wounds.

But a part of me still regrets not calling Alan that day.

I hear a key against the lock, slap shut my journal and tuck it away in the bottom of my duffel. Nope, this journal is now a private journal. I don't want Neil to see that last entry. It wouldn't piss him off, he would want to talk to me and understand it, but I'm not ready to do that. Not yet. Someday.

Neil crosses the room, kisses me lightly on the cheek, and then sinks down to sit on the bed. His expression and posture says everything. He is not happy after his meeting with Ernie Levine.

"What's wrong?" I ask.

Neil runs a hand through his hair. "We were going to take some time together, figure out what we're doing, and Ernie booked me for a show taping next week in New York. A bunch of other bullshit publicity things for the next month that I don't want to do. And when I'm done, studio."

I make a pout. "No big deal. We've got a week to kick back and do nothing. I'm not angry. Why are you?"

He gives me the *stare*. "You agreed to discuss the possibility of getting married."

I laugh. The way he says that makes me sound ridiculous. I make a face. "What? A week is not enough time to finish a discussion on the possibility?"

I give him a silly smile and reluctantly he laughs.

"No. With you, Chrissie, there is no such thing as enough time to discuss anything."

My brows hitch up. "That was kind of mean."

Smiling green eyes lock with mine. "Nope. Not mean. Accurate." He sighs heavily. "Fuck, Chrissie, I want something in my life defined and certain. I want us to get married."

"OK. Not mean. Frustrated." I cross the room and sink down beside him on the bed. "So what do you want to do about being frustrated?"

He starts working his hand under my dress and I shove it away.

"I didn't mean that kind of frustrated."

He laughs, wraps me in his arms and pulls me with him until we're lying on the bed. I don't know why we're laughing. But it feels good. Really, really good.

"Do you know where you want to take me?" he whispers. "We've still got a week. We'll go where you want to. Let's get the hell out of here. I don't want to waste any of our alone time."

I turn on my side facing him and fight back a smile. Jeez, he's so sexy even when he's aggravated and disappointed and fighting to be patient with me when he doesn't want to be. I lean in and kiss him, and when I pull back, the color darkens in his eyes in that way that's wonderful. Emotion and want join in lock-step in a jolt of clarity that rockets through me in an inescapable way.

"I know where I want us to go," I say.

Neil shakes his head in that way that says he's not buying it. "Staying here in West Hollywood doesn't count as you making a decision, Chrissie. It's a lack of decision."

I choke on a laugh. *Damn, the guy does know me pretty well. Wrong this time. Logical assumption.*

"I've never been to Vegas before. I want to go to Vegas," I announce.

He's looking at me like I've lost my mind.

"Really. I hate Vegas. And you hate the desert. Why the hell would you want to go there?"

I stare at him. "Because in Vegas we can get married today."

~~~

We step out of the over-air-conditioned county clerk's office into the overheated Vegas sun. Crap, it's scorching today and it is only April.

"Are you sure you want to do this?" Neil asks for about the hundredth time. "It's only a three-day wait in California. We can get married in Santa Barbara. Have Jack and my family there."

I peek up at Neil. He looks a little bemused that I'm actually insisting we elope.

"Nope. This is a limited-time offer. Today or never."

Neil smiles and then his expression takes on a more serious edge. "You're not having second thoughts, are you?"

The way he's looking at me makes my heart overflow. *God, how can he think that? I dragged him here.*

"Do you remember our A-through-C marriage agreement?"

He taps the side of his head with an index finger. "Burned into my memory forever. A: *You want to live in Santa Barbara. You want a house there and only there.* B: *If we have kids you won't travel with me and I promise to never ask you to.* C: *You don't want to wait to start a family.*"

I kiss his arm. "No second thoughts. You remembered the agreement."

He frowns. "Let's get married in Santa Barbara."

"No. Today. That's what I want."

He shakes his head and stares down the street. "Supposedly we can get married anywhere. Pick a place. They all look the same. Awful."

He's right, they do.

I point. "Let's just go there."

I pick the Heart of Vegas Wedding Chapel, because it's the nearest one and they all do look the same.

Neil pulls back the door and I enter first. I quickly inspect the room. Awful just converted to hideous. Pink. I've never seen so much pink anywhere before.

I look at Neil's reaction to this and it takes every ounce of control not laugh.

A middle-aged woman, short and bouncy and over-tanned, comes from the back and pauses at the counter. "Can I help you?"

"We'd like to get married," I say.

She smiles in that *duh hidden behind fake politeness* sort of way since that's pretty much all they do here, but she still asks what we want.

We're given more papers to fill out.

I watch as Neil labors over the forms.

"Why does everything take so much paperwork?" I ask.

He doesn't answer. He's concentrating. I stare into the glass case I'm leaning against. Shit, they think of everything here. Rings. They even sell rings here. Your one-stop marital shop. I note a sign on the wall. Crap, you can even get a divorce, too.

My gaze anxiously moves around the chapel. God, it's tacky here. Maybe this is a mistake. Maybe I'm being lame and not spontaneous and romantic.

I lean into Neil and bring my lips close to his ear. "We don't have rings."

He shakes his head. He continues to write. "I don't have a ring. You do."

My eyes widen, and he smiles into my questioning gaze, hands the required papers and our licenses to the clerk and pays.

OK, why so secretive, Neil?

A registry of some kind is shoved under my face. The lady points at a line. "Sign here."

After we finish signing, the clerk goes into the back for the justice of the peace.

"What do you mean I have a ring?" I ask.

Neil reaches into his pocket for his wallet. "You're a size six ring finger, right?"

I nod, alertly watching as he rummages in his wallet for something.

"I'm glad I got it sized right. No chance to fix it now."

I try to see what he's grabbing and he makes little motions so I can't. He starts lowering to a knee.

Tears sting behind my lids.

"I've been carrying this for six months," he says. "If you don't like it, we can get something else. It was my grandmother's wedding band. My mom wanted me to have it for you."

I don't want to cry, but I can't stop it.

"Christian Parker, will you marry me?"

~ ~ ~

A strange sound pulls me from sleep. There is a moment of confusion before my eyes lock on the tacky Vegas strip hotel room, and I wonder where Neil is, and why there is the sound of sloshing water near the bed.

Then I see Neil. There are candles all through the room, surrounding that ridiculous Jacuzzi tub that for some reason isn't in the bathroom. He is sitting in the center, the champagne we didn't drink at dinner and two glasses resting on the tile edge.

I laugh at the nonsensical picture he makes and rub the sleep from my eyes. "How long have you been up?"

He smiles at me, his eyes lustrous and mildly dissipated at once. I flush. That was a poor choice of words.

"We have an early plan tomorrow," he says, filling the champagne glasses. "I thought we should probably use the tub before we're out of here. We've never done it before in water."

I watch him rise, comfortable in his long-limbed body. He's a gorgeous guy. It's like I'm seeing him for the first time, or maybe differently now that I know he really is mine. No wonder all the girls at CAL were crazy over him.

He is fucking gorgeous.

He leans in, claiming my mouth with his. His tongue dances with my own, bringing my senses fully awake. He eases back. Against my lips, he says, "I love you, Mrs. Stanton."

The look in his eyes. The way he says that. That he wants to say that overwhelms me.

He scoops me up from the bed and carries me to that obscene tub. It's suddenly absolutely perfect. There is a beautiful view through the wall of glass. Lights twinkling at night can make any city look beautiful, even Vegas.

I watch him, bathed in the soft glow of candlelight, as he lowers me into the water and then against him. His long-boned fingers start to roam my flesh as his lips return to mine. His head dips toward me, his lips a teasing presence on my neck, his hands a knowing glide across my flesh. I watch him move across my body, kissing and touching and cherishing me. He lifts me up, bringing me down to glove his erection. His mouth is greedily working at my breast. His cock is hard in my body, moving with delicious intensity. Fully filling me. His fingers are stroking me wondrously.

I wrap my limbs tightly around him and melt into his touch. I can't recall a time I've ever been this happy or felt this consumed by Neil.

~ ~ ~

We are dangerously close to missing our plane.

I stare at Neil's long fingers holding mine as we run down the ramp toward the waiting plane. I'm struggling to keep pace with Neil.

"Hurry up, Chrissie. If we miss the plane we'll miss Jack's party. We should have left last night."

"I didn't want to leave last night. And I'm trying to hurry, but I have to take two steps for each one of yours. And you fucked all the energy out of my legs."

He pulls me against him. "You want to start a family right away, that's how you do it. Marathon fucking."

I flush, hoping that no one near us heard that, and then crinkle my nose since *marathon fucking* isn't the least bit romantic of a phrase.

Jeez, why are guys such jerks at times?

Before I can stop him, Neil has my black bag under an arm and is lifting me in the air to set me on his shoulder.

"Put me down, Neil. This is humiliating."

"We're not going to make it at your speed."

He carries me at a jogging pace to the boarding gate. He is panting by the time we reach it. He helps me slide down to the floor, but his strong arm keeps me close against him. He is kissing my neck, my hair, and pushing me forward in line with the lower part of his body.

Yuck, we are being watched, even stared at. I try to pull away and Neil holds me in place.

"You have to excuse us. We just got married," Neil says loudly, to no one in particular.

I flush, embarrassed, but suddenly people all around us are smiling. Somehow he manages to kiss my neck, hand the boarding passes to the attendant and continue the gentle massage of his lower body pushing me forward.

We run down the ramp, barely onto the plane before the door shuts, and drop into our seats.

Once we're in the air, I curl into Neil, and put my cheek against his shoulder.

"I don't want to tell my dad we got married during the party. I want to wait until tomorrow, OK?"

Neil gives me an exasperated look. "You should have called Jack before, like I told you to. It might have been picked up by the wire services. He might already know. We should tell him when get there."

Crap, I hadn't thought of that.

"Today, but after the party. Privately. Not surrounded by people."

He gives me the look, the *Chrissie is being confusing and a pain* look, but he nods and sets back his head, closing his eyes.

"I don't want to stay at the party very long," I add. "And I definitely don't want to stay at my dad's house. Let's get a room down by the beach."

"Fine, Chrissie."

I kiss him on the jaw and close my eyes.

Ninety minutes later, we're in the Santa Barbara Airport terminal, grabbing our bags and rushing for the rental car counter.

Once we're on the road, I grab my black bag and freshen up my makeup in the visor mirror. I shove my stuff back into the bag as we pass beneath the black metal arch of Hope Ranch.

I turn to face Neil. "Do I look OK?"

"You're beautiful, Chrissie. You always look beautiful."

We pull into my dad's driveway and are stopped by a

valet. Shit, there are a ton of cars here, valet parking and people everywhere. Jack went all out for the foundation fundraiser this year.

A guy in a red vest and black pants taps on our window. Neil rolls it down.

"You can't park in the driveway," he says.

I lean across Neil and stare at the valet. "Can you move that barrier so we can park in the garage? This is my house. I'm Christian Parker."

The guy flushes, embarrassed, and pulls back the sawhorse blocking the driveway. We park and climb from our seat.

I take in a deep breath. "We made it. We're here."

Neil laughs, lying his arms on my shoulders. "God, you are crazy today. What's up with that?"

"This is a really big thing for my dad. He doesn't do parties. He does one party a year to raise money for the foundation. The inner city music programs were my mom's work. I think it's Jack's way of making everyone remember my mother. It's important to him. He was really upset I didn't come last year."

Neil's face grows sweetly sympathetic. "Then I'm glad we made it in time for the party, too. And I won't mention we got married, though I want to. And I won't try to maneuver you into a bedroom during the party to make love to you today." His eyes do a rakish once-over of me. He grins ruefully. "Nope, won't do that either, even though you are wearing that little black dress that drives me insane."

He takes my hand and I'm laughing as we rush to the

front door.

CHAPTER SEVENTEEN

I sit on a white-cushioned rattan couch, part of one of the intimate groupings scattered all across the lawn. Everywhere there are people, a band on the stage, long buffet tables and bars, lawn lights lit, and fire pits near the seating to heat up the misty air of early evening rolling inland from the Pacific.

It's a magnificent party. Jack went all out this year. He was so happy when he spotted us crossing the lawn, his magnificent blues twinkling. He cut out of the circle around him to immediately trot across the grass to give me a hug. It made me smile that he hugged Neil, too.

I take a sip of champagne from the flute dangling from my fingertips, and my gaze rests on Neil. He's enjoying this party almost as much as Jack is. We've been sitting with the Delmos, laughing and talking for four hours.

It's just been that kind of thing. A pleasant kind of industry party. These strange personalities pulled together for a cause, checkbooks open, everyone having a good time, laughing and talking and crowding the dance floor.

I love that Jack put it near the cliffs this year. My gaze fixes on my dad. Jeez, he's dancing with Linda Rowan. It was a shock to arrive and find the Rowans here. I didn't even know that they were friends with Jack. Maybe they are not friends. When Delmo arrived he stared at the gathering and called them the fat wallet club.

I don't know. It's strange that Jack has spent so much of the evening with Linda, and more strange that he's dancing. And even stranger, the Rowans came without any of the others from the Blackpoll mob. They're such a cliquish circle. Though I should be relieved none of the others are here. If I ever see Kenny Jones again it will be too soon.

Neil breaks in his conversation with Vincent, leans back into the cushion and looks at me. "What's wrong? You've got the strangest look on your face."

I shake my head to chase away that kind of *irked and don't know why* feeling. I smile. "This is going to sound lame. But I've never seen my dad dance before."

Neil looks in the direction of my stare. "So Jack's dancing. What's the big deal?"

"He doesn't even know Linda Rowan and they've been dancing together most of the night."

"Jack's probably trying to be a good host. It doesn't look like Len is interested in anything but that brunette practically sitting on his lap."

I look across the lawn at the couch Len Rowan hasn't moved from all evening, and make a face. *Poor, poor Linda.* I don't know how she puts up with Len, his roving hand and his dedication to fuck everything that moves right in her face.

"Shit, don't ever let us become like them, Chrissie. I don't know why some people get married."

"I don't know why anyone gets married," Nicole announces and then shudders.

I bite my lip and then Neil gives it a playful tug. My

gaze moves back to the dance floor against my will. I don't know why I'm bothered by this.

Neil notices my preoccupation again.

"I tell you one thing, if anyone ever danced with you the way Jack is with Linda, I'd punch them, Chrissie."

Startled, I turn to stare at Neil. "What? What do you mean by that?"

He gives me a look. "The way they're holding each other isn't an *I don't really know you* kind of thing."

I make a face at him. "You're crazy."

"Fine. I'm crazy." He brushes back the hair from my shoulder and leans in to kiss me lightly on the side of my neck. Into my ear, he whispers, "Can we leave now? I am really ready to leave."

I blush and pull back. "How ready are you?"

He brushes my ear with his thumb and then with his teeth does a light nip on my lobe. "Very, very ready."

"What's up with you two?" Delmo asks suspiciously. "You've been acting weird all evening, like there is something going on that only the two of you know about."

"Stop giving them a hard time, Vinny," Nicole exclaims, stomping out her cigarette in an ashtray. "If they wanted us to know they'd tell us."

Neil shrugs by way of answering them.

I climb from the couch. "Stay here. I won't be long. And then we're leaving."

"Where are you going?"

"Maria hasn't been at the party all night. I didn't even get a chance to see her before we got caught up in this. I'm just going to go to her room and check on her. I won't be long. I promise."

I drop a kiss on Neil's mouth and hurry away. I maneuver through the guests and then I'm past the low fence markers that keep the house and pool blocked off from the party.

I rush around the side of the pool house and run straight into a body. I look up and my insides drop to the floor.

No. No. No. What is Alan doing here?

"If you run, I will humiliate you," he warns, his voice icy and clipped.

I take a hurried step back from him. It feels like I've just brushed up against fire and by the way he's staring at me there isn't a shred of doubt he'd humiliate me. Disjointed pictures of the party in New York flash in my head. Every muscle in my body stiffens at once.

He takes my hand in a grip that hurts and before my mind can catch up with what he's doing, I'm locked in the pool house with him. He moves away from me and I lean back against the door, breathing heavily.

He stops on the far side of the room and turns to stare at me. He rakes a hand through his dark, wavy hair. He looks coiled with frustration and something else I can't decipher.

It feels like hours instead of seconds passing with him saying nothing. *Why the hell doesn't he say something?*

I swallow down the lump in my throat. "What are you doing here?"

He arches a brow, amused. "I was invited, Chrissie. I'm invited every year. I don't come. I send a check. This year I came. You are a very difficult person to reach these days."

"I'm not difficult at all. I don't want to talk to you."

He settles on the sofa beside the fireplace and takes his cigarettes from his pocket. He lights one. He shakes his head and his posture changes, a loss of intimidation and aggressiveness.

"You don't have to stand there hovering against the door like you might need to run," he says softly.

I lift my chin. "I'm not. I'm just trying to figure out why you're here."

Those potent black eyes lock on mine and I can see it. The way I'm behaving hurts him, and in spite of how he started this, it's not *Mean Alan* sitting in here with me.

"Chrissie, you're behaving ridiculously. Sit down. A few minutes of your time. That's all. You'll never hear from me again."

Never hear from me again. My heart reacts unexpectedly severely to that and I fight to keep how that one hurts me from my expression. I slowly move from the door and settle in a chair across the coffee table from him.

"What do you want?"

He runs his hand through his hair and then holds the black waves in the clutch of his fingers. He lets out a long exhale of breath. "Christ, I wish you'd read my letter. I don't know how to say the things I have to say to your face."

My brows shoot up. I've never heard Alan sound so anxious and unsure before. I feel a crack in the wall around my heart and I don't want to.

"Then don't say them. Whatever you think you need to say to me, Alan, don't. I'm happy. I don't want to hear it."

He looks amused again. Amused *and* sad. His expression confuses me and I lower my gaze to focus on my hands resting in my lap.

"I don't doubt you don't want *this* any more than I want to be the one to do it to you," he says quietly.

Oh no, what does that mean? Do what?

"I care about you, Chrissie. No matter what's happened between us, I will always care about you. I would never want to hurt you. And I would never lie to you. You believe that, don't you?"

My thoughts are spinning and I nod. I don't know why, It's crazy and I don't even know why he's here after all this time, but I do believe Alan. When he talks to me this way I know in the center of my being it is the truth.

"I will regret not calling you back last year as long as I live," he says in a rough, desperate sort of way. "I've hurt you in inexcusable ways. I was angry. I was hurt. I behaved horribly to you, but not one time did I ignore you because I'd stopped loving you."

I don't look at him, and I stare hard into a vacant space in the pool house because I can feel myself weakening. If I look at him, I will fall to pieces.

"You're the only person in my life that matters to me," he says. "It's why I'm here, Chrissie."

I take in a deep, shuddering breath to steady me. "Only I'm not in your life, Alan. Not anymore. You shouldn't have come here. It would have been better for us both if you hadn't."

"Better for me, yes. Better for you, no, love."

I feel on the verge of tears and I don't trust my voice to ask him what that one means.

"There is not a thing that happens in your life, a thing you do, that I don't know about," he says.

Everything starts to run frantic and loose inside me.

"I never meant for my anger to hurt you," he continues. "If I had known before I would have stopped you."

Oh no. Is that why he's here? He knows about last April? How does he know?

I can't breathe. I can't feel my legs, I can't feel my arms, but somehow my body rises from the chair and moves toward the door.

"It doesn't matter, Alan. If you had called me I wouldn't have changed my decision," I whisper with more injury in my voice than I want to show. "I don't want to talk about this with you. Not now. It's too late."

I'm almost to the door when he stops me. He whirls me around to face him. Those potent black eyes lock on mine directly and the lockbox breaks open. It all tumbles out. My hurt. My regrets. My love for him. In leveling waves, real and present and consuming me.

He takes my face in the palms of his hands. "Please, stop hurting yourself because you hate me. I can't bear knowing that all this has happened because you hate me."

I say it before I can stop myself. "I don't hate you, Alan. I love you."

"Then don't marry Neil. It's in all the trades. It's why

I came here today. Don't marry Neil because you hate me. Don't hurt yourself again because you hate me. I couldn't live with that. I swallowed my pride to come here. I couldn't let *you* hurt *you* again."

He pulls me against him, surrounding me with his flesh, and he is trembling with his emotions, as frantic and despondent and in pain as I am.

I don't know why I do it. Maybe it's because this is goodbye. Maybe it's because I want to stop this. Maybe it's because Alan is crying.

I lean into him and join my mouth with his. His mouth moves on mine tentatively at first, only gentle contact. Then it deepens on its own, and I can feel it changing, that we are both changing what this is.

I pour all my hurt and heartbreak of the last year into our kiss, and it happens as it always did—the second I touch him, I am lost in him and we are lost in each other.

I shouldn't do this... And then the words in my head are silenced as Alan puts me on the bed.

CHAPTER EIGHTEEN

We lie together, not touching or kissing. Disconnected and yet really connected in that way we share and haven't shared for too long for the both of us, I think. It is *us*. Connected in the disconnect. Sexually spent, emotionally messy and raging internally.

I turn in Alan's arms so I can see him. His eyes are midnight black and guarded, and he is unnerved by what we just did, too. I can tell he didn't intend this. *This* was not why he came to the party to see me.

My confusion and distress kicks up. No longer able to meet his gaze, I roll away and my eyes lock on my ring. My simple gold band on my left hand.

"I've got to go," I whisper, barely able to push the words past the lump in my throat.

I pull from his arms, climb from the bed and gather my clothes. My shaking hands make feeble attempts at securing my clothing back into place. Why did I do this? How could I be unfaithful to Neil? What power does Alan have over me that I could forget everything good in my life just to screw him in the pool house? That in a flash, everything inside me is turned upside down. That the strongest impulse I can feel raging through my veins is to trash my marriage and go back to Alan?

Alan sits up and settles on the edge of the bed. There

is something on his face that makes me anxious and afraid. The room fills with heavy silence.

"Stop dressing, Chrissie," he whispers, his raspy voice with an edge again.

More heavy silence. I continue to move, dressing like I'm numb. The lump in my throat is strangling and I can't look at him because if I do I won't ever be able to say and do what I have to.

"I have to go, Alan."

"I don't want you to leave," he whispers, his voice raw. He crosses the room, stopping my hands, stopping me. "You are not walking out that door until I've said everything I came here to say to you. Not this time, Chrissie. It is too important."

"I love you," I whisper, almost unable to push the words out of me. "I always will. But whatever you have to say to me doesn't matter. Not anymore. Let it go, Alan."

I lock gazes with his intense black stare. His face changes in a flash from passion-kissed to alarmed. "Doesn't matter? What the fuck are you trying to tell me, Chrissie?"

I struggle not to drop my gaze. I step back from him and continue tidying my clothing.

He grabs my arms again. "What are you saying, Chrissie? Answer me."

I twist out of his hold. I quickly step back. If I stay too close to him, I will crumble. I have to get out of this room and away from Alan. *Soon…or I will crumble…*

Alan scrambles from the bed. "You are not leaving, Chrissie. I have not said everything I need to say to you.

Baby, don't go."

I move to the door. My fingers tighten around the doorknob. "You're too late, Alan. I'm married."

The look on his face—*what am I seeing in his eyes?*—is not the reaction I expect to see and the way those black eyes stare at me catapults my world into a shaky, shadowy mess.

Quickly, before Alan can say anything else, I slip through the door.

There is no one on the patio and, while I'd rather run into the house and hide there, I hurry back to the party, desperate to get Neil away from here.

I spot Neil still sitting on the white couches where I left him. I cross the yard to him, unable to look up even though people occasionally speak to me as I pass.

I don't wait for a break in conversation. "I want to go, Neil. I'd really appreciate it if we could leave now."

He sets his drink down, and when he looks at me his eyes fill with alarm. "What's wrong? Are you OK, Chrissie? What's happened?"

The worry in his voice makes shame flood my veins and I can feel that I'm starting to shake. Damn, I just want to hold it together until I'm out of here. Then figure out *somehow* how to explain to Neil what I've done. Beg him for forgiveness. I don't know. My thoughts are spinning out of control, and all I can think of is to get away from *here*.

My shaking intensifies and I can feel heavy stares on me and I know I must look more of a mess than I thought.

"Stay right here," Neil says in an urgent and anxious way. "I'm going to tell Jack we're leaving. Don't move,

Chrissie. Wait here."

I stand there numb for a few minutes, but it feels like an eternity. Finally I see Neil cutting through the party guests back toward me.

He places a hand on the small of my back and starts guiding me across the lawn.

"What happened?" he asks. "Can you tell me that?"

I'm so ashamed.

"Not now, Neil. I promise I'll tell you everything. Just not here. Not now."

He shakes his head in aggravation. "Fuck, Chrissie, what is going on? You're scaring me."

I ignore him. I can't talk. Not now. I'm going to break down if I do and I don't want to do it surrounded by people. That would be even crueler than what I just did to Neil and our marriage.

We're almost to the patio when Alan exits the pool house. The two men lock eyes, and Neil's body goes rigid beside me.

I look up at him and I know with sinking dread that Neil has put the pieces together. He knows I was alone in the pool house with Alan and what happened is why I'm dragging him from the party now.

Panic overwhelms my senses and I feel him start to move away from me. Frantically, I lock my hands onto his arm to try to hold him back.

"What the fuck did you say to her?" Neil shouts, enraged.

Alan calmly arches a brow and locks simmering black eyes on green. "We didn't get a chance to talk, if that's what you're worried about, Neil," he snaps in a pointed and dismissive way.

The earth falls from beneath my feet. There is absolutely no way to misinterpret *that* statement. Not from Alan. Not with how he says it.

I try to keep hold of Neil, but my fingers lose their clutch on him. Before my anxious eyes, I see him shoot across the yard toward Alan.

"You asshole," Neil hisses. "Do you have to fuck up every life around you? You stay away from her."

My heart stills in my chest. I have never seen Neil look like this. Not in his most angry moments. Oh no, not like this. If there was a speck of doubt in me before today that Neil fucked up Andy as severely as the rumors claim, it died with what I see on his face. If he lets loose a punch it won't end with one punch. He's going to screw up his life again, only this time it will be my fault.

Oh fuck. Oh fuck. Oh fuck.

I move quickly, trying to get to them before Neil hits Alan, and then, out of nowhere, Len Rowan appears between them, his hands planted on Neil's chest. Even through my panic-dulled senses, I can tell by the motion around me and the stir in the air that everyone at the party is fully aware of this hideous confrontation.

"Settle down," Len says, struggling for air as he quickly maneuvers to hold Neil back. "You don't want to do this. Not here. Not now. You'll fuck up your life. One punch. Everything you've worked for gone, over. Get it?"

Neil shoves him back, but it looks like some measure of control has returned to him. He is shaking with rage, raking a hand through his hair over and over again, but he's not charging at Alan anymore.

"Would you please go?" I whisper anxiously, my eyes imploring Alan.

He looks at me and something in his gaze turns me ice cold. He starts walking away.

"I'm sorry, Chrissie," he whispers as he passes me.

Neil erupts again, moving his body between me and Alan. "You don't fucking speak to her. Not now. Not ever."

Alan stops walking. *Oh shit. Neil, why didn't you let him go?* I try to move between them again, but Neil won't let me.

"How could you marry her?" Alan exclaims, his timbre carrying to the four corners of the yard without effort. "How the fuck do you live with yourself?"

Numb with disbelief, I frantically try to make sense of what I'm seeing in Alan's eyes and hearing in his words, but before I can do either he turns to leave.

Then everything happens all at once, so quickly my mind can't keep up: Neil grabbing Alan by the shoulder; whirling him around; the sound of his fist landing in Alan's jaw; the explosion of flashes as the press runs toward us, cameras snapping pictures with each step; the shouted questions from every direction.

"You fucking stay away from her," Neil growls, standing above Alan. "You don't talk to her. You don't try to see her. You stay the fuck away from my wife and from me."

Stunned, I can't find my words.

For some reason my gaze desperately moves to Alan and not Neil. Our eyes lock. Alan says nothing. He stares at me and my heart jumps into my throat. Why are those great black eyes so full of pity and anguish as they look at me?

Before I can make reason of it, Neil is dragging me to the house, shouting *no comment* with every step. Inside he pulls me with him to a bedroom, slams the door and locks it. I stare at him, afraid and unsure how to manage this.

His fingers drop away from my wrist and he moves to the bathroom. *Oh crap, he's bleeding. What have I done?*

"We should go to the hospital, Neil. You might have broken something."

His jaw clenches and unclenches as he holds his hand under running water. After a few minutes he shuts the tap off and wraps his hand in a towel.

In the bathroom doorway, he stops, staring at me with eyes wild with pain and something else I've never before seen. The knot in my throat becomes strangling.

"I don't ever want to talk about this," he says with a quiet voice that makes me jump. "I don't want to know what you did in there with him. Not ever."

I nod, even though I'm not sure where he's going with this.

Those green eyes lock on mine. "Do you want our marriage, Chrissie? Or do you want him?"

Neil waits for my answer, and the expression on his face turns my mind blank. I speak without even attempting thought. "I want you, Neil. I want you."

CHAPTER NINETEEN

I sit on a chaise lounge in the hot July sun, watching Neil and Jack side by side deep in conversation as my dad flips burgers on the grill.

As awful as that scene was with Alan at the party three months ago, after the press furor died down—I push from my mind the avalanche of terrible tabloid press each and every one of us got after *the punching incident*—everything in our life has somehow jelled in a wonderful way. Whatever small doubts I still had the day I married Neil, they are gone today.

As impossible as it seems, the events have only brought Neil and Jack closer to each other. It's almost as if my dad's respect for Neil has deepened, their bond strengthened in mutual disregard for how they *think* Alan Manzone unfairly treated me. It would serve none of us if I explained that I was the one who behaved badly and had been unkind to Alan.

Some secrets are meant to be kept forever.

Another snippet of that day claims my thoughts. The look in my dad's eyes, standing stunned and silent, staring at Alan sprawled out on the grass and Neil snarling in his face. I could see when the pieces connected in Jack's head, the look of anger mingled with shock, when he figured out the abortion I had last year was mine and Alan's. I was so ashamed, I never wanted Jack to know this, and it was definitely a betrayal to Alan, but it all smoothed out on its own.

Alan left the scene like a gentleman. I never expected that one. He apologized to Jack, didn't press charges against Neil, and quietly went away. I haven't heard a peep from him since that day, and something in how he looked at me that last time has stuck with me. I can't define it, it was a strange kind of thing, and yet it made me sharply aware that Alan and I didn't end that day. We are still connected by life in way I can't label yet. Connected and always will be. I don't know how, but I am certain of it.

Strange, even knowing that isn't an internally messy thing for me.

As for my dad, in what should have been the ultimate Chrissie low moment, somehow it wasn't. Jack remained calm through it all and I often wonder if, in the silent chambers of Jack's mind, he really enjoyed someone slamming a fist in the face of that *fucker* for a change.

I don't know. It's strange. But Neil and I have been in a really good place since the *Alan incident*. Jack and Neil have been really good. Life is simple if you let it be. You can be happy if you let yourself be.

My gaze floats around the patio, taking in the rowdy Stantons lounging everywhere. It's nice that Jack included them for Neil's send-off on the road, and to keep the party casual so they'd feel comfortable in the Hope Ranch house.

I laugh and lower my gaze to fix on my glass of ice tea. A family of law enforcement on the same lawn as Jack. Jeez, I would have never believed this one would work well, but even the Stantons have effortlessly folded into our tiny Parker clan. One giant family surrounding me in Santa Barbara when the house was always too quiet here.

Life is good. Very good. I'm happy.

I hear my name and, startled, I look up. "What, Neil?"

Neil gives me an affectionately chiding look. "The second we got married you stopped listening to me."

I roll my eyes.

"Welcome to marriage, son," I hear Michelle Stanton heckle from across the pool and her husband, Robert, explodes in laughter beside me.

Neil gives a pointed stare to his dad, and then looks at *my* dad. "Why don't you help me out here? Why don't you talk to your daughter? Tell her that it's better for our marriage if she goes out on the road with me."

Jack shakes his head. "Nope. Not doing it. I'm staying out of this one."

"I'm not traveling with you anymore, Neil," I announce firmly. "Not ever. Never. Done."

He stares at me, exasperated. "We had an agreement when we got married. They were your rules, Chrissie. Not mine. And now you're breaking them."

"Yep, that's marriage," Robert Stanton says under his breath. All the Stantons laugh again and I laugh with them.

Jeez, how could I have forgotten how delightfully obnoxious the Stantons are? I love having them here. I love that they give Neil such shit. What an incredible family to be a part of.

I sink my teeth into my lower lip. Neil is so adorable when he's frustrated and everyone is ganging up on him.

He may be a bright rising star in the recording industry, but *here*, he's just Neil.

I can feel my eyes are sparkly when I look back to him. "We need to buy a house. We need a home, Neil. We can't live out of a suitcase forever."

He shakes his head, raking his messy waves back from his face with a hand. "We don't need a house. We're going to be on the road the next fifteen months. When we're not on tour we can stay here with Jack."

Jack looks up from the grill. "Like hell you can."

There is more laughter all around us.

"I'm not going, Neil, I *can't*," I repeat with more emphasis, more meaning.

Neil grows perfectly still. His eyes become enormous as he stares at me. "Can't? What do you mean you *can't*?"

I feel my cheeks color and my heart warm as I meet his gaze. "I mean I'm not breaking our agreement. I'm keeping our agreement. I can't go on tour with you. And we really do need a house, Neil."

He rushes across the patio, dropping to his knees in front of my chaise. Those lush green eyes are wide, hopeful, and excited.

"Are you sure?" he asks anxiously.

I nod. "Pretty damn sure."

In a second I'm in his arms and he's kissing me sloppily, and we're both laughing and crying simultaneously.

"Fuck, I shouldn't be squeezing you like that. I just can't believe it happened so soon."

He sits back on his heels and stares at me. I touch the

moisture from his cheek.

"Well, you better believe it, because we can't change it now."

Neil's arms encircle my waist again and he places a light kiss on my stomach *there*. I can tell by how everyone is smiling and staring that they've pretty much figured this one out.

My gaze shifts to my dad. My heart jumps in my chest. I've never seen Jack look so happy. He looks almost as happy as Neil.

"Don't worry, Daddy," I say. "I'm not moving in with you. I'm having a baby."

Jack lets out a ragged breath. He's crying and for once I've made my dad cry in a good way.

"You can stay as long as you want, baby girl," Jack says lovingly. "That's my grandchild you're having."

~ ~ ~

I stare at myself in the full-length mirror and make a face. Whoever said black was slimming is a liar. But then there is no way to hide this. I run my hands over my month seven baby bump. It's been forever since Neil's been home and I don't know what he's going to think about this.

I turn sideways. Crap, it would be nice if I wasn't quite *this* big, and I could still manage to pull off a little bit of sexiness. Shit, we haven't had sex for five months. I attempt a provocative stance and expression. I crinkle my nose. Nope, I'm all waddle and belly these days.

I make my way from my bedroom down the hallway, checking the rooms as I pass. Perfect, even though not completely done even after two months here. I need to paint Kaley's nursery, but at least the recording studio downstairs is finished, thanks to Jack. Neil is going to love that. The kitchen is almost together, and the living room is done.

I stare out the wall of glass and smile. A pretty nice homecoming for Neil, even if I'm going to be a less-than-spectacular sight. He's going to love it here.

I make my way carefully up the short rise of stairs to the foyer, noting that I really need to put a banister here. Who builds a house and doesn't put a banister and a rail on an upper landing? It may look dramatic, but it's a nightmare. Someone is always accidently dropping off into the living room.

I laugh. It is definitely a weird house. Neil will probably think it's strange, but it is so *us*. It is exactly the kind of house I want to raise Kaley in.

I grab my purse from the console table, go into the garage, hit open the door, and then climb into my black Range Rover. Thank God it has four-wheel drive. The driveway definitely needs improvement.

At the end of the drive, I stop and check traffic. I pause for a moment to look left. Devil's Playground is only a short hop up there. Smiling, I go right toward the highway. I slowly maneuver down the narrow one-lane tree-lined road, the forest so thick here that the sun is completely blocked, and keep a careful eye on the moss-covered boulders.

I merge onto the two-lane highway to the city. How funny it is that I used to be afraid of the mountain pass, so afraid I used to make Neil drive it for me, and now I drive it every day.

Twenty minutes later I pull into the Santa Barbara airport and park at the loading curb. I start to unbuckle my seatbelt, and then wonder if it would be better to wait here. I don't look as fat when I'm sitting. Grabbing my purse, I pull the key from the ignition and climb out of the car anyway.

I walk through the nearly empty Spanish-style building that acts as the terminal. I exit onto the patio and sink onto a bench close to the entrance from the runways.

I check my watch and my legs starts to jiggle anxiously. Any time now, Neil. I'm more than ready to see you. My gaze floats around the patio. There are a couple of other women here. I wonder if they're waiting for their husbands, too. It's a nice feeling, waiting on Neil. I smile.

People start entering from the runway, and I struggle to stand up. I anxiously search the small line of arriving passengers. My heart jumps against my chest. Green eyes, smiling, and looking for me.

Neil drops his bag, scooping me up in his arms, and gives me a passionate embrace. "God, I've missed you," he whispers between kisses.

"I've missed you, too."

He steps back as if seeing for the first time the dramatic change in me. The color in his eyes darkens.

"How's my baby today?"

I sink my teeth into my lower lip to hold back my emotions. Then he leans forward, kissing my belly, and I give him a gentle push away from me.

He looks at me, a teasing glint in eyes. "What?"

"I thought you were asking how I was. I can see how it is. You're completely obsessed with Kaley and have totally forgotten me."

He slips his arm around my waist and whispers in my ear, "Nope, I just can't greet you the way I want to here."

I flush, and we start walking out of the airport. I can tell when someone in the terminal recognizes Neil by how they stare, and I ease close into him in that *this guy is mine* kind of way.

He tosses his bag in the back of the car as I climb into the driver's seat. "You want to drive?" he asks, surprised.

I nod. "Yep. I am taking *you* to *our* house for the first time. I'm driving."

He climbs into the passenger seat, buckles his safety belt, then I pull from the curb. We drive for a while in silence with him just staring at me.

"You look so beautiful, Chrissie. I'm so glad to be home."

"Beautiful, huh? I'm enormous, or haven't you noticed that?"

"You're beautiful, Chrissie. Stop it. I wish I'd been here with you. Seeing the change all at once brings it home how much I've missed with you already."

I focus on the road, fighting back my tears. "Well, you're home now. You can make up for it."

He leans in and kisses me lightly on the shoulder. "I plan to. I don't care what you have on your calendar. We're not leaving the bedroom for a week."

I laugh and turn onto the mountain pass.

Neil frowns. "Where are we going?"

"Home, Neil."

He stares at me, surprised. "You bought a house on the mountain? *You* picked a house on the mountain?"

I nod. "Don't say it that way. I wanted the perfect home for us and I found it. Up here."

Fifteen minutes later, I'm slowly making my way down our driveway. Neil's expression is priceless. He's savoring being in the forest, but looking at me like I'm crazy.

I stop before the Spanish-style structure hugging the side of the mountain. There is not another house in sight, the acres around us are lush natural forestland, nothing but indigenous plant life here, but everywhere there's blue sky and a magnificent view of the Pacific Ocean. It's so quiet. The only sound is us and the comfortable quiet of the forest.

Neil stares. "You bought this?"

I keep my expression carefully neutral. I can't tell if he's happy, disappointed, or confused. I climb from the car and unlock the front door.

I kiss him. "Welcome home."

I step into the entry foyer. I point.

"I don't have a railing or banister yet," I say, dumping my things on the table. "That first step is a big drop if you go the wrong way. I need to fix it soon. Jack fell down it yesterday."

Neil laughs, then freezes and stares. He sinks on the red painted concrete floor of the landing, his legs dangling over the side. He's just staring.

His eyes widen. "Jesus Christ, Chrissie. I can't afford a house like this."

"Too late. We already bought it. You told me you didn't have to see it. That it was my choice. I bought this."

"Chrissie," he says in an exasperated growl. "Rich-girl you are. Rich-boy I am not. I can't afford this house."

"Oh, stop. We're married. Whatever we have belongs to the both of us, and that includes this house. I love this house. We're not moving from here."

I grab his hands and pull him onto his feet and kiss him on the cheek. I point at the door on the far side of the living room.

"That goes downstairs," I explain. "There are guest bedrooms. And Jack helped me convert some of the space into a recording studio. You have everything you need to work from here."

His brows lift. "You did that for me?"

"I did that for us. Our entire life, everything we love, all is here. We don't ever have to leave the mountain unless we want to."

I pull him with me to the wall of glass and his eyes widen even more as he looks out.

"This house is us, Neil," I say. "It's you. It's me. It's where I want to raise Kaley."

"Chrissie, what did it cost?"

I ignore the question.

I point to the left. "Over there is a trail to Devil's Playground. And look, there is Judgement Rock, the edge of the earth, and we can see it from our living room. We can hike there every day once I'm able to go uphill again. And there, you can see the beach. And I can see Hope Ranch and the islands and downtown. From every room

281

we can see the Pacific. Everything we love is right there out our back window for both of us to see every day. It's *us*, Neil. Perfect. I walked into this house and I never wanted to leave."

He turns me, taking me in his arms and his lips start moving on my flesh. "It definitely has everything. Does it have a bedroom?"

I laugh. Between kisses and touches I start pulling him through the kitchen toward the master suite.

"Neil, we have everything. It couldn't be more perfect if we had it custom-made."

~~The End~~

.

For all my current and future releases visit my website: http://susanwardbooks.com
Or like me on Facebook:
https://www.facebook.com/susanwardbooks?ref=hl
Or Follow me on Twitter: @susaninlaguna

Continue the Half Shell Series with the final book, The Girl in the Comfortable Quiet (June 2015), and read more of the Parker Saga with the first book of the Sand and Fog Series, Broken Crown (June 2015).

Enjoy one of my current contemporary romance releases:

The Girl on the Half Shell

The Girl of Tokens and Tears

The Girl of Diamonds and Rust (Releasing April 2015)

The Signature

Rewind

One Last Kiss

One More Kiss

One Long Kiss (Releasing March 2015)

Or you might enjoy one of my historical romance releases:

Susan Ward

<u>When the Perfect Comes</u>

<u>Face to Face</u>

<u>Love's Patient Fury</u>

<u>Love me Forever: Releasing Summer of 2015</u>

PREVIW THE GIRL IN THE COMFORTABLE QUIET

I can't stop shaking. God, I wish my body would be still. But nothing in my life could have prepared me for this. Maybe there are some shocks so severe that they reverberate through you, and you can't do anything except wait until they quiet on their own.

I stare down into my wine. This is definitely one of those shocks.

Rene sinks to sit on her knees across the coffee table. She just stares and I can see this has leveled her as much as me. She doesn't know what to say. It is as if this crisis is so enormous she's afraid to speak. A Rene first.

My eyes fix on her, stricken and wounded. "I can't believe this. How could it be true? Shouldn't I have known? How could I not know? I'm married to the man."

Rene flushes, something flashes in her eyes and then she looks away.

Oh my God.

"You knew!" I accuse harshly. "You knew and you didn't tell me. How could you do that, Rene? How could you do that to me?"

"No, no, no. I didn't know, Chrissie. I swear. I had suspicions and you were so certain about Neil. I ended up thinking I was wrong. Crazy. I thought I was wrong so I didn't say anything because I didn't want to hurt you."

"Why didn't you tell me? What kind of friend are you?"

She eases forward in a posture simultaneously aggressive and defensive. "I did try to tell you, Chrissie. When we lived together in Berkeley. I told you I didn't like Neil. I told you there was something about him I didn't like. You just didn't hear me."

Flashing snippets of old memories soar through my head. Oh God, she did tell me. I just didn't understand. I refused to see what Rene could see, but deep down, I think I always knew.

I jump to my feet and run to the bathroom, slamming the door behind me. Everything is running loose and frantic in me and I can't bear to look at Rene, not for another moment. I haven't gotten a single thing in my life right. Every decision I've made *hasn't* been right or left turns. It's been right or *wrong* turns, and the wrong path is the one I invariably take.

I let Alan go, over and over again, and he's the only man I've ever truly loved. That is the truth. Why do I hide from it?

I married Neil and I shouldn't have. That is the truth and I hid from that as well. That nagging voice deep inside me told me not to do it, I ignored it, and I refused to listen. My life is in shambles, I have no one to blame but me, and I don't know how to fix any of it

PREVIW BROKEN CROWN

I shut off the shower deciding not to call Chrissie. I dress for an excursion on my bike. Traveling the rural splendor of the United States on a Harley is one of the few things left in my life I still enjoy. The decision this time has nothing to do with savoring the scenery. The days it will take to travel from New York to California will give me a chance to back out if sanity decides to return. The call ahead of time will do neither of us any good if I decide not to see her.

I sink down onto my bed to make two phone calls. I tell my assistant to clear my calendar for the next month. I hang up as she bellows every reason why that isn't possible. Then I call the garage to get my bike ready.

I tuck into a backpack only what I need for the journey to Los Angeles. I almost leave the bedroom when I recall the lump in my sheets. Tucking the bracelet into my pocket, I reach out a hand and shake the body in my bed. "You need to get dressed and get the hell out of here, love. I'm going to California. If you're a whore, I'd like to pay you first. If you're a nice girl, leave me your number."

The brown-eyed beauty sits up, pulling with her the blankets to cover her naked flesh. Morning after modesty, another farce since my memory isn't so dim that I forgot what we did last night. Those pouting red lips smile.

Ah, Boston bred. The girl isn't ruffled by any of it.

Smoothly charming, she says, "I'll bill you. Though it's often considered a blurry difference, I'm not a whore. I'm your attorney. One of your divorce attorneys. I brought the finalized settlement contracts, and though you missed our meeting, I waited ten hours in this apartment for you to return to sign them since your ex-wife has an irritating proclivity to change her mind. I thought it best we jump on the offer and settle it fast since you didn't have a pre-nuptial agreement. When I tried to explain, you jumped on me. I thought what the hell, it's been a slow day and I'm earning five hundred bucks an hour for this. Why shouldn't my job have an occasional perk? You have been interesting. I've never been laid by a man who holds an infinity band while he fucks me. I think it's better I don't tell you the things you mumbled. I'll only warn you that you should be relieved it's covered under attorney/client privilege since my meter ticks until you sign those documents. The contracts are on the dresser. Please sign them so I can shower, dress and go. It's Saturday, in case you don't know what day it is, and I play racquetball at six. *That* I didn't expect you to know. It was a subtle attempt to speed you up in the signing."

I laugh softly. My attorney is charming. I go to the dresser and do a quick study of the contracts. "Thank you for not boring me with whatever I mumbled and thank you for promising to bill me so it's privileged. You can, however, bore me by letting me know how much this is costing me."

Panties and bra in place, my attorney scrambles from my bed, gathering her clothes then snatches the signed contracts from my hand.

"Me, I cost you seventy-two hundred for this meeting. You're ex-wife cost you one-hundred-sixteen million two hundred-twenty-seven thousand, a combination of cash, future cash, and an interesting assortment of personal property. You did, however, manage to retain the Malibu house, that against my advice you battled her over, the bill from me five-hundred thousand over the value of it."

I clutch her chin a little roughly and give her a hard kiss. "You, love, were a bargain."

I leave her, half dressed, staring at me from my bathroom doorway. It sounded theatrical even to me. Chrissie would have given me such shit for those theatrics, but the girl seemed to be expecting something like that so I played along.

Thank you for reading. You might enjoy a sneak peek into Chrissie and Alan's future, with Rewind **A Perfect Forever Novella.**

He doesn't laugh. Instead, his gaze sharpens on my face. "I am being nice, Kaley. I came to you. I got tired of waiting."

What? Did I just hear what I think I heard?

Before I can respond, he says, "How's your afternoon looking? Do you have time to take off and come see something with me?"

My afternoon? There is something. I'm sure of that, but I suddenly can't remember a single thing.

"What do you have in mind?"

"I want to show you where I've been living. What I've been doing. I think you'll find it interesting."

Interesting? Why would I find it interesting?

"So, do you think you can cut out for a few hours?" he asks, watching me expectantly.

I focus my gaze on the table, wondering if I should go, wondering why I debate this, and what the heck I have on the calendar that I can't remember. God this is weird, familiar and distant at once, and I haven't a clue what I should do here.

I stare at his hand, so close to mine, on the table. Whoever thought it would be so uncomfortable *not* to touch a guy? It doesn't feel natural, this space we hold between us, spiced with the kind of talk people have who know each other intimately. What would he do if I touched him…?

His fingers cover mine and he gives me a friendly squeeze. The feel of him runs through my body with remembered sweetness.

Suddenly, nothing in my life is as important as spending the afternoon with Bobby and for the first time, in a very long time, I don't feel like a disjointed collection of uncomfortably fitting parts. I feel at ease inside me being with Bobby.

I stop trying to access my mental calendar. I smile up at Bobby. "I've got as much time as you need."

Bobby chuckles and his hand slips back from me. He rises and tosses some bills on the table. "Just a few hours, Kaley. I'll have you back before the end of the day."

I rise from my chair and think *not if I figure out fast how not to blow this.*

Or enjoy the first novel in the Perfect Forever Novels: The Signature. **Available Now. Please enjoy the following excerpt from The Signature:**

She became aware all at once how utterly delightful it felt

to be here with him, alone on the quay, with the erotic nearness of his body.

She closed her eyes. "Listen to the quiet. There are times when I lie here and it feels like there is no one else in the world."

"No one else in the world? Would that be a good thing?" he asked thoughtfully.

"No. But the illusion is grand, don't you think?" she whispered.

Krystal turned her head to the side, lifting her lids to find Devon's gaze sparkling as he studied her. He shook his head lazily. "No. The illusion wouldn't be grand at all. It would mean I wasn't here with you."

It all changed at once, yet again, and so quickly that Krystal couldn't stop it. The ticklish feeling stirred in her limbs. Devon's words, as well as the closeness of their bodies, should have sent her into active retreat, and instead she felt herself wanting to curl into him. *What would it feel like if kissed me? Would I still feel this delicious inside? Or would that old panic and fear return?*

Laughing softly, Devon said, "I'm not used to relaxing. Can you tell?"

"I wasn't used to it before Coos Bay, either. There is a different pace of life here. At first I thought there was no sound. That's how quiet it seemed to me. Then I realized that there is music, beautiful music in this quiet."

After a long pause, he murmured, "You'll have to bring me here every Saturday until I learn to hear music in the quiet."

Krystal smiled. "Once you hear the music it's perfect."

"It's perfect now to me." His voice was a husky, sensual whisper.

He was on his side facing her. *When had that happened?* An inadvertent thrill ran through her flesh, and she could see it in his eyes—the supplication, the want, and an unexplainable reluctance to indulge either.

Devon was no longer smiling, his eyes had become brighter and more diffuse. His fingertips started to trace her face with such exquisite lightness that her insides shook. For the first time, in a very long time, she felt completely a woman, and wanting.

Was it possible? Had she finally healed internally as her flesh had done so long ago? Was she finally past the legacy of Nick? Was what she was now feeling real? Should she seek the answer with Devon? Or was it better to leave it unexplored?

"You are a very beautiful woman," he whispered.

She watched with sleepy movements as his mouth lowered to her. It came first as a touch on her cheek, feather soft between the play of his fingers. Her breath caught, followed by a pleasant quickening of her pulse. She was unprepared for the sweetness of his lips and the rushing sensations that ran through her body. His thumb traced the lines of her mouth, as his kiss moved sweetly, gently there.

His breath became rapid in a way that matched her own, and his mouth grew fuller and more searching. The fingertips curving her chin were like a gentle embrace, but their mouths were eager and demanding. Flashes of desire rocketed through her powerfully. Urgency sang through her flesh, a forgotten melody, now in vibrant notes. She found herself wanting to twist into him. Reality begged her to twist back.

Susan Ward

ABOUT THE AUTHOR

Susan Ward is a native of Santa Barbara, California, where she currently lives in a house on the side of a mountain, overlooking the Pacific Ocean. She doesn't believe she makes sense anywhere except near the sea. She attended the University of California Santa Barbara and earned a degree in Business Administration from California State University Sacramento. She works as a Government Relations Consultant, focusing on issues of air quality and global warming. The mother of grown daughters, she lives a quiet life with her husband and her dog Emma. She can be found most often walking at Hendry's Beach, where she writes most of her storylines in her head while watching Emma play in the surf.

Spare a tree. Be good to the earth. Donate or share my books with a friend.

Printed in Great Britain
by Amazon